THE TAILOR'S THREAD
An Italian - American Legacy

Johanna DiMaria Saladini   Pasquale Saladini

By

Vincent Rocco Saladini, Sr.

ISBN: 1-4107-9580-2 (e-book)
ISBN: 1-4107-9581-0 (Paperback)
ISBN: 1-4107-9582-9 (Dust Jacket)

Library of Congress Control Number: 2003096844

This book is printed on acid free paper.

Printed in the United States of America
Bloomington, IN

1stBooks – rev. 12/16/03

Step back in time and experience the poignant, heartwarming odyssey of Vincent Rocco Saladini, Sr., from his humble beginnings as the third youngest child of Italian-American immigrant, Pasquale Saladini, a West Virginia limestone miner, to his successful rise in the field of fashion and education. Experience life through Vincent's eyes and learn as he did that you, too, can realize your dreams if you persevere and never stop believing in yourself.

This book is dedicated to my dear father, Pasquale Saladini.

CONTENTS

FORWARD

The purpose of this book is to help preserve the culture and history of a small but brave group of Italians, who at a very early age and without any formal education in their native language, came to America at the turn of the century. They had left their families and friends behind to work at the Standard Lime and Stone Company in Martinsburg, West Virginia.

This book traces the many daily hardships and sacrifices that these people had to endure in order to survive. In addition, it celebrates their bravery in accepting the challenges of the unknown in order to make a better life for themselves as well as their families. They never gave up the fight to survive. As a result, their perseverance and determination enabled them to achieve personal success and become stellar members of the community in which they lived.

In addition, this book contains a variety of interesting and useful information that ranges from favorite family recipes to "How to get the most value for your money if you use a little care in selecting your wardrobe." Such information will enable readers to have a better understanding of the multi-talents and skills of these brave Italian-Americans, who, though forced to wear many hats in order to survive, eventually achieved success, despite being subjected to the cruelest and most adverse conditions imaginable.

Moreover, readers should find this book inspirational in that the author traces his experiences from the time of his birth to the present. Along the way, they will be given a rare glimpse into the past and how its impact influenced the present. This book is a further testament to the fact that although a person is born into poverty, it is possible to achieve success and personal gratification through hard work, dedication, sheer will, and determination. Success is within the hands of anyone who is willing to believe in himself and is determined to work hard to achieve his dreams.

I salute the bravery, courage, and dedication of the hard-working Italian-American men, women, and children of Big Springs, West Virginia, because their lives are an inspiration to those around them. They have proven that nothing in life is impossible to achieve and that no dream is unattainable if you are willing to work hard to make it happen. Their contributions have helped lay the solid foundation for the many benefits we all enjoy today. They were and still are a truly remarkable group of pioneers.

VINCENT ROCCO SALADINI, SR.

ACKNOWLEDGEMENTS

I wish to acknowledge all of the wonderful members of my family who contributed to the success of my book and who offered me moral support and constant words of encouragement in my pursuit of achieving my dream of writing this book. I am forever grateful to my precious and loving wife, Viola Esther Saladini, my daughters, Denise Ann Ceurvels and Deborah Jean Saladini, Esquire, my son, Vincent Rocco Saladini, Jr., M.D., my daughter-in-law, Linda Victoria Saladini, M.D., my sisters, Minnie Saladini Manspeaker, Rosie Saladini Crabtree, Lucy Saladini Cutrone, and my brother, Angelo Peter Saladini, Sr. I also wish to thank my grandson, Matthew James Ceurvels, for his technical assistance in editing the book as well as his beautiful photographs that grace it, and James Di Liberto, for his technical assistance with the computer graphics for my book. I would also like to thank my daughter, Denise, for her valuable assistance in editing my book.

In addition, I would like to acknowledge the contributions of my father, Pasquale Saladini, my biological mother, Johanna DiMaria Saladini, my stepmother, Cesarina Saladini, my father's first wife, Teodolinda Angelucci Saladini, and all of the other 13 families who lived in Big Springs, West Virginia. The men, women, and children of Big Springs, West Virginia, are examples of the true pioneers who suffered extreme hardships and who made many sacrifices which laid the foundation for the many benefits that we enjoy today. I am deeply proud and most honored to have been a part of their culture and heritage for they exemplify the true American pioneer spirit.

Furthermore, I would like to thank the Langsdale Library at the University of Baltimore, Maryland, the West Virginia Division of Tourism, the Bell Atlantic West Division of Tourism in West Virginia, and Martinsburg High School for their valuable contributions to my book.

Finally, I would especially like to thank my daughter, Deborah, who dedicated countless hours typing and editing the entire manuscript of this book while running a busy private law practice at the same time. Through her untiring effort, my lifelong dream of writing this book has now become a reality.

VINCENT ROCCO SALADINI, SR.

CHAPTER ONE

COAT OF ARMS

The Coat of Arms first began as a way of distinguishing knights in full armor as they paraded and fought in medieval times. The fighting man of the Middle Ages wore a metal suit for protection. Since the head was covered with a helmet, a knight in battle dress was unrecognizable. In order to prevent friends from attacking each other, it became necessary for the knights to be able to identify each other.

Many knights decided to paint colorful patterns on their battle shields. These patterns were also woven into their surcoats, which were worn over a suit of armor. Thus was born the term "Coat of Arms."

Coat of Arms

Saladini

In order to prevent the knights from using the same insignia, records were kept that granted the right to a particular pattern to a particular knight. His family also shared that same right to display these particular arms. In some instances, these records have been preserved and/or compiled in book form. The records list the family names

1

Vincent Rocco Saladini, Sr.

and an exact description of the "Coat of Arms" that was granted to that family.

Interest in heraldry is becoming increasingly popular as more and more people desire to preserve their heritage. A "Coat of Arms" is one of the rare remaining methods that provides an incentive for an individual to preserve his family heritage.

The source for the Saladini Coat of Arms is Halbert's, 3687 IRA Road, Bath, Ohio 49210.

CHAPTER TWO

BIRTHPLACE OF PARENTS

My father, Pasquale Saladini, was born on July 3, 1888, in Trisungo, Italy, a small village in the Commune of Arquata del Tronto, Province of Ascoli Piceno, Region of Le Marche (The Marches), Italy. He was one of four children including two brothers, Luigi and Emidio, and one sister named Delia.

The particular part of Italy that marked my father's birthplace was an extremely rugged and mountainous area. The main occupation of the village was farming. The people literally lived off of the land. They raised sheep and other animals for food and clothing. Chestnuts were plentiful in that area and as a result, chestnuts were considered one of the staple foods. The people of Trisungo were a close- knit group who would often share in chores such as sheep shearing and the butchering of hogs.

The women of the village would make beautiful

Salerno, Italy
Uncle Angelo DiMaria

3

clothing from the sheep's wool. They were all taught the various survival and farming skills from the time they were very young, and they were expected to meet their responsibilities of contributing to the family's survival. There were few opportunities available to the village people during those trying times. As a result, many of the young people eventually left the village for other lands and for other opportunities. Some came to America while others traveled to many different parts of the world. The Italians seemed to adapt to their new surroundings quite readily.

Salerno, Italy

Left to Right
Tony DiMaria, Catherine DiMaria
Louise Saladini, Angelo Saladini

My mother, Johanna DiMaria, who was born on February 1, 1894, in Casa Sottano, Province de Salerno, Italy, was one of six children. She had three sisters named Catherine, Louise and Carmela, and two brothers named Angelo and Anthony. My mother's birthplace was a picturesque area located near the Mediterranean Sea. The climate there was always pleasant and mild. In fact, it was an ideal climate for growing fruits and vegetables.

The property that my mother lived on consisted of a well constructed stone house and 200 acres of fertile land on which they grew olive, fig, lemon, and grapefruit trees. The women did all of the manual chores in cultivating the land. My uncles would go fishing in the Mediterranean Sea. Because fish were so abundant, there was always a plentiful supply for food.

My uncle, Angelo, joined the police force and continued this occupation as his career. In fact, he spent over twenty-five years on the police force before retiring with the rank of Chief of Police. My uncle, Anthony, remained at home with the three sisters who never married.

As a young child, I can recall my parents' sending clothing and other items to our relatives there. Although they had ample food supplies that they raised on their own, money was very scarce in the family. They always thanked my parents for the kindness and help that they gave to them. As a token of their deep appreciation, my relatives would, in turn, send us boxes of figs that they grew on their property. The figs were delicious and plentiful. My brother, Angelo, was the only member of our family to have ever visited our relatives in Casa Sottano, Italy. He visited our relatives there in 1955 while he and his bride, Louise, were on their honeymoon. My brother, Angelo, was first introduced to his future bride through our stepmother, Cesarina. My brother, Angelo, traveled to Trisungo, Italy, to become acquainted with his future wife. They seemed happy and compatible with each other right from the onset of their first meeting. Her family was very pleased with my brother and the prospect of his marrying their daughter and coming to America.

After several weeks of courtship and after getting to know each other, they decided to get married. Louise's family gave her a huge Italian wedding and they invited many of their friends and relatives from the area. It was truly a blessed and memorable occasion. My brother Angelo and his bride, Louise, enjoyed a six- week honeymoon visiting friends and relatives in Casa Sottano, Italy, and forming lasting relationships.

Since my brother Angelo and his bride, Louise, did not own a car, my brother rented one for the six weeks that he was in Casa Sottano, Italy, during which time he took many of their friends and relatives for a scenic tour of the area. They drove to Naples, Italy, where they visited our uncle, Angelo. Since Uncle Angelo was a policeman, he was able to give them a guided tour of the area. This was the first time that my aunts and Uncle Anthony had ever visited Naples. They were grateful for the opportunity to visit such an enchanting city as Naples.

My brother Angelo and Louise also enjoyed a pleasant visit to my mother's birthplace. The relatives treated them with much kindness, generosity, and respect. They prepared delicious meals for them from the food that they had grown and produced on their own land. Their meals consisted of fresh fruits, vegetables, fish, and chicken. Beef and pork were very rarely eaten during that time, due to their scarcity and high cost.

Fortunately, the people of the area were very healthy and seldom in need of medical care, although they would go occasionally for a check-up. My brother, Angelo, was introduced to the town doctor by our relatives. The doctor remarked that while he did not earn very much money, he was happy and content to care for the people of the town. Because money was scarce in my family, our relatives would often pay for their medical care in the form of produce, chickens, vegetables, and fruits.

Unfortunately, all of our relatives from Sottano, Italy, are now deceased. My aunt Catherine, who was the oldest survivor, died several years ago. She lived to the ripe old age of 92. Since her death, the property upon which she lived has been sold. Despite the passage of time, however, the area remains relatively the same and the people still live the age- old basic lifestyle of relying on the land for all of their needs. It is as though time there has stood still.

CHAPTER THREE

FATHER'S IMMIGRATION TO AMERICA

The first thought that comes to one's mind when mention is made of Italian immigration to America is that all Italians settled in the following large cities of the United States: New York, Chicago, New Orleans, and Newark. However, little is known about the Italian immigrants who migrated to other sections of the United States. One such area is Martinsburg, West Virginia.

As fate would have it, an Italian by the name of Thomas Cherrino, who later changed his name to Thomas Cherry, also came from my father's hometown of Trisungo, Italy. He had gone to Canada to work for a mining company. An exceptionally intelligent young man, Thomas Cherry was able to draw and write down the complete operation of the entire plant from memory.

Thomas Cherry came to America where he met a wealthy businessman named Newton D. Baker. Mr. Cherry presented his plans of the mining plant to Mr. Baker and finally persuaded him to open a mining company in Big Springs, West Virginia, an area approximately 2 1/2 miles south of Martinsburg, West Virginia.

Mr. Cherry assured Mr. Baker that securing the necessary manpower to work the mines would not pose any problem. He would be able to recruit able-bodied young men from Italy to come to America to work in the mines. Mr. Baker liked what he heard and agreed to Mr. Cherry's proposal.

Mr. Cherry traveled to my father's hometown of Trisungo, Italy, and several nearby villages where he was able to recruit thirteen men to come to America to work the mines. My father, Pasquale, was one of the thirteen men selected. As an added incentive for the men to come to America, Mr. Baker agreed to pay for all transportation costs and build each man a house to live in, free of charge, in exchange for each one's agreeing to work for the Standard Lime and Stone Company. Mr. Baker further agreed to build a grammar school for the children of the village of Big Springs, West Virginia. Mr. Baker encouraged the single men to find a wife and to settle down. Once he established the mining operation, Mr. Cherry eventually returned to Italy.

Mr. Frank Allesio, a well- educated Italian immigrant, spoke English fluently. He was held in high esteem by the Italian immigrants. He was the "galantuomi" (gentleman) who worked for an Italian Steamship Line. He was responsible for introducing *Il Progresso-Italiano Americano*, which became the leading Italian newspaper in the Italian community. In addition, he formed an Italian-American Club in Martinsburg, West Virginia.

The Italian immigrants from Big Springs, West Virginia, were given an opportunity to socialize with the Italians from Martinsburg, West Virginia, and the other neighboring towns. The men would gather together and play cards or bocce. A pool table was also available for their entertainment. In addition, one could always enjoy a friendly glass of homemade wine with the fellow members.

The majority of the Italians who belonged to the club who did not live in Big Springs, West Virginia, resided in Martinsburg, West Virginia. Among these men were Joe and Paul Leporini, Carmen and Virgil Quaglio, John and Carmen Ferro, Philip Chirelli, Carmen Fierro, Frank and Carmen Cicone, and others. All of these Italians were self-employed as shoemakers, tailors, barbers, bakers, butchers, and grocery store workers.

Mr. Frank Allesio was very helpful in giving sound and trusted advice to the immigrants, which ranged from politics to the stock market. I can recall one incident when Mr. Allesio suggested to my father and several other immigrants that they invest $800.00 in the stock market. He assured them that they could make a profit since the stocks were of the highest of blue chips. As it turned out, they invested as suggested and made a nice profit since the stocks had gone up.

Mr. Frank Allesio was also responsible for encouraging a large Italian grocery store owner in New York City to make one or two trips a year to Big Springs, West Virginia, to bring olive oil, spaghetti, grating cheese and other Italian specialties for them to enjoy. Although the village had a company store, it did not offer a wide variety of Italian products. We all looked forward to having the grocer from New York City come to our village.

Unfortunately, Mr. Frank Allesio did not remain in West Virginia for any length of time because his home base was in New York City and further, because his wife was confined to a wheelchair and needed special medical care that was offered in New York City. We all dreaded his departure and missed him dearly when he finally left West Virginia. His departure left a void that was never quite filled again by anyone else.

Mr. Luigi Botti was a well- educated, Italian immigrant and a very shrewd businessman. He was able to speak English fluently.   Mr. Botti owned a large cola bottling plant in Martinsburg, West Virginia. He was the person whom the Italian immigrants would contact in case of any legal problems, funerals, passports, and weddings. He was paid a fee that was frequently padded. Although he was not well liked, the Italian immigrants would turn to him because they were desperate. Mr. Botti recognized their desperation and responded accordingly, much to his financial gain.

During his lifetime, Luigi Botti amassed a fortune through his prosperous business and the often exorbitant fees that he charged the Italian immigrants. He died a broken man, however, much in keeping with the old Italian saying "Money that you do not honestly earn, you do not enjoy."

In 1904, my father, Pasquale, was among the first Italian immigrants to settle in this small sleepy mining village called Big Springs, West Virginia. It was a village consisting of fourteen houses, located 2 1/2 miles south of Martinsburg, West Virginia. Arriving in America at the tender age of sixteen, lacking a formal education, and without having any marketable skills, my father was forced to accept the lowest paying, back breaking jobs imaginable. In fact, my father was among one of the first workers employed by the Standard Lime and Stone Company in Big Springs, West Virginia.

After my father settled down, he sent for his brothers, Luigi and Emidio. Unfortunately, Uncle Luigi died in a boating accident shortly after arriving in America. Apparently he was trying to get across the river in a small boat when it capsized and threw him into the raging water. He was unable to swim and consequently drowned.

Uncle Emidio could not adapt to the rugged life of a miner. He eventually pulled up stakes and moved to Wilmington, Delaware, where he met and married a young lady named Alba. Uncle Emidio found a job in a tannery and seemed to be quite happy with his new job and way of life. He made new friends and enjoyed the company of the many Italian workers who were also employed at the tannery.

Uncle Emidio had three children: Sammy, Noemi, and Virginia. I would often visit my Aunt Alba and Uncle Emidio in Wilmington, Delaware, where I would have an opportunity to enjoy my Aunt Alba's excellent Italian cooking. She prided herself on preparing elaborate Italian feasts for me whenever I came to visit.

I have many fond memories of my Uncle Emidio. He reminded me so much of my father. He had a similar physical build and his mannerisms mirrored those of my father. He was also a pleasant and likeable man who made friends easily.

I would enjoy playing horseshoes for hours on end with my cousin Sammy out in the open air. We also enjoyed playing catch. Cousin Sammy was always so full of life and fun to be around. I enjoyed his company very much and always looked forward to our visits together.

Eventually, my Aunt Alba grew weary of living in Wilmington, Delaware, and longed to move to New York City where she believed there were more opportunities for advancement. In 1952, Aunt Alba, Uncle Emidio, and their children, moved to Bronx, New York. Aunt Alba quickly found a job as a seamstress. She was a very creative woman and an expert in clothing construction and design. Uncle Emidio found work in a thread manufacturing factory where he seemed to be quite content. I would often visit my Aunt Alba and Uncle Emidio in the Bronx where I was always treated with kindness, respect and a meal fit for a king. I always looked forward to my visits with them.

One of my fondest memories of their Bronx, New York, home was the huge fish pond in the back yard. It was so relaxing and peaceful and a welcome change from the bustling city life just outside their yard.

Eventually Aunt Alba and Uncle Emidio decided to move to Somerset, New Jersey. Aunt Alba also had several sisters who lived in and around the Somerset area. By this

Sammy Saladini

Dolly Saladini

Virginia Saladini

July 4, 1947 Riverview Beach, NJ

time, my cousins Sammy, Noemi and Virginia were all married and had started families of their own. Aunt Alba and Uncle Emidio shared a home with my cousin Virginia and her family. My cousins Sammy and Noemi purchased homes in the same neighborhood, which enabled all of them to maintain close contact and to continue to share in each other's lives.

I would often visit my Uncle Emidio and Aunt Alba in Somerset, New Jersey. Each visit would bring back a flood of fond memories of the times that we had enjoyed each other's company in the past. Whenever my Uncle Emidio saw me, his eyes would light up and he would hold onto me as though he never wanted me to leave. He always said that I reminded him of my father, Pasquale, who is his brother.

Although the area of Somerset was pleasant enough and my Uncle Emidio was enjoying his retirement, he was homesick for the Bronx, where he left behind many of his close friends and acquaintances and a way of life that he could never recapture in Somerset. While living in the Bronx, Uncle Emidio had made friends with many of the Italian immigrants who, like himself, shared a way of life and a system of values that were unparalleled. Uncle Emidio enjoyed socializing with his Italian friends there.

Unfortunately, in Somerset, there were few Italians with whom Uncle Emidio could socialize, and he longed to be with his old friends once again. In fact, Uncle Emidio would walk two miles just to be able to speak to an Italian barber. Uncle Emidio was never really quite the same after he left the Bronx, for sadly, he had lost much of the sparkle and enthusiasm that he once had.

Uncle Emidio and Aunt Alba have long since passed away. With their passing we all felt a deep and lasting loss not only for the love and zest for life that they possessed, but also, for the tradition and values that they instilled in all of us.

Left to Right
Sammy Saladini, Vincent Saladini,
Louie Nardinicchi   April 6, 1947

My cousins Sammy, Noemi and Virginia continue to reside in Somerset, New Jersey, with their children, who now have families of their own. I am proud to be blood relatives with such a fine group of people, and I value our time together and the memories that we share.

CHAPTER FOUR

FATHER'S THREE WIVES

Teodolinda Angelucci (1882-1920)

In 1908, after working in Martinsburg, West Virginia, at Standard Lime & Stone Company for four years, my father, Pasquale, decided to return to his hometown, Trisungo, Italy, to marry his childhood sweetheart, Teodolinda Angelucci. However, his plans were altered when he was drafted into the Italian Army. He spent the next two years in Ethiopia. Upon his discharge from the Army, he returned to Trisungo, Italy, and married, Teodolinda. They returned to the New World on December 21, 1910, via the ship "America." They settled in Big Springs, West Virginia, where my father returned to his mining job. Teodolinda was very happy to come to America

because she was truly in love with my father and had four brothers and two sisters who were also living in the West Virginia and Pennsylvania areas.

Living conditions in the West Virginia area in which they settled were extremely difficult. The winters were cold and severe. The homes lacked indoor plumbing and central heat. The only source of heat for the homes was a wood burning stove which provided little more than a minimal source of warmth against the cruel and chilling winters. In spite of all the hardships, four children were born out of this marriage. They were named Amelia, Venanzio, Guiseppi, (Joseph) and Teodolinda. Unfortunately, Venanzio died during childbirth. However, my family was united and determined more than ever to enjoy a successful life in America.

After ten years of life in America, my family became adapted to the rugged living conditions. Unfortunately, tragedy struck once again. In 1920, my father's wife died during the great influenza epidemic. Having no one to care for his children posed a very serious problem for my father. The West Virginia State authorities threatened to place the children in a foster home. My father was heartbroken over the prospect that the family would be separated. He spent many sleepless nights worrying about the fate of his beloved family. The oldest daughter, Amelia, was forced to quit school and care for the rest of the children. Although it was very difficult, my father struggled and was able to keep the family together for the time being until he was able to remarry.

Pasquale and Teodolinda Saladini were among the 2,650 passengers aboard The America December 21, 1910
Photo: Andreas Hernandez Collection

Photo courtesy of the Steamship Historical Society of America Collections, Langsdale Library, University of Baltimore

Johanna DiMaria (1894-1929)

My father was desperate at this point in time. Taking care of four children and trying to raise a family was becoming increasingly difficult. It was at that time that he decided to have a neighbor write a letter to a friend of his in Salerno, Italy, to explain his situation and to make it known that he wished to remarry if he could find someone who was willing to come to America and help him raise his children. The friend recommended a young woman named Johanna DiMaria. After a brief exchange of letters, Johanna DiMaria arrived in America to accept my father's marriage proposal.

It was very difficult for my mother because all of her relatives remained in Italy. She was the only member of her family to come to America. She soon grew extremely homesick but remained strong and willing to suffer her pangs of separation from her family because she truly believed that she would eventually enjoy greater opportunities in America.

Johanna DiMaria Saladini   Pasquale Saladini

Life was a constant struggle and monies were scarce despite the fact that my father worked night and day just to survive. The scarcity of money coupled with the poor and often depressing living conditions made every day a struggle. My mother had to adapt to the cold climate, a far cry from the mild and pleasant weather that she had always enjoyed in Casa Sottano, Italy.

Out of this marriage were born six children: twins Minnie and Rosie, Lucy, Vincent, Angelo, and Mary, who died tragically shortly after birth. I am the fourth oldest of the six children born to my father and mother. According to my family, my mother was ecstatic when I was born because they had had three daughters and had hoped for a son. My mother would spoil and pamper me. I was her son, her pride and joy, and she showered me with endless love and care. In fact, I was breast-fed until I was two years old.

Sadly, I have very few memories of my dear mother because she died when I was only five years old. She apparently died of breast cancer and pneumonia. During that time, little was known about the horrible disease of breast cancer and my mother, who was raised to be strong and independent, never complained to my father about her illness until it was too late.

While visiting Martinsburg, West Virginia, several years ago, I happened to meet a taxi driver named James Perry, who used to drive my parents all the way to Baltimore, Maryland, from Martinsburg, West Virginia, in order for my mother to receive cancer treatments. He explained how my poor mother would cry because she was so ill and how she constantly worried about my father and her children. Mr. Perry said that he would try to offer my mother words of encouragement during this tragic and painful time. I knew Mr. Perry when I was a young child working in Martinsburg, West Virginia. He had nothing but praise and kind words for my parents. He indicated that I had a strong physical resemblance to my mother and father.

Upon my mother's death, life became increasingly difficult for my father and my brothers and sisters. As in the past, my oldest sister, Amelia, was once again forced to take care of the rest of the children while my father went to work.   Once again, the West Virginia State Agency threatened to take away the children and place them in foster homes. The neighbors tried to assist my father as much as possible so that we would not have to be separated.

As I look back in retrospect, without the mutual respect, love, and kindness of our neighbors, we would have had a very difficult time remaining together as a family. The neighbors came to the aid of my family by helping to care for the children, cooking for us, and seeing to it that we were fed properly. My oldest sister, Amelia, was unable to handle this monumental task alone; however, there was no doubt that she was the glue that helped to hold the family together. I will always have the utmost and highest respect and admiration for my sister, Amelia, and I shall always be grateful to her for the many sacrifices that she unselfishly made on behalf of the family so that we could remain together as a family with our love for each other in tact.

Our sister, Teodolinda (also known as Dolly), was taken to Sardegne (Sardinia), to live with her godparents. My father was heartbroken, but he had no choice but to allow her to leave. Her godparents were a very pleasant, respectful, and trustworthy couple who treated my sister as though she were their own daughter.

My father would send her financial assistance so that she could receive an education. She did, in fact, succeed in obtaining an excellent education. She also learned to play the mandolin and the guitar.

In 1937, prior to World War II, my father decided to return Teodolinda to America. Her godmother had died, and the political climate of Italy, which was under Benito Mussolini at the time, made it unsafe for her to continue to remain in Italy. My father feared that if she remained in Italy during such an explosive time, she would not be able to leave Italy. He, therefore, quickly made arrangements for her to return to America.

Teodolinda finally arrived in America when she was seventeen years old. She found life here in America to be much better than it had been in Italy. She was united with her biological family once again and soon adjusted to life in America. She eventually learned the English language and was able to find a job in a cardboard manufacturing factory. She has long since retired after having worked there for many years. Her employers hated to see her leave because she had always been a devoted, conscientious, and reliable employee.

Teodolinda is presently living with our brother Joe's family in Martinsburg, West Virginia, where she has resided for many years. While she never married, Teodolinda seems to be very content, and comfortable with the life that she has made for herself here in America.

Cesarina Rossi Saladini (1888-1967)

Left to Right
Pasquale Saladini, Cesarina Saladini

After the death of my mother, my father was extremely lonely. He missed my mother very much and found it difficult to go on without her by his side. My father began to become desperate once again. He wanted to remarry for the sake of his children and to keep the family together.

A neighbor, Cesarina Rossi, who was the godmother to my two older sisters, Minnie and Rosie, was a widow. She had one son named Carlo. Cesarina had a very difficult life. Her husband had died during World War I. She originally had four children, but three of them died from childhood diseases. Cesarina was truly a

Left to Right
Carlo Rossi, Cesarina Saladini
Big Spring, West Virginia

remarkable woman. My father proposed marriage to her and she graciously accepted the challenge of coping with a very difficult situation. She had to care for nine children from different mothers. She was a very compassionate, kind, dedicated and capable mother who showered all of us with love and a sense of belonging. My fondest memory of Cesarina was that of her

22

reading prayers to us at bedtime. It was so comforting, reassuring, and soothing to me to have her close to us during these trying moments when life seemed its bleakest. Cesarina would always offer us encouragement and hope and above all else, she provided us with the love and nurturing that we so craved in a mother. We were truly blessed for having her love and warmth in our lives.

Left to Right
Lucy Saladini, Cesarina Saladini
Lincoln Park, Newark, NJ
May 2, 1948

Cesarina taught all of my sisters to cook and sew. They made all of our clothing and did all of the baking for us. My father had built them a special outdoor oven that could hold twelve loaves of bread. My sisters and mother would make potato bread and wheat bread. The aroma of baking bread would fill the house and linger there long after we enjoyed the fruits of their labor. Our neighbors could smell the baking bread a half a block away. Of course we would always share what little we had with our neighbors, and they were always appreciative of such a treat.

My mother also taught my sisters how to make dresses out of old flour sacks and sweaters from sheep's wool. The finished products turned out to look most professional, and my sisters prided themselves on their ingenuity and talent.

My mother would purchase the fleece from the nearby sheep farm and then go through the entire process of preparing and then weaving the yarn to make clothing. My father would wear these homemade sweaters to work because they kept him warm and comfortable in the damp, cold mines.

Unfortunately, my mother, Cesarina, became seriously ill with kidney problems. She was forced to be constantly under a doctor's care, which was extremely expensive, especially since my father did not have any type of medical coverage to help defray these costs. My father would struggle to pay the doctor in cash, as he required. Sometimes the doctor would accept fresh fruits and vegetables in exchange for medical services. I can vividly remember how my poor father opened up his small wallet and held his head with a look of despair on his face. He had so many expenses and so little money with which to pay for them.

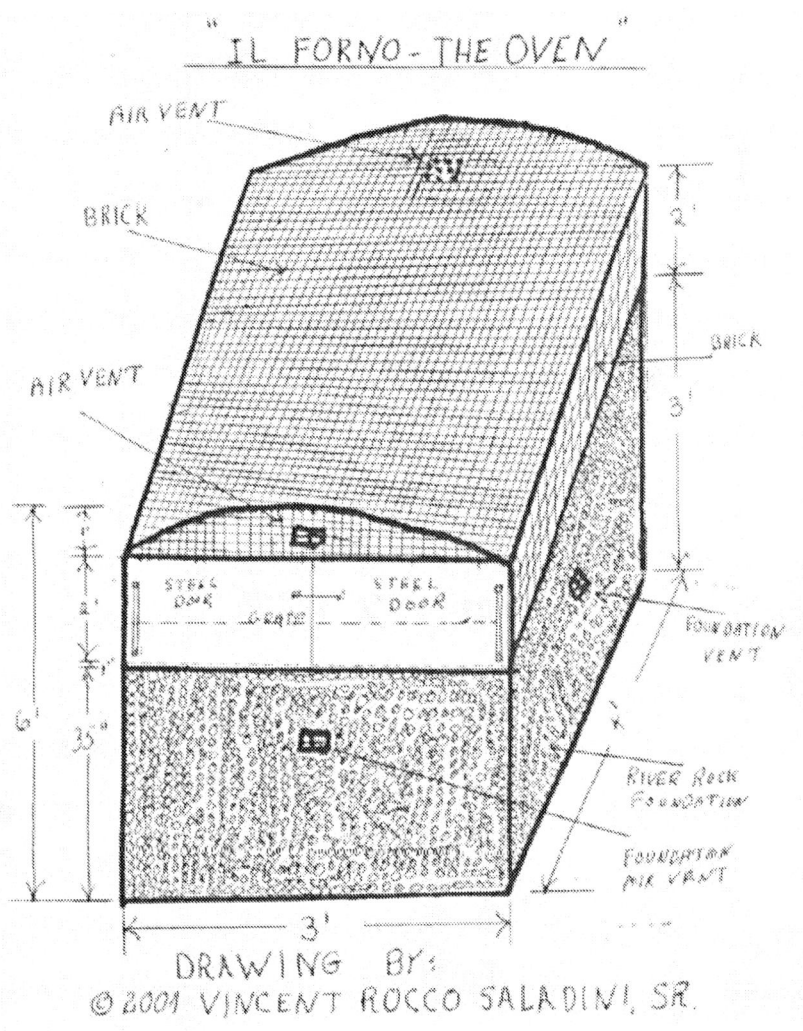

"IL FORNO - THE OVEN"

DRAWING BY:
© 2001 VINCENT ROCCO SALADINI, SR.

This is an original drawing of "IL FORNO: THE OVEN" at Big Springs, West Virginia.
I drew this from my recollection of observing my father, Pasquale, building it in our backyard.

25

To earn extra money, my father would work a part-time job on the nearby farm after having spent all day working his fingers to the bone in the mines. I can remember how he would come home totally exhausted from working both jobs and feeling frustrated over the fact that monies were still so scarce.

My father was a proud man who would not accept any type of welfare assistance even though we more than qualified to receive it. He always said that he would rather work ten jobs than take welfare assistance.

Left to Right
Vincent Saladini, Cesarina Saladini
Lincoln Park, Newark, NJ
May 2, 1948

I can recall an incident when I was fourteen years old. One hundred bags of flour and food were delivered to Big Springs, West Virginia. None of the inhabitants of the village would accept the handouts, however. I can vividly recall my father's saying proudly and most unselfishly, "Give it to someone more deserving." I greatly admired and respected my father. He would literally give someone the shirt off of his back without a moment's hesitation. If someone asked him for something, he would give it unselfishly to him without any questions asked. He was extremely kind, compassionate and generous.

Another example of my father's kindness and generosity occurred when a neighbor needed money to visit his family in Italy. Without any hesitation, my father gave him $500.00 on just a handshake. In the village of Big Springs, West Virginia, a man's word was his honor. The neighbor returned the borrowed money in due time without my father's ever having to mention it again.

Left to Right
Vincent Saladini, Cesarina Saladini
Minnie's Farm, Hagerstown, Maryland
August 11, 1947.

Another time my Uncle Emidio needed money as a down payment to buy a home in Wilmington, Delaware. Although my father did not have very much money, he willingly loaned my Uncle Emidio the money he needed. My uncle repaid the money to him in due time.

My parents' kindness and generosity have left a lasting impression on me. In spite of having very little monetary wealth, they always tried to help others who were less fortunate and in need. They taught me that true wealth is not determined by how much money a man has in his wallet, but rather, by how much love, compassion, and understanding he has in his heart. I have never forgotten that philosophy and have continued to embrace it throughout my life.

CHAPTER FIVE

BIRTHPLACE OF THE SALADINI CHILDREN

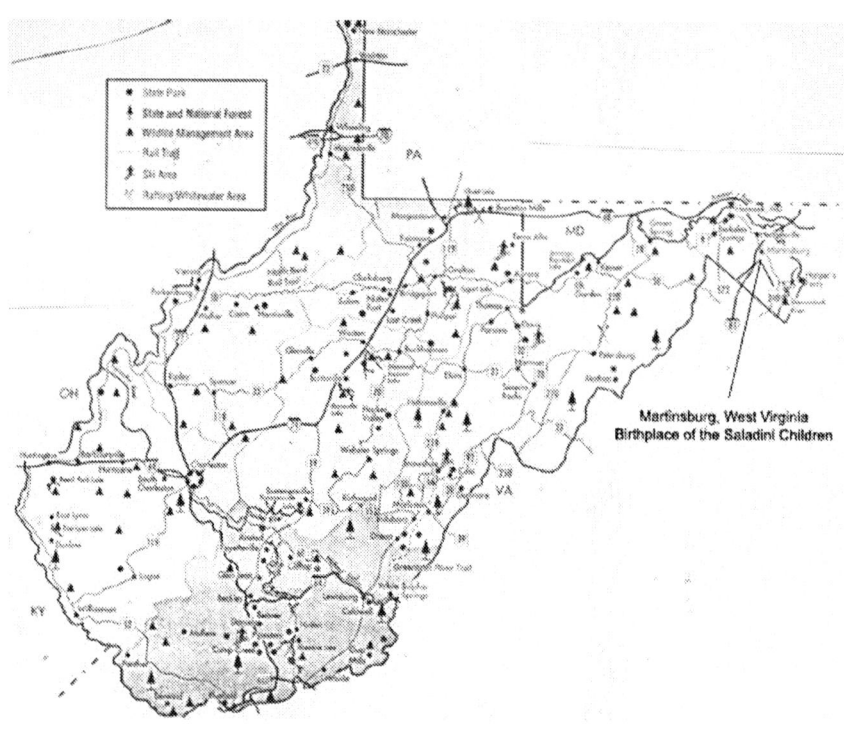

Martinsburg, West Virginia
Birthplace of the Saladini Children

West Virginia Outdoor Adventure Guide – Courtesy of West Virginia Division of Tourism

All of the Saladini children were born in Martinsburg, West Virginia, as follows:

Amelia: January 14, 1912; died August 27, 2000
Venanzio: 1914, died at birth

Guiseppi: March 21, 1916; died November 3, 2001
Teodolinda: October 14, 1918
Rosie: August 1, 1922
Minnie: August 1, 1922
Lucy: November 8, 1923
Vincent: December 23, 1924
Angelo: June 25, 1926
Mary: 1928, died at birth

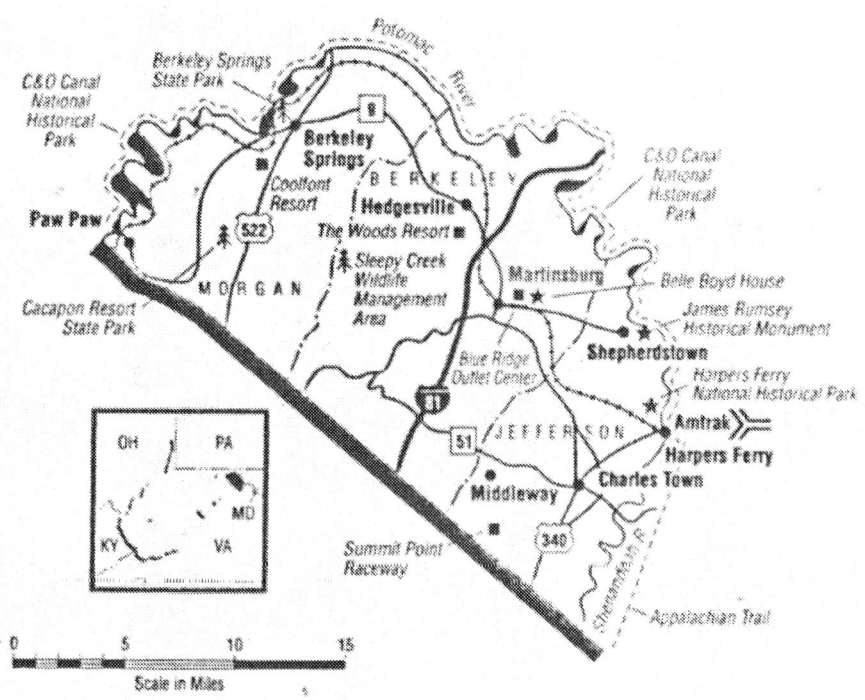

West Virginia State Official Travel Guide – Courtesy
of Bell Atlantic West Division of Tourism

With a population of approximately 15,000 people, Martinsburg, West Virginia, founded by General Adam Stephen, is located in the eastern panhandle of West Virginia. It was incorporated in 1778 and later flourished as a railroad town. It was home to the B & O Railroad Engine Shop. The General Adam Stephen home, the period-furnished colonial era home, is open to the public on weekends and by appointment.

Courtesy of the 1942 Martinsburg High School yearbook, The Triangle

Martinsburg, West Virginia
The monument to Adam Stephen

Martinsburg, West Virginia's central location in the panhandle as well as its easy access to Interstate Highway 81, make it a center for commerce and recreation in the area. Known far and wide as a shopper's paradise, Martinsburg, West Virginia, is home to the Blue Ridge Outlet Center, where brand name merchandise sells for factory outlet prices in more than fifty shops. The shops were housed in a complex of 19th century woolen mills, one of which was the famous Interwoven Woolen Mills.

During the Civil War, Martinsburg, West Virginia, was coveted by both sides. The Union Army held it for thirty-two months while the Confederate Army held it for sixteen months.

As a native of Martinsburg, West Virginia, I am proud and honored to call it my hometown. Because Martinsburg was a relatively small town, most of the inhabitants knew each other and enjoyed a close- knit bond that enabled them to survive the often harsh and difficult times. I shall forever remember how friendly the people were and how they were always willing to lend a helping hand to a neighbor in need. Chance meetings in and around town were always greeted with a cheerful hello, all of which gave one a sense of pride, belonging, and self-worth. I shall always have fond memories of my hometown of Martinsburg and all of the wonderful people who touched my life in a most immeasurable way.

We recognize Martinsburg from the air by the familiar landmarks.

Courtesy of the 1942 Martinsburg High School yearbook, The Triangle

CHAPTER SIX

THE VILLAGE OF BIG SPRINGS

The village of Big Springs, West Virginia, which had a population of eighty-eight, was owned by the Standard Lime and Stone Company. It consisted of fourteen, seven room wooden houses that were occupied by the Italians who came to America to work in the mines. One exception was an Irish family who occupied the house at the south end of the village. Although the Smiths were of Irish decent, they spoke Italian very well and blended in very nicely with the rest of the Italians. The Smiths even adopted many of their customs.

Because the houses lacked proper insulation and indoor plumbing, they were no match for the harsh and frigid winters which were brutally uncomfortable. Our only source of heat was a wood burning pot-bellied stove, which was located in the kitchen. In order to stay warm at night, we would heat bricks, wrap them in cloth, and lay them at the foot of the bed. We also slept three in a bed in order to keep warm.

Vincent R. Saladini
1943 Big Springs, West Virginia

Since we lived in a cold water house, we did not have an inside bathroom or any indoor plumbing. Instead, we used an outside bathroom also known as an "outhouse" or "backhouse," which was located about one hundred feet from the rear of the house. The "backhouse" was extremely inconvenient and uncomfortable during the cold winter months, especially when it snowed, since we would have to shovel out a path before we could use it.

If we wanted water, we had to travel to one of several water pumps that were located throughout the village. Then each family had to carry the water in buckets to their houses. It was strenuous and tiring work, but we had no other choice if we wanted water. I can vividly recall seeing my mother and the other women in the village frequently carrying buckets of water balanced on their heads while struggling to hold other buckets of water in their hands.

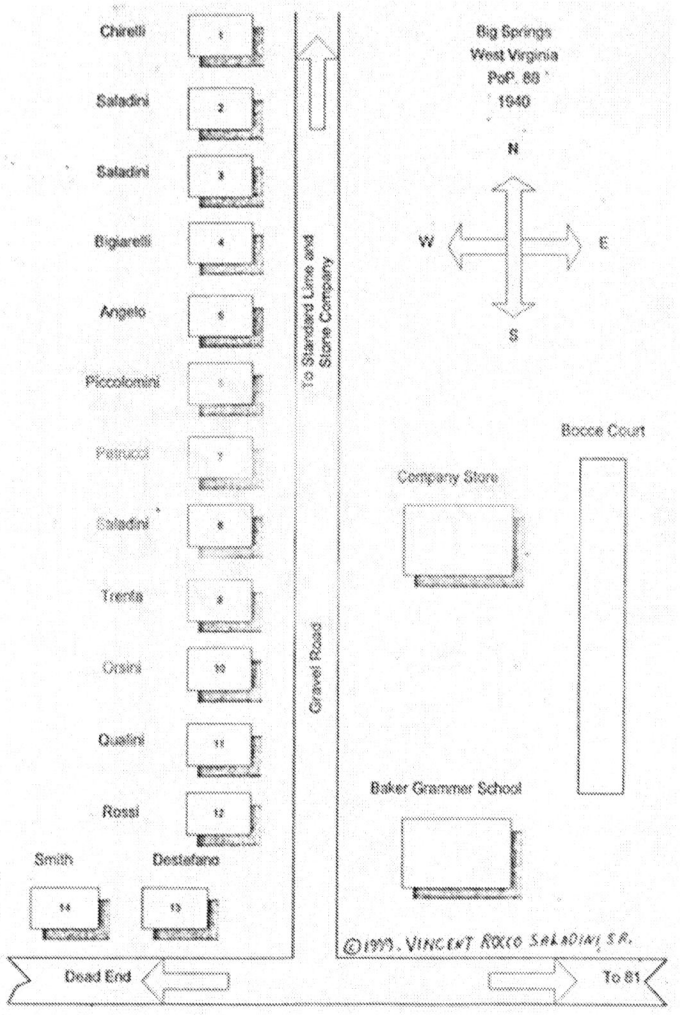

This is an original drawing of the layout of Big Springs, West Virginia. I drew this from my recollection of living there for 22 years.

In order to take a shower, we would have to walk one and one-half miles to the shower room located at the mines. Several of us would get together once a week, usually on a Saturday, to take our weekly shower. Because the mining company was aware of our situation, they would allow us to use their shower room. Unfortunately, this privilege did not extend to the women and children of the village. Instead, the women and children had to bathe at home, using a basin filled with warm water that they would heat on the wood burning stove. Despite these harsh and crude living conditions, however, the women and children made certain that they would bathe at least once or twice a week.

I can recall experiencing another example of our harsh living conditions when I was thirteen years old. I developed a severe cold which resulted in my contracting pneumonia. My family summoned Dr. Powers, our family physician, who immediately came to our house. My father had placed a small electric heater next to my bed to keep me warm, but it really did little to help me. It was so cold in the room that when I took a breath, I could see the cold vapors pouring forth from my mouth. Upon examining me, Dr. Powers suggested that more heat was needed to keep me warm. At this point, I was shivering uncontrollably. Supplying more heat was simply impossible as this was our only available source of heat. I can still recall Dr. Powers' reaction when he was told that we had no other source of heat. He just shook his head in sadness and disbelief while my mother and father worked

Birthplace of the Saladini Children

feverishly to layer several homemade woolen blankets upon me. I was also given a new pair of woolen long johns to wear as well as plenty of homemade chicken soup and other fluids to drink.

August 1943
Lucy Saladini, Louise Saladini

Dr. Powers also gave my parents some medication to give me, but I refused to take it unless my sister, Minnie, took some of it first. Poor Minnie was my guardian angel and the one I would always run to in such desperate times. After much prodding from my parents and only after Minnie first tasted the medicine, I then took my medicine. As a result of my parents' constant love and care, I made a complete recovery within a week's time. Much to the delight of my family, I was soon back to doing my regular chores.

Fortunately, the inhabitants of Big Springs, West Virginia, were very healthy and required little medical care. We consumed fresh vegetables, all home grown without the use of any chemicals, and we enjoyed good home cooking. We also drank plenty of fresh, pure spring water and kept active by hiking, walking, bicycling, and engaging in other such types of sports.

All in all, it was a true honor and privilege for me to have grown up in Big Springs, West Virginia. Despite the fact that we were financially poor, we were all like one big happy family and shared a special bond of love and a sense of community that no amount of money could buy. We cared about each other, looked out for each other, and helped each other, always with a strong sense of pride, trust, and mutual respect. I shall always cherish my memories of life in Big Springs for were it not for the hardships that we shared, I would never have known such loyalty and goodness.

Vincent Rocco Saladini, Sr.

1943, Big Springs, West Virginia
Vincent Saladini   Elio Bigiarelli

1943 Big Springs West Virginia
Tito Orsini   Vincent Saladini

Angelo Saladini
1943 Big Springs, West Virginia

June 2, 1946
Big Springs, West Virginia
Rose Marinni
Vincent Saladini   Elio Bigiarelli

38

Burney Petrucci

Vincent Saladini   Tito Orsini

July 7, 1946 Big Springs, West Virginia

July 4, 1948 Big Springs, West Virginia
Angelo Saladini, Dolly Saladini

Clara Saladini

Angelo Saladini
(holding Mary Joe Saladini)

July 4, 1948
Big Springs, West Virginia

Left to Right
Vincent Saladini, Lucy Saladini
June 2, 1946 Big Springs, West Virginia

39

Vincent Rocco Saladini, Sr.

Left to Right
Rose Wolfensberger, Minnie Smith, Ello Bigiarelli, Mary Bigiarelli

June 2, 1946
Big Springs, West Virginia
Stanley Wolfensberger, Joseph Saladini

July 7, 1946
Big Springs, West Virginia
Angelo Saladini, Dolly Saladini

Adam Caparotti Jr.

Rose Wolfensberger

June 9, 1946 Big Springs, West Virginia

40

June 2, 1946 Big Springs, West Virginia   Rose Wolfensberger

Lucy Saladini

June 2, 1946   Big Springs, West Virginia
Lucy Saladini, Rose Wolfensberger

Vincent Rocco Saladini, Sr.

BIG SPRINGS, WEST VIRGINIA
POPULATION 88

HOUSE# 1
Sam and Antoinette Chirelli
Angelina Chirelli
Ned Chirelli

HOUSE# 2
Pasquale and Cesarina Saladini
Amelia Saladini
Joseph Saladini
Teodolinda Saladini
Rosie Saladini
Minnie Saladini
Lucy Saladini
Vincent Saladini
Angelo Saladini
Carlo Rossi

HOUSE# 3
Angelo and Mabel Saladini
Kay Saladini
Sherry Saladini
Joan Saladini

HOUSE# 4
Umnberto and Regina Bigiarelli
Italo Bigiarelli
Elio Bigiarelli
Enase Bigiarelli

Mary Bigiarelli
Adolph Bigiarelli

HOUSE# 5
Henry and Mariana Angelo
Louie Angelo
Angelo Angelo
Mariana Angelo

HOUSE# 6
Sam and Ottava Piccolomini
John Piccolomini
Chris Piccolomini
Paul Piccolomini
Sam Piccolomini, Jr.
Yolanda Piccolomini
Angelina Piccolomini
Eva Piccolomini
Antoinetta Piccolomini

HOUSE# 7
Raymond and Mary Petrucci
Elizabeth Petrucci
Anthony Petrucci
Frank Petrucci
Bernard Petrucci
Tom Petrucci
Raymond Petrucci, Jr.

HOUSE# 8
Agostino and Francesca Saladini
Clemintine Saladini

Vincent Rocco Saladini, Sr.

Ralph Saladini
Angelo Saladini
Louise Saladini
Albina Saladini
Rose Saladini
Clara Saladini
Patsy Saladini
Elizabeth Saladini
Joseph Piccolomini

HOUSE# 9
Joseph and Cora Trenta

HOUSE# 10
Sam and Rachel Orsini
Tito Orsini
Jenny Orsini
Theresa Orsini
Uncle Alfredo Ferramini

HOUSE# 11
Mr. and Mrs. Qualini
Americus Qualini
Grace Qualini
Elizabeth Qualini

HOUSE# 12
Mrs. Carmela Rossi
Louie Rossi
Angelina Rossi
Frances Rossi

HOUSE# 13
Domenick De Stefano
Louie De Stefano
Orlando De Stefano

HOUSE# 14
Jim and Annie Smith
Tom Smith
Bob Smith
May Smith
Mary Smith
Edna Smith

There were 27 adults and 61 children.

CHAPTER SEVEN

SOCIAL LIFE AND ACTIVITIES

Although we lacked money, there were always plenty of activities for us to do at the village. The men would gather together on Sundays to play bocce, cards, horseshoes, and a game called "mota." In this game, two or more people would form a circle. They would then try to outguess the opponent as to the correct matching of the number of fingers thrown. For example, if I threw out two fingers and my opponent threw out two fingers, and I called out the number four, I would win a point. The object of mota was to match the total number of fingers thrown.

Music was another important activity in Big Springs. Once a month, Mr. Tony Marino, an accordion player from Hershey, Pennsylvania, would be invited to Big Springs, West Virginia, to play an array of Italian songs. Mr. Marino was a truly gifted and talented musician. The men

Hagerstown, Maryland
Rosie Saladini Crabtree

and women would enjoy dancing to their favorite Italian songs. Mr. Marino's visits would constitute an all-day affair with plenty of food, drinks, and laughter. A good time was always enjoyed by all, and the music served to bring all of us even closer together during these often harsh and trying times.

Each family would make homemade wine for family consumption based on the laws of the State of West Virginia. We were allowed to make several hundred gallons. When a neighbor or friend would visit, wine would be served as a gesture of hospitality. Wine was also served at mealtime. The men of the village were excellent winemakers. A favorite wine that they would make was from dandelions that grew wild in the area. Dandelion wine was a clear, yet powerful drink. One could only drink a small amount at a time due to its potency. Families would compete to determine who made the best wine. The men of the village also made wine from grapes and cherries. They would share each other's wines and then offer comments and suggestions on how to improve the taste, quality and texture of the wines.

Hagerstown, Maryland.
Minnie Saladini Smith

Each member of a family was assigned to perform certain chores in the household. My job was to milk two cows each morning and evening before and after school. We would supply enough milk to the inhabitants of the village. We would charge ten cents per quart. Our cows produced several gallons of milk per day.

I can recall an incident that occurred one day when I was milking the cows that caused me to become greatly upset at the time. I was milking one of our cows when my brother, Angelo, came into the barn and began talking to me about getting ready for school. The cow became so excited and nervous that he kicked the bucket of milk thus causing it to spill all over the floor of the barn. I began to cry and

April 24, 1944 Big Springs, West Virginia
Angelo Saladini

become upset because I thought that I would be short milk that day for our customers. Fortunately, I had already gotten enough milk from the cow before the incident to take care of all of our customers for that day. This was the only time that such an incident ever happened. I made sure from that point forward that when I milked our cows, no one would interrupt us ever again. My brother, Angelo, felt terrible about what had happened, however, I assured him that he should not worry since it was a freak accident and really not his fault.

I really loved my cows and treated them with a great deal of compassion. I would place my arms around my cows' necks before milking them and speak softly to them while stroking their heads and back. They were very kind and gentle animals, and I looked forward to our quiet time together.

1947 Big Springs, West Virginia
Lucy Saladini

My brother, Angelo, was in charge of helping to clean out the barn, to take care of the vegetable garden, and to help cut the firewood. He also helped to deliver the milk to our customers. Each member of the family was kept quite busy each day, and each of us knew our place and did as we were told. We recognized at an early age that we had to cooperate with each other if we were to survive the difficult times, and we all did out best to obey and to do as we were told. One of the social activities that I especially enjoyed was going down to the village square to listen to Sam Chirelli, who would read the *Italian-Progresso Newspaper* to the men who had gathered around him. He would read the newspaper aloud from cover to cover and explain every detail of the news along the way. I found this to be an extremely fascinating and educational experience as did the other men in the village.

It was during these times that the men of the village would open up to each other and share tales of their experiences in Italy as well as in America. Sharing in such tales was my way of catching up on world and local news. Unfortunately, Sam Chirelli was one of the few people in the village who was literate. Most of the other men in the village only had a second-grade education when they came over from Italy.

Vincent R. Saladini Sr.
Spading the garden
Big Springs, West Virginia, 1946

My mother, Cesarina, was an educated woman. She completed eight years of study in Italy. She would read all of the mail that the neighbors received from their family and friends in Italy. She would also write letters for the neighbors to send to their family and friends abroad. My mother was always so happy to be able to help out the other neighbors. She never asked for anything in return because she did it out of the goodness of her heart. She derived a great deal of pleasure out of being able to bring some joy into their lives and delighted in being able to help them maintain contact with their friends and loved ones in Italy.

Left to Right
Angelo Saladini, Vincent R. Saladini, Dolly Saladini
1943 Big Springs, West Virginia

The people of the village of Big Springs, West Virginia, were a self-sustaining and self-reliant group. They grew their own organic vegetables and raised hogs and chickens for meat. They also raised cows and goats for dairy products. My family made a variety of cheeses: mozzarella, ricotta, and smoked cheeses. They also made delicious ice cream and butter.

At butchering time, the neighbors would gather and help each other with the chores. Everyone always had a wonderful time sampling the various sausages and pork cuts for proper seasoning and taste.

Left to Right
Sherry Saladini, Tommy Petrucci, Madeline Angelucci
July 7, 1946 Big Springs, West Virginia

A large kettle would be placed over an open fire to boil the fat to make lard for preserving the various cuts of meat. While the fat was boiling, we would throw a chunk of meat into the boiling kettle. When the meat had browned to a crisp, we would remove the cooked meat and then place it between two towels to absorb the excess fat. The meat would be crisp on the outside, yet tender and succulent on the inside. We would then serve the meat

Rosa Wolfensberger (holding son Stanley) Hagerstown, Maryland 1943

51

on fresh baked slices of bread and eat to our heart's content.

Sausages would be preserved by placing them in a five gallon crock. The fat from the kettle would be poured over the sausages until the crock was filled to the top. The crock was then placed in the dry basement and allowed to cool. During the winter months the sausages would be removed as needed for meals when no other foods were available.

In addition to utilizing domesticated animals for food, the men of the village also hunted rabbits, squirrels, and quail. They were excellent hunters and experts in handling firearms. Hunting and survival techniques were taught to the males in the village at an early age in order to enable them to provide for themselves and their families when they reached adulthood. I must admit that I could never bring myself to hunt animals and did not partake in such activities.

Instead, one of my favorite activities was to gather walnuts. My brother, Angelo, and I would begin our day early in the morning, often at the crack of dawn. We would hike for several miles deep into the woods, each of us carrying a one hundred pound sack for the walnuts that we would gather. We would remain in the woods until we filled each sack. We would then shuck the walnuts right out in the

Left to Right
Mabel Saladini, Lucy Saladini
1948 Martinsburg, West Virginia

open woods before heading for home. When we arrived home, we would spread the walnuts out to dry. During the cold winter months, my mother and sisters would bake mouth-watering walnut pies and cakes, which we would enjoy all winter long. I can still remember the aroma of freshly baked walnut cinnamon cakes as it wafted through the rooms of our house filling every room with warmth and comfort.

My brother, Angelo and I also enjoyed gathering apples, peaches, and berries when they were in season. My mother, Cesarina, and my sisters, Amelia, Teodolinda, Rosie, Minnie and Lucy would make delicious fruit preserves as well as succulent fruit pies, which we would enjoy throughout the year. A special treat for us was a piping hot slice of fruit pie from the oven topped with a dollop of fresh homemade ice cream. We would all huddle together in the warmth of the kitchen and share stories while enjoying each other's company. Such comforting times shall remain with me forever.

Left to Right
Vincent R. Saladini, Patsy Saladini
April 5, 1948 Big Springs, West Virginia

Another of my favorite activities was hiking. Usually five or six boys from the village would gather together and decide on a place to hike. We would normally pack a light lunch to carry along on the trail. Whenever we grew thirsty, we would drink the cool water right from the flowing river since, in those days, the water was safe to drink. From time to time, we would rest alongside the river and share stories with one other before we resumed our hike.

One of our favorite spots to visit was an old abandoned warehouse, which was about six miles from my home. Since all of the windows were broken in the building, birds and other different animals such as squirrels, raccoons, and owls would make their homes there. Sometimes late at night when all was quiet, I could hear the faint rustling of the animals inside the warehouse as they scurried about to keep warm in the empty stillness. The warehouse reminded me of an old haunted house. It was covered with cobwebs and dust after many years of being unoccupied by humans, yet it held a special magic for us whenever we would gather there.

Eventually the warehouse was demolished because it was deemed to be unsafe. The walls were beginning to crumble and the beams were rotted beyond repair. I can remember feeling sad when I first returned to the empty spot where the warehouse once stood and hordes of animals once sought shelter. I could not help but feel emptiness and longing for our familiar landmark. Without a doubt, the homeless animals echoed my sentiments as they scurried about for a new home.

During one particular four- mile hike around Thanksgiving, when the weather became increasingly cold, we came upon a river which had high vines cascading from the trees above. I could not resist the urge to play "Tarzan." I decided to swing across the other side of the river using the vines to propel me. In my hurry, however, to grab one of the larger vines, I did not get a firm grip and my hands slipped, thus leaving me suspended over the center of the river. Unable to hold on any longer, I fell into the icy water below crying and saying to myself as I plummeted downward, "One dead fish!"

I was soaked from head to toe in the icy cold water. As my friends struggled to pull me from my four foot descent into the river, icicles had begun to form on my clothes. With the prospect of becoming a human Popsicle weighing heavily on my mind, I gathered the little strength that I had left and began running the four mile trek back home, all the while shivering uncontrollably.

When I arrived home my mother asked me what had happened. She immediately told me to stand in front of the wood burning stove in the kitchen while she wrapped me in warm woolen blankets. She then gave me a change of clothes and handed me a steaming hot cup of tea and clover honey. Eventually I warmed up and was able to stop shivering, but not before I vowed never again to play "Tarzan" over an icy cold river. The whole experience was not only totally humiliating, but also, dangerous as well.

Later that same day, my friends came over to offer me some comfort and plenty of friendly teasing. Fortunately I made a full recovery with no serious side effects other than an occasional reminder from my friends of that fateful day that I decided, most unsuccessfully, to become "Tarzan."

Another activity that I enjoyed very much was that of sledding with my friends during the icy cold winter months when there was a freshly fallen crest of snow blanketing the earth. My friends and I would gather together at the huge hill at Mueller's Farm, which was located about one half of a mile from the village. We would build a roaring campfire at the bottom of the hill, and then gather around the warm flames to sing and tell stories.

One sledding incident shall remain ingrained in my mind forever. The sled that I owned did not have any steering mechanism. Instead, I had to steer the sled using only my legs. One day while sledding down a steep and particularly icy hill, my sled began to pick up speed to the point where I was flying over the rough terrain, unable to control my sled as it headed straight for the bottom of the hill. I knew in an instant that I was in serious trouble because at the bottom of the hill was a barbed wire fence that had been installed to prevent someone from falling into the nearby pond.

Tomato Patch at Big Springs, West Virginia August 11, 1947

Kay Saladini   Madeline Angelo

Normally, I would have been able to stop in time to avoid the barbed wire fence. On this particular day, however, I was unable to stop my sled and proceeded to put my head down and brace myself for the nightmare that lay just ahead. In a matter of seconds, my sled crashed through the barbed wire fence and ensnared my upper lip before sending me hurling across the frozen pond. To this day I still bear the facial scars of that fateful day that my sled ran amok down the hill.

After washing the blood off my face in a nearby stream that still flowed freely, my sister Minnie who had been sledding with us that day, wrapped my face in bandages before we all headed back to the campfire to keep warm. Fortunately, we always carried a safety kit with us in case of an emergency, so we were prepared for my frightening accident.

I did not do any more sledding for the rest of the day. Instead I resigned myself to enjoying the warmth of the campfire and the company of good friends. A sign warning others of this dangerous condition was later posted. I was extremely grateful that my injury was not serious. I was not discouraged, however, from sledding in the days to come. Eventually my parents bought me a new sled that had a steering mechanism and was much safer to operate than my make-shift sled.

June 9, 1946
Big Springs, West Virginia
Vincent Saladini

Lucy Saladini, Vincent R. Saladini Sr.
Big Springs, West Virginia, 1946

57

Over the years my friends and I continued to enjoy sledding on the old hill until the land was eventually sold to make way for new homes. I still own and cherish my sled to this day; in fact, over the years my children have also enjoyed using it.

Another favorite activity enjoyed by all was that of dating. Unfortunately during the time period that I was growing up, dating girls or boys of non-Italian descent was looked upon most unfavorably by our parents. Some of my friends did ultimately marry girls and boys from other ethnic groups with some degree of success; however by and large, these relationships were total failures. The majority of the men in the village married girls from the village and raised their own families in and around the area.

January 12, 1948   Jamaica, New York City
Lucy Saladini

Another one of my favorite activities was called "pushing the rim." This game involved using a bicycle rim and a Y-shaped wire that we constructed ourselves. The goal behind this game was to steer the rim without losing control of it. This game required a tremendous amount of self-control, stamina, endurance, patience, and coordination. My friends and I would spend hours playing this game. Sometimes we would cover several miles in our quest to see who could travel the longest without losing control of the rim. Not only was this activity healthy for our minds and bodies, but also, it was inexpensive, challenging and just plain fun to do!

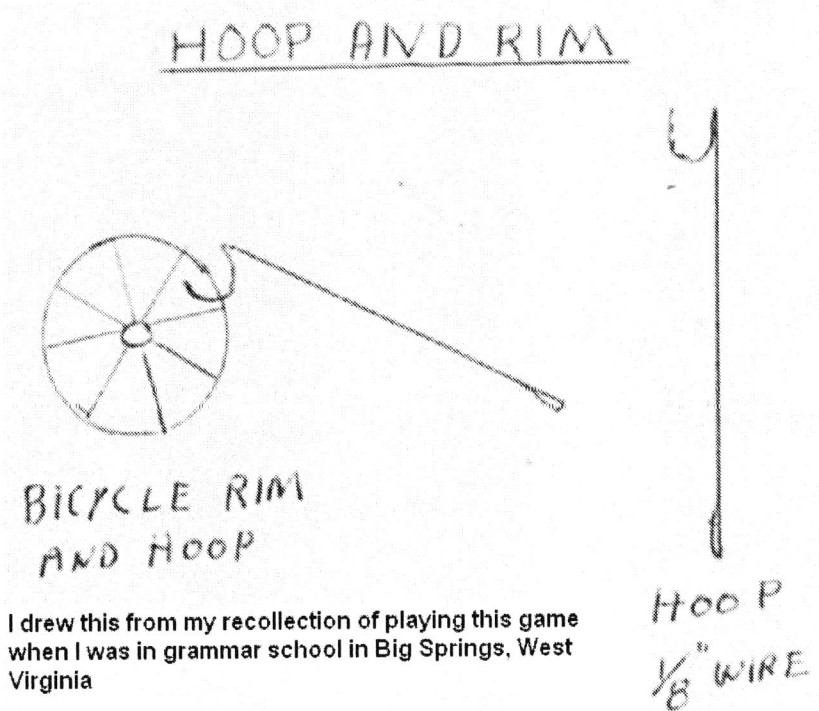

HOOP AND RIM

BICYCLE RIM
AND HOOP

I drew this from my recollection of playing this game when I was in grammar school in Big Springs, West Virginia

HOOP
1/8" WIRE

CHAPTER EIGHT

VILLAGE EDUCATION

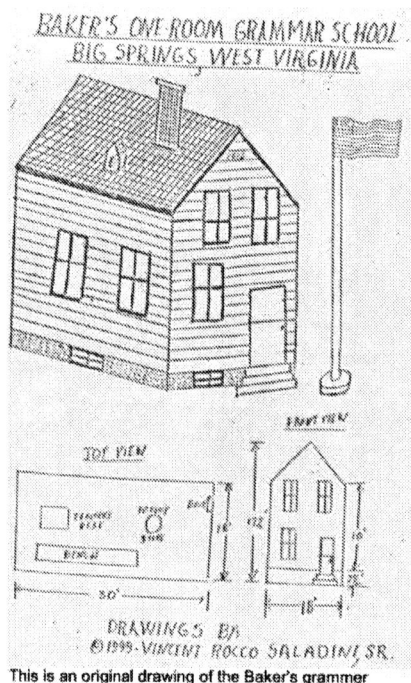

DRAWINGS BY
©1999-VINCENT ROCCO SALADINI SR.

This is an original drawing of the Baker's grammer school house in Big Springs, West Virginia. I drew this from my recollection of when I attended 1930-1938.

The village of Big Springs, West Virginia, consisted of a one-room wooden schoolhouse with outside plumbing. The school was heated with a wood burning, potbellied stove. My brother Carlo and I were responsible for keeping the stove burning. We would have to arrive one hour before classes were scheduled to begin in order to start the fire so that the schoolhouse would be warm and comfortable by the time the other students arrived at 9:00 a.m. We were paid $2.00 each per month.

Unfortunately, the schoolhouse was not equipped with a library or magazines. We did, however, have the most essential ingredient of all for an outstanding education—a group of devoted and caring professional teachers. I have always believed that it is not the outward beauty of the building that ensures an excellent education, but rather, the devoted staff members who run the school that truly counts.

Martinsburg, West Virginia
Interior of St. Joseph's Catholic Church

One of my fondest memories is that of our teacher, Ms. Clary. She always showed a genuine interest in teaching us not only what we needed to learn from books, but also, what we needed to learn from our life's experiences outside of the classroom. Although the teaching conditions were less than ideal, Ms. Clary achieved success with us because she was a highly motivated and organized woman who had a true love for her profession.

Martinsburg, West Virginia
AN EARLY PICTURE OF ST. JOSEPH'S CHURCH

The older children would assist the younger children whenever possible. We would have a music teacher come to our school once a week to teach us how to play the trumpet and trombone as well as how to read music.

In addition to receiving our public education, we were also taught our catechism and religious studies by nuns from St. Joseph's Roman Catholic Church in Martinsburg, West Virginia. Every Sunday after mass, the nuns would come to Big Springs, West Virginia, to give us our religious instructions to help prepare us to receive our First Holy Communion and Confirmation.

The nuns were very devoted and conscientious women who made our religious training a time of joy and fulfillment. They would peak our interest in the world around us through the eyes of the church. The nuns were held in high esteem, and they were deeply respected by all. Father Lackey, Pastor of St. Joseph's Church, would

Left to Right
Frank Larkin, Lucy Saladini, Sammy Piccolomini

occasionally come to Big Springs, West Virginia, to meet and converse with the children. We would enjoy his company since he was always such a kind, compassionate, and caring person. He always seemed to understand us and presented himself in such a way that we felt comfortable confiding in him.

In spite of all of the hardships that we endured, we always had the one thing that money could not buy— the love, trust, and respect of our parents. They instilled a strong sense of pride and self-worth in each of us and they helped us to cope with the many struggles that we were forced to face during the difficult times.

I firmly believe that the early childhood bond of love and trust that I shared with my parents and family helped me to overcome many of the difficulties that I encountered in my later years. Not only did I enjoy a sense of trust with my family members, but also, I felt a similar bond of trust and closeness with the other families in our small Italian community that had a population of eighty-eight people. We were all experiencing similar fates and we all stuck together and helped each other to make it through the difficult and trying times.

Unfortunately, many of the older children dropped out of school, as a result of a dying economy, and were forced to help support their families. The older boys went to work in the mines while the older girls remained at home to help care for the other members of the family who could not fend for themselves.

July 4, 1945 Big Springs, West Virginia
Vincent Saladini

In addition to taking care of the home, the women of the house were involved in performing many outside chores. For example, it was not at all uncommon to see the women of the village outdoors mixing the cement by hand when cement work was necessary. I can recall how my sister Lucy helped Joe, Angelo, and me mix cement in preparation for laying down a sidewalk.

In spite of the hard work, the women never complained. They also helped to spade the garden and prepare the soil for seeding. Because of the sacrifice and hard work by the women, we were able to survive such difficult times. I have always had the utmost respect and admiration for the women of the village of Big Springs, West Virginia. The older women of the village did not receive a formal education. Instead, they received an education in life. Such an education enabled them to endure the difficult times and to overcome whatever obstacles came their way.

In spite of a lack of a formal education, the people of Big Springs, West Virginia, had a natural ability to survive, and they used good common sense to solve problems. I can recall one particular incident that was a true testament to the stamina and ingenuity of my family. One day my cousin Pee Wee (Angelo) and my brother, Joe, had completely disassembled a Model A Ford and laid out all of the pieces on a table in a systematic order. I could not believe the number of parts that comprised one car. I asked them if they would be able to assemble the parts in the proper order so that the car would run once again.

Judging from the network of pieces before me, it seemed impossible that anyone could put the car back together again. Joe and Angelo remarked that they had placed the parts in the order that they removed them, and they would assemble the car engine in the same order. Much to my delight and amazement, after several hours of diligence and hard work, all of the parts were inserted into the car, and it was up and running in perfect order.

Most of the men in the village of Big Springs, West Virginia, seemed to have a natural talent for the arts and crafts. They were also very versatile in many trade areas, which enabled them to foster independence and a strong sense of self-reliance. It is astounding to think what these men might have accomplished if only they had been given the opportunity for formal, professional training.

Working in the mines enabled the men to become involved in many facets of construction and engineering. They had to work with precision while being mindful of the dangers that could result if their estimates were even slightly inaccurate. Just one mistake could mean the difference between life and death. In a way, their on-the-job training enabled them to acquire and hone their skills because Italians who were masters in the field of mining were supervising them.

My brother, Joe, was able to make any repairs required on our family car, a 1937 Chrysler, which was built as solid and sturdy as a Sherman tank. The metal on

Bigiarelli Family Car: 1939 Dodge

Saladini Family Car: 1937 Chrysler

the car was extremely thick and the engine was as sound as ever, especially since my brother, Joe, prided himself on keeping the car in top running condition.

Driving that car was one of the highlights of my youth. I learned to drive at a very early age as did the rest of the men of Big Springs, West Virginia. Back then it was essential to be as mobile as possible, especially since the job market was ever-changing, and we all had to be ready to grab hold of whatever opportunity for employment came our way.

I can recall one particular man, Frank Larkin, who would deliver groceries to the village on Saturdays. We would anxiously wait for his arrival so that we could take turns driving his pick-up truck from one house to the next. Mr. Larkin never seemed to mind since we saved him from having to make each individual delivery stop, and no harm would come due to very little traffic in that area.

I will never forget how happy and excited I was the day I officially received my driver's license. All of my brothers and sisters took the driver's test on the 1937 Chrysler. There was no automatic drive or power steering in the 1937 Chrysler. Instead, there was only a stick shift. Driving the 1937 Chrysler required tremendous skill and stamina. One had to have excellent driving skills to pass the road test that was given back then because the West Virginia State Troopers accompanied the driver during the road test to make certain that he/she was proficient and capable of driving in a safe and cautious manner.

When I took my driver's test, the trooper made me drive up a steep hill and then required me to pull over to the side of the road and come to a complete stop. I was then asked to start up the car and proceed up the hill, which required tremendous skill because I had to be mindful of the clutch and the gas pedal, all the while knowing that a trooper was sitting right beside me the entire time.

Fortunately, like the rest of my brothers and sisters, I passed the driver's test without any difficulty. I knew at this point that I had truly earned my driver's license. Knowing how difficult it is to pass the driver's test in West

Virginia instilled in me a deep respect for West Virginia drivers.

One might find it unusual to hear such names as "Minnie" and "Lucy" for Italian children because they were not their true birth names. The Italians living in Big Springs, West Virginia, gave their children American names upon their children's enrollment at the Baker Grammar School. While it was a common practice during those days to Americanize a child's name whenever possible, the Italian children largely preferred to maintain their Italian birth names because they were proud of their heritage at an early age.

There was really little choice, however, since the school authorities back then would automatically change our names from the Italian to the American version on all legal documents once we were enrolled to attend school. Such a practice was thrust upon us with little regard for our wishes since it was believed that the American versions of our names were easier to pronounce than the Italian versions. At home, however, our families continued to address us by our Italian names so that we would never forget our heritage and would continue to be proud of our Italian background and who we truly were.

CHAPTER NINE

LIFE AT THE MINES

Photo of the mines at Martinsburg, West Virginia
June 19, 1945

Life at the mines consisted of long hours which ranged anywhere from twelve to fourteen hours a day, generally seven days a week. The men had to walk several miles each day just to get to the job site, all the while carrying with them such heavy equipment as jack hammers, shovels, picks and any other necessary equipment. The work was exhausting and draining, and it required a tremendous amount of physical and emotional stamina on the men's part.

My father first started to work for the Standard Lime and Stone Company in 1904. At that time, the mining site consisted of a large open field. Over time and after many years of digging, the men finally dug far enough into the earth to form a huge pit. Once the men dug down approximately fifty to sixty feet into the earth, they were able to start tunneling into the side of the hole that they had dug. Eventually, they ended up with seven different mine entrances that extended several miles under the earth.

In those early days, the men were required to walk into the mines to the jobsite as in previous times. They did not begin to receive any pay until they actually reached the jobsite, which usually took one hour or more.

As time passed, the men became extremely proficient in mining technology. They were very capable and they learned their skills quickly. My father, Pasquale, actually became a foreman, but he was eventually removed from that position because of the language barrier.

Elio Bigiarelli, Enase Bigiarelli, Vincent Saladini
The mines at Martinsburg, West Virginia

Nevertheless, my father, Pasquale, was an exceptionally talented and intelligent man. I can remember his doing complicated mathematical calculations in his head without writing them down. He was also most adept at pioneering new technologies to make mining more efficient and less hazardous to the men without sacrificing the quality of the work performed.

My brother, Joe, went to work for Standard Lime and Stone Company after graduating from Martinsburg High School around 1934. Since he had worked on Mr. Burkhart's farm in Martinsburg, West Virginia, Joe was familiar with handling horses. His first job assignment was to handle the mules that were used for pulling the carts at the mines. Joe had these mules highly trained.

I can recall one particular mule by the name of Fanny. My brother, Joe, would give the command, and Fanny would automatically back up to a cart filled with rock. She would then remain there until she was hitched up to the cart. Fanny would then pull the cart to the holding center where the cart was unloaded. She would then return to the original site to wait for the next cart to be pulled. Fanny was truly a highly disciplined and intelligent animal.

Elio Bigiarelli
The mines at Martinsburg, West Virginia

My brother, Joe, was made foreman, a position that my father previously held. Joe had an excellent command of mining skills as well as a keen mechanical mind. He always excelled in school. As a result of dire financial circumstances, however, Joe was unable to attend college and become an engineer. I can recall many instances when my father and Joe would discuss different job opportunities. My father would offer his views and suggestions and

71

each would always keep an open mind as to future possibilities for employment.

Not only was Joe very successful on the job, but also, he was well liked and equally respected and trusted by the management. He was able to relate to the management as well as to the workers, and he took pride in sharing his mining skills and knowledge of mining technologies with his fellow workers. Joe had the benefit of supervising the Italian miners from Big Springs, West Virginia, where he was raised. They shared a special rapport and mutual respect and admiration for each other that strengthened over time. The miners had the highest respect for Joe's keen mining skills and for his knowledge of mining technologies.

The mines at Martinsburg, West Virginia

Italo Bigiarelli

Elio Bigiarelli

The men of Big Springs, West Virginia, had many different skills and abilities, which enabled them to adapt to many different situations. Sam Chirelli was in charge of keeping the pump house in running order, which was crucial to the proper function of the mines. He was responsible for making certain that the water was pure and that the pumping system was working properly. Sam Chirelli successfully undertook this challenging position and displayed his skills and capabilities evey step of the way.

Ralph Saladini, my cousin, worked in the chemical laboratory. There they analyzed the quality of the cement that was being produced in the mines. The rock that was mined was used for making cement products as well as for producing steel. Many tons of rock were shipped to the steel mills throughout the country. According to my father and brother, the rock mined there was of the highest quality and as such, was in high demand at that time.

My cousin, Angelo Saladini, was a scaler who was capable of climbing great heights. He would climb up a one hundred foot ladder and then scale loose rock in order to prevent anyone from becoming injured from the falling rock. This particular job required a person who was in top physical condition. In order to maintain the physical stamina and conditioning required for such a job, Angelo would climb a twenty-five foot flagpole without any ropes for support. Even though he weighed only 130 pounds, Angelo was exceptionally strong and agile, and he had extraordinary stamina. Like my brother Joe, Angelo was also highly respected and well liked by the management as well as by his co-workers. During his mining career,

Angelo received many commendations from the management for his excellent work history.

Interestingly enough, the first and only woman from the village ever hired by the company to work in the mines was Mariana Angelo, the widow of Henry Angelo, who worked in the mines for over fifty years. She worked as the maintenance woman for the company. Despite the hard work, Mariana was happy with her job and she took great pride in her work. Born and raised in Italy, Mariana did not receive a formal education. As the maintenance woman for the company, Mariana was able to receive all of the benefits offered such as medical care and free housing.

Mr. Umberto Bigiarelli was recognized as one of the best ladder makers in the country. His ladders were sturdy and well constructed. He used only the finest wood. His ladders were also well known for their safety features. His talent for making ladders was recognized throughout the mining industry. Mr. Bigiarelli was also recognized as being an exceptional carpenter.

I would enjoy many long and informative conversations with him. He was a very intelligent man as well as a pleasant individual who delighted in sharing his love of his craft with others. He took great pride in his ladder making and never missed an opportunity to improve upon the many safety features that he created to make the task of mining less dangerous for all concerned.

The remaining group of Italians, because of their language barrier, did general mining. They would work wherever they were needed. I would go down to the bank of the mine and watch the men working in the open cut (pit). They had to be experts in handling explosives since they were required to blast out large rocks using explosives and then break them into small pieces so that they could actually be loaded on small trucks and transported to a holding place for crushing.

I can recall my father's saying that he had loaded seventeen trucks and had received nineteen cents per truck. The work was grueling and backbreaking. Fortunately, all of the men were young, healthy, and strong, which enabled them to meet the challenge. While engaging in such labor, the men needed to drink plenty of water because the pit (cut) became extremely hot, and they did not have any protection from the blazing rays of the sun. Since dehydration was an ever- present problem for the men, it was necessary to provide them with plenty of fresh water to drink while they were working.

I would occasionally go to the mines where my father was working. I would help him to load rock onto the cars. Although I was only twelve years old at the time, no one complained because I was physically big and strong for my age, and I could easily pass for sixteen years of age.

In the early days, the workers had very few benefits for themselves and their families. They lacked medical services and benefits. They were largely at the mercy of the mining company. I can recall one incident that occurred on Christmas Day. My father was off from work. He had planned on staying home to enjoy the holiday with his family. His plans were soon altered when a worker from the mines came to our house and informed my father that he was needed on the job.

I could see the look of disappointment on my father's face at the prospect of not being able to spend Christmas with our family. He was not in a position to protest because if he did, he would lose his job, and he could not afford to be without an income, however small it might be.

Reluctantly, my father went to work. To make matters even worse, my father was not given any extra compensation for giving up his holiday with his family. Instead, he was paid only straight time for his efforts; overtime pay was non-existent at the mines in those early days. The workers endured many hardships and abuses that today would never be permitted. Back then, there was no one to look out for the rights of the miners. Times were hard and the miners lived under the constant threat of losing their jobs if they so much as dared to challenge the rules and regulations set up by the mining company.

The miners' lives were on the line every day that they worked. Little if anything was done to ensure their health and safety. I can recall seeing the men exit the mines at the end of a long and exhausting day. They were completely covered with lime dust to the point where they looked like snowmen. There was no protective gear for them to wear, and no precautions were taken by the mining company in those early days to ensure their health and safety. The quality of life meant little if anything to the mining company whose sole purpose was to see that the job was done at any cost, even if the miners had to suffer health problems in order for the job to get done.

Good medical care was completely lacking in those early days. One particular incident that clearly illustrated this point concerned my brother, Joe. One day while working, Joe got his hand caught between two rocks, severely crushing his fingers. He went to the company doctor who simply bandaged his hand without ever taking any x-rays. As a result of this type of primitive medical care, Joe's fingers sustained permanent damage.

Unfortunately, there was no recourse to remedy this tragic situation for there was no one to complain to or turn to for help. Instead, Joe was forced to live with the consequences of such poor medical care. Perhaps the greatest tragedy of all was that Joe was no longer able to play the musical instruments that he loved due to his failure to receive the proper medical care for his injuries.

When the workers were no longer able to tolerate such deplorable working conditions, they organized a union. In the early stages of their organizing such a union, the workers met a tremendous amount of resistance from the company. They were threatened with the loss of their jobs if they joined the union and were treated with complete disrespect. After many years of struggle and hardship, the workers succeeded in forming a union to protect their rights.

Unfortunately, the workers' efforts did not come without a price. I can remember "Goon Squads" coming to Big Springs, West Virginia, to threaten and intimidate the workers. The "Goon Squads" would throw rocks at our homes and threaten us with bodily harm if we joined the union or persisted in forming a union. The Italian workers resisted these threats and fought back as hard as they could to protect their rights. Eventually, after many years of struggle and perseverance on the workers' part, things began to calm down and return to normal. The workers had prevailed and a new era was born for the workers' rights. It was a difficult time, but it was also a proud time for the workers.

The men who remained behind at Big Springs, West Virginia, all worked at the mines, including my brother, Joe Saladini, my cousin, Angelo Saladini, and my friends, Italo Bigiarelli, Americus Qualini, John Piccolomini, Chris Piccolomini, Louie Rossi, and Chris Angelo. Those who remained behind did not have many options since job opportunities were extremely scarce and monies were hard to come by in those days. A college education was also an impossibility because of the lack of financial resources and scholarships available to the people at that time. Because all of the men were young, eager, and talented, they did not have any difficulty performing their jobs successfully.

Conditions at the mines improved somewhat with the coming of the union. Wages were increased, and the working conditions were better. The workers also had more job security and some medical benefits.

As previously stated, it was extremely difficult for the men to organize the union during the early years of the labor movement because of the constant resistance by the management and their ever present threat to terminate any worker who joined the union. It took a tremendous amount of courage and perseverance by the men of Big Springs, West Virginia, especially because they were constantly being threatened by the scabs who did not want to organize such a union. After much struggle, the union was born, and peace and harmony eventually prevailed among all concerned.

The improvements in working conditions were encouraging. Instead of only being paid by walking to the jobsites, as was the former practice, the workers were now paid from the moment they clocked in at the mines. Moreover, instead of having to walk to the jobsite, the workers were now driven down with their equipment. There was a vast improvement in working conditions from the time my father first began to work in the mines.

The company continued to strengthen its relationship with the employees. For example, the company would hold a picnic every summer and invite all of the families and employees from Big Springs, West Virginia. Everyone always had a good time, and the workers would look forward to this pleasant and enjoyable gathering each summer.

We would spend the day eating homemade meals prepared by the women of

This is the drill for producing rock material.

Mines were closed in the late 1960s. Then they started to quarry stone on top of the mines.

Quarry that provides stone from which all cement products are made and shipped.

the village. We would also take part in events such as: horseshoes, potato sack racing, the one hundred yard dash, and rope pulling. In addition, we also enjoyed fun contests such as: pie eating, apple bobbing and watermelon eating. The delicious pies were usually homemade. No one could resist such delicacies, and there were rarely any pies left over by the end of the picnic. At the end of the day, all of the children and their parents would gather around the campfire, roast marshmallows, sing songs, and tell stories under a blanket of stars that seemed to stretch forever. Such special moments made all of the struggles worthwhile, and a feeling of unity, love, and caring filled the air. The company would also sponsor a softball team during the summer season. The employees would participate after all of their work was done for the day. Although I was only approximately fifteen years old at the time, I was allowed to play on the team whenever my tight schedule would allow. I was an excellent catcher and the men, cognizant of my talent as a catcher, were eager to have me play on their team.

The Standard Lime and Stone Company had an outstanding team whose members participated in the sport and played for the sheer love of the game. We did not receive any type of financial reward for playing on the team. I was especially fond of playing softball as well as hardball.

Unfortunately, I could not spend too much time playing ball since I worked in the tailor shop during the summer. My employer, John Ferro, however, recognized my deep love for the sport and gave me time off to play on the team whenever possible. I shall always be grateful to Mr. Ferro for his understanding and compassion towards me during those years. He was truly a fine, upstanding gentleman whose deep sense of caring and compassion allowed me to still be a boy, even though I was forced to work like an adult in order to help support my family.

CHAPTER TEN

FOND CHILDHOOD MEMORIES

As I reflect upon my early childhood days spent at Big Springs, West Virginia, I never realized how poor we actually were back then. While we could not afford the material riches that so many others enjoyed, we were wealthy beyond words where love was concerned. My family and I shared a special bond of love, loyalty, and genuine concern that filled our lives with warmth and instilled in each of us a sense of being that was unsurpassed and beyond any monetary value.

Growing up in the absence of material riches was difficult at times, but we always made the best of every negative situation. I can recall one time as a young ten year old child, when the local ice cream company, in order to induce people to buy Popsicles, would inscribe the word "FREE" on certain Popsicle sticks. Unfortunately, we were too poor to indulge in such a luxury as being able to purchase a Popsicle.

Instead, my friends and I would gather together around the roadside deli on Highway 81, which was about one and one-half miles from our home. We would scout the area for discarded Popsicle sticks, each one hoping to find the one lucky stick that would allow us to receive a free Popsicle. Sometimes we would search the highway for hours before finding one "FREE" stick. When we were lucky enough to find a "FREE" stick, we would race to the deli and share our good fortune with each other. This was always a real treat for us since we could not afford to buy a Popsicle.

What often made matters worse was when we would see the wealthy people in town drive up to the deli in their fancy cars with their dogs. They would buy Popsicles for their dogs, and we could only watch with our mouths watering as the dogs hungrily devoured the icy cold Popsicles.

We would all stand around hoping that when the dogs were finished with their Popsicles, their owners would throw away a "FREE" stick so that we could have a Popsicle, too. We made a pact that we would remain until each of us got at least one free Popsicle or until each of us was at least able to share our Popsicle with a friend who did not find a "FREE" stick.

We kept our Popsicle game a secret from our parents because we knew that they would not have approved of our activities. We also did not want them to feel hurt because they did not have the money to give us to buy a Popsicle. It was many years later before we finally told our parents about our little game. As we guessed, they clearly did not approve!

Another fond memory of my early childhood days was playing baseball on an open cow pasture, which we had converted into a ball field. The farmer who owned the land was a kind and compassionate man who realized our love of baseball and who happily allowed us to use his field. The ground was rocky and rough. We would collect all of the rocks and lay them aside. We would use old bed cushions for our bases. I recall some of the older boys' playing baseball on a cool summer afternoon and can still smell the fragrant scent of hay and flowers wafting on the breeze as the boys raced around the bases to score a homerun. The older boys were always eager to teach us baseball techniques, and we happily accepted their assistance.

My brother, Joe, would play catch with me for hours on end. He would throw the ball to me at full speed. Fortunately, I was capable of handling his curve ball and his fast ball without incident. I really learned so much about the game of baseball from him. Moreover, my friend, Italo Bigiarelli, would hit fly balls in batting practice so that we could gain some experience. Ralph Saladini would also give me catching tips since he was an excellent catcher.

Johnny Piccolomini, a master pitcher with a natural talent for throwing the ball, delighted in offering us pitching tips to improve our game. I can recall one particular game against Martinsburg, West Virginia, when Johnny struck out twenty-one batters in a row to the cheer of the roaring crowd. Unfortunately, Johnny never pursued a professional baseball career, for like the rest of the young men in the village, his work in the mines came first.

The older boys found time to form a baseball team called "Big Springs." The team included Johnny Piccolomini as pitcher, Ralph Saladini as catcher, Joe Saladini as centerfield, Angelo Saladini as shortstop, Paul Piccolomini as third baseman, Louie DeStefano as left field, Americus Qualimi as right field, Chris Piccolomini as second base, Italo Bigiareli as first base, and Orlando DeStefano as relief pitcher. Since the team only had ten players, it was critical that no one missed even one game. If a player could not be present for any reason, I was called in to substitute for the missing player; it was a challenge which I met with the greatest enthusiasm imaginable.

Another fond memory of my early childhood concerned the manner in which my father handled discipline problems. With a large family including eight children, one had to be creative and patient in order to keep discipline problems to a minimum. My father had a unique method of getting the children's attention. For as long as I can remember, my father always wore a large brim hat. Whenever he placed his hand on his hat, it meant that he was about to use it.

I can vividly recall one particular time when I had disobeyed my father's orders, and he was about to reprimand me. As he started to approach me, I figured that I could outrun him, an error in judgment on my part that cost me dearly. As I started to run, I looked back at my father just in time to see him raise his hand to his hat. As quick as a flash, my father flung his hat at me like a frisbee, and with pin- point accuracy, his hat landed directly on the back of my head. If hat tossing had been an Olympic sport, there is no doubt in my mind that my father would have taken home the gold medal!

I immediately stopped running and meekly walked back towards my father. I knew that I had been outsmarted and that his message was rather loud and clear. When I reached my father, he reprimanded me for having disobeyed him and for having tried to run away from him. He then put his arms around me, hugged and kissed me, and told me that he still loved me no matter what. I soon realized that my father did not have to chase me at all to get my attention. He simply had to touch his large brim hat as a gentle reminder that he could not be outsmarted and that he expected to be obeyed.

When we were youngsters, we found many different activities to keep us occupied and out of trouble. One of our favorite pastimes was to go down to the nearby highway, sit on top of the grassy knoll, and watch the various cars go by for hours on end. We would count the various license plates of the different states that were represented by the cars that traveled along the highway. The person who had the largest variety of states would be the winner. We always found this activity to be fun and challenging as well as educational. We reached a point where we were able to recognize the names and license plates of every state in the Union as well as the make and model of the cars being driven.

Still another fond memory of my living in Big Springs, West Virginia, was visiting the company store that was owned and operated by the Standard Lime and Stone Company. The company store was ideally located in the center of the village. This made it accessible as well as convenient for everyone.

The building that housed the store was a quaint one story wooden framed structure that was heated by a wood burning pot-bellied stove. Like all of the homes in the village, the bathrooms were located outside. A faucet was installed for the purpose of drinking water and for washing hands before handling food.

Ned Orsini managed the company store. He was a huge, strapping man who was 6'4" tall and weighed about 220 pounds. He was also well-built and extremely muscular. Mr. Orsini, the father of six sons, was a well-respected and revered member of the village. He was not only pleasant, compassionate, kind, and understanding, but also, trustworthy and honest when dealing with the people of the village. Many times he would offer the children of the village free candy because he knew how scarce monies were in those days, and he also knew how special such a treat was to the children whose parents could not afford to buy such a luxury.

The company store itself was picturesque, like a painting on a wall, so typically country, so typically Italian. I can vividly recall the barrels filled with sugar, nuts, rice, beans, salt, and other fine and tempting products. The shelves were always stacked with huge cans of olives, boxes of pasta, and jars of spaghetti sauces. The company store also carried a variety of household products such as soaps, brooms, detergents, and other such items.

As a young child, I would marvel at the interior design of the store, and the neat and orderly manner in which all of the inviting items were so meticulously displayed. Everywhere I looked, there was some new and interesting item to see and experience. I shall also never forget the sweet, fragrant smells that filled the air inside the store including cinnamon, dried herbs such as basil and parsley, and scented candles of rich vanilla and strawberry filling my senses.

Since all of the families of the village baked their own bread, the company store always stocked plenty of 100 pound sacks of flour. The cloth flour bags would later be used by the women of the village of Big Springs, West Virginia, to make clothes for their families. The company store also carried a variety of dried and fresh cheeses. Among them were mozzarella, parmesan, and provolone.

In addition to selling fine Italian delicacies, the company store also functioned as a warm and informal gathering place where the men of the village would meet and reminisce about the good old days in Italy. The women of the village would occasionally meet there as well to discuss their children and families although most of the time they were too busy caring for their families to frequent the store.

Sadly, the company store was demolished in or around 1931 and a grand tradition was lost forever. Mr. Orsini moved to Bunker Hill, West Virginia, a small village about three miles south of Big Springs, West Virginia. He purchased a small dairy farm and eventually sold milk to the people in the area. His sons also assisted him with the many chores required to properly work the dairy farm. Mr. Orsini and his wife have long since passed away. Unfortunately, his oldest son, Angelo, was killed in a bulldozer accident. Many of his remaining descendants, however, still live in the area. In fact, some became prosperous and highly respected business owners who long remained active in their communities.

Another fond memory that shall always remain with me was getting together with a group of my friends and relatives to share good times. Whenever we did get together, we comprised a large group consisting of Elio Bigiarelli, Tito Orsini, Jenny Orsini, Patsy Saladini, Mary Bigiarelli Caponi, Minnie Saladini Manspeaker, Rosie Saladini Crabtree, Lucy Saladini Cutrone, Elizabeth Saladini Bigiarelli, Angelo P. Saladini, Sr., Sammy Piccolomini, and Angelina Piccolomini.

We would form a huge circle on the lawn and take turns telling stories. Our gatherings were always a huge success and extremely fun to attend. The women would serve tea and fresh homemade breads, pies, cookies, and cakes. We would sit and talk for hours. We had the utmost love and respect for one another, and we shared a bond of trust and closeness that could not be broken despite the ravages of time. We could truly confide in one another, and we knew that we could always rely on the love and trust that we shared to help us cope with the difficult times that we often faced.

While we may not have been materially wealthy, we shared a love and bond of loyalty that no amount of money could ever buy, all of which made us far richer than the richest man. It was our deep sense of love for one another that gave us the emotional stability to endure the many hardships that often befell us during those trying times. Whenever we had a problem, there was always someone there ready and willing to listen and to lend a helping hand without being critical or judgmental. I shall always cherish the warm memories of my family and friends, and I shall be forever grateful for having been blessed to share in their love and trust.

Another fond memory was the first of May. It was always a happy occasion for the children of the village of Big Springs, West Virginia, because it marked the official day when we would take off our shoes and go barefoot until school re-opened in September.

I can recall that after going barefoot for several months, my feet would become so calloused that I was able to walk over the roughest terrain without feeling any pain whatsoever. We would have races in our bare feet to see who could travel the fastest through the open fields. The sheer joy of experiencing the dewy earth beneath my feet made me feel like a king. Another unexpected benefit of going barefoot for several months was the fact that it gave our parents a break from having to buy us new shoes. More importantly, we cherished every moment of being allowed to go barefoot and dreaded the thought of having to wear shoes again once school started. Luckily, we never had any health problems with our feet, and always looked forward to our yearly tradition with joy and delight.

When I was a youngster, I would enjoy going down to the chemistry lab at the mines to chat with the workers. I will always have fond memories of speaking with Mr. Drysbox, the head chemist. The lab was responsible for making certain that the products produced at the mines were of the highest quality. The Standard Lime and Stone Company was well recognized and highly respected throughout the area for its quality cement products. I was always fascinated each time that I visited the lab, especially when I was able to speak with Mr. Drysbox. He was a very understanding and intelligent man whose warm, inviting personality made it a pleasure to speak with him. Mr. Drysbox would always allow me to observe him while he worked, and he would explain, along the way, what he was doing and why he was performing each particular task.

One day while I was visiting the lab, Mr. Drysbox asked me what career I intended to pursue and what plans I had for the future. I was twelve years old at the time and had just begun an apprenticeship program as a custom tailor with John Ferro in Martinsburg, West Virginia. I worked after school, on Saturdays, and during the summer months.

I told Mr. Drysbox of my hopes and plans for the future. As I explained to him, I always dreamed of attending college, but deep down inside, I knew that it would be impossible for me to do so because of my family's impoverished financial situation. My second choice was to become as highly skilled as possible in the useful trade of custom tailoring. As I spoke to Mr. Drysbox, his face lit up, and he looked me straight in the eyes as he gently placed his hands upon my shoulders. He said to me, "Son, whatever career you choose to follow, just always make sure that you become the very best in your choice." I have never forgotten his advice.

Mr. Drysbox left a deep and lasting impression upon me. His sincerity and heartfelt wisdom were a great source of comfort to me during difficult times. I always looked upon him with the utmost respect and admiration and have always tried to follow his advice by working hard to become the very best at whatever I set my mind to accomplishing. Mr. Drysbox was an inspiration and an unparalleled role model for me, and I shall never forget what he taught me.

Another of my fond memories as a youngster was enjoying the many school picnics that we had while attending Baker's Grammar School. We would all gather together with our teacher, Mrs. Clary, and head down to the creek for a cookout. She would bring hotdogs, marshmallows, and hamburgers for us to eat. Our parents would supply freshly baked buns, hot and aromatic right from the oven.

We would quench our thirst with refreshing homemade lemonade and homemade root beer. We would then make a huge campfire out of twigs and dried branches that we gathered in the nearby woods. We took great pride in finding just the right size twigs for roasting the hotdogs and marshmallows over the open fire. We would grill the hamburgers over an open barbecue pit that was permanently installed at the campsite.

Whenever sweet corn was in season, we would boil it in a five- gallon can over the open fire. The farmers in the area would allow us to pick the corn right from the stalks free of charge. The fragrant aroma of the sizzling meats and freshly baked buns would waft through the air as it whet our appetites all the more.

For entertainment our teacher would have all of us sit around the campfire and sing songs and tell stories. We would delight in coming up with the scariest tales imaginable. When we had our fill of spooky tales, we would then take part in running contests and three-legged races in order to determine the fastest runner.

As the afternoon wore on and the summer heat became increasingly unbearable, we would race down to the creek and jump in to cool off. Since we had dammed off a part of the creek, it was several feet deep, which was more than deep enough for swimming. The creek also had a mud bottom that we delighted in stirring up with our feet as we frolicked and splashed about to ward off the summer heat.

I will forever cherish the precious memories of my childhood days at Baker's Grammar School. Ms. Clary was a wonderful role model for all of us. She was more than a teacher. She was also a friend and confidante. She instilled in us a sense of pride in who and what we were, and she helped us to recognize our potential to become whatever our hearts desired. She made us realize that the only limitations that we had were those that we imposed upon ourselves. It is no wonder that Ms. Clary had won the love, trust, and respect of the children as well as the parents of the village of Big Springs, West Virginia.

In spite of the many hardships that we were made to endure at the mining village, we enjoyed an equal number of pleasant memories. My early childhood experiences taught me to be honest, trustworthy, and loyal, and respectful of the feelings and rights of others. I enjoyed a childhood that was rich in love and filled with warmth and a strong sense of security. We trusted and respected one another, and we were always there for each other emotionally as well as spiritually. As I moved into adulthood, the values that were so deeply instilled in me as a child enabled me to pattern my own life in the same manner and to bring to my own family and friends the values that meant so much to me as a young child growing up in Big Springs, West Virginia.

Another memorable experience that I recall as a young child occurred when I was approximately eleven years old. My brothers and sisters and I had walked from our home in Big Springs, West Virginia, to Martinsburg, West Virginia, to attend Mass at St. Joseph's Church. It was customary for us to walk since we did not own an automobile at that time.

We attended Mass and then set out for the long trek back home again. When I had walked about fifty feet from the church, I spotted a five-dollar bill on the sidewalk. I picked it up, believing it to be play money at first. When I realized that it was a real five-dollar bill, I raced all the way home to give it to my father. When I handed him the bill, he asked me where I had gotten the money. Excitedly, I told him how I had found it. Only then did he accept the money. In those days, five dollars equaled two days' pay for my father. Being the generous man that he was, my father shared our good fortune with our family and friends.

I shall be forever grateful to my parents for being the wonderful role models that they were. My brothers, sisters and I all had the utmost love and respect for our parents. I can recall one warm summer night when my father decided to take a nap outside on a bench that was surrounded by fragrant honeysuckle blossoms. The aroma was simply exquisite.

I knew my father was exhausted from working so many long hours at the mines. I decided to kiss him quietly on the cheek so as not to awaken him from his peaceful slumber. As I bent down to gently kiss him, he opened his eyes and gave me a big smile and a warm, tender hug. He then fell softly back to sleep. As I sat down beside him and watched silently for a few moments, I could not help but feel the utmost love and tenderness for my father. Even now when I recall this precious moment in my life it brings tears to my eyes, and for a moment, I am once again that little boy of long ago sitting beside my father amidst the fragrant honeysuckle blossoms that perfumed the air that warm summer night.

Another fond childhood memory was watching my mother and sisters bake fresh cakes, pies, cookies, and bread. My mother would always be sure to leave extra swirls of chocolate in the bowl when she was through baking so that we could all gather around to lick the bowl. That delicacy was an added bonus to the real treat still to come. We would all wait around anxiously for that first tantalizing morsel to come out of the oven so that we could all have a taste while it was still hot and gooey. My mother never seemed to mind our eating half of her baked goodies before they ever had a chance to cool. The aroma of freshly baked pastries throughout the house on baking day was indescribable and ever so pleasurable. My mother would use only the freshest ingredients: fresh milk, eggs, and creamy butter, which we mostly produced ourselves.

Sunday mornings were a particular favorite of mine. Because our bedroom was directly over the kitchen, we enjoyed the added pleasure of smelling the delightful aromas of mother's Sunday dinner which always included a huge simmering pot of meatballs, sausage, and gravy. My mother would prepare the meats and sauce early in the morning and then let the pot simmer slowly for several hours. The aroma was mouth-watering.

Once that delectable scent wafted its way upstairs, we knew that before long we would be sitting down to another delicious meal of homemade pasta, meat, and tomato sauce. I could not wait to dunk chunks of freshly baked bread into the leftover sauce. My mother was an excellent cook, who was constantly creating new and different ways to prepare delicious meals with whatever foods were on hand.

Each meal at our home was like a banquet. All of the children would gather around the large wooden table to be fed. Meals were almost always served family style with huge platters of food placed in the center of the table. We would start with one platter, take our share from that platter, and then pass it along to the person sitting next to us. We would continue this pattern until everyone had a chance to sample all of the foods being served. My mother always made sure to prepare plenty of food so that no one ever went hungry. There was always enough food for our family as well as for whatever friends might happen to stop by from the village for a bite to eat. My family always welcomed them with open arms. In fact, my mother always said that good food and good friends went together like bread and butter.

Lunchtime at our house was always memorable. I recall one particular day when my mother was preparing sandwiches for lunch. My nine brothers and sisters and I were eating the sandwiches as fast as my mother could prepare them. My mother kept making sandwiches until we were all happily fed. One of my favorite sandwiches was an omelet made with fresh eggs, peppers, and prosciutto (ham), served with freshly baked pizzelle. My mother would prepare the dough for the pizzelle from scratch. She would make a pizza-like shape about eight inches in diameter and about one inch thick, which formed the pizzelle. She would then place this dough in a pot of boiling vegetable oil to brown. After the pizzelle was cooked, she would then remove it from the oil and place it between sheets of paper towels to drain off all of the excess oil. Once cooked, the pizzelle was split down the center. The omelet was then sandwiched between the layers and ready to be enjoyed. This was one of the tastiest meals that my mother ever made. I loved an omelet and pizzelle sandwich so much that I would often take it to school for lunch. Not only was it succulent and delicious, but also, it was filling and nutritious.

Breakfast was also a fun time to remember, especially when my mother would whip up her special pancakes. As with the sandwiches, we would gobble up the buttery pancakes as fast as my mother would lift them from the sizzling hot griddle. My mother would make several varieties of pancakes including blueberry, buckwheat, oat bran, and golden wheat pancakes which were served with fresh honey from our own beehives. Mealtimes were always healthy and delicious, especially since only organically grown, natural ingredients were used.

Another fond memory was gathering around the table with my family to enjoy a meal of polenta corn meal. My mother and sisters would stir the corn flour on the stove until it became soft and creamy. Once the polenta was fully prepared, and the sauce, sausage, and meatballs were cooked, my father would place a large board on the table. My mother would then pour the steaming hot polenta over the board and spread it out until it was three quarters of an inch thick. She would then spread the sauce over the rolled out polenta. The last step was to place the meat at the center of the board.

Each individual was assigned a wedge of polenta from the board. It always gave me a warm, comforting feeling inside to watch all of my hungry brothers and sisters eating away at the polenta on the board. In order to reach the meat in the center of the board, we each had to eat the wedge of polenta that was assigned to us. The meat was the last delicious morsel that was eaten. Any leftover polenta was heated up the next day and served for either lunch or dinner. A small glass of wine was served at each meal to those who chose to have some with their dinner. However, I was never much of a wine drinker and preferred to have a big glass of ice cold milk with my meals.

Music was also an important part of our lives. My father played the accordion. My brother, Joe, played the harmonica, guitar, and mandolin. My sister, Teodolinda played the mandolin and I played the guitar. We would all gather together on the front porch during cool, spring nights or warm, breezy summer nights and play to our hearts' content.

Our friends from the village would join us, and for hours we would sing and play all of our favorite songs. I truly enjoyed these precious moments when we were all together for they were soothing and relaxing times for all of us. During those times together, all of our troubles seemed to disappear, and there was only love and laughter filling the air. The joy and happiness in my father's face as he played the accordion shall remain etched in my mind forever. Sometimes even now if I close my eyes and listen closely enough, I can still hear the melodious music of my father's accordion filling my heart once more.

Although we were poor growing up in Big Springs, West Virginia, there were many scenic and educational places that we could visit that were relatively inexpensive, yet beautiful. Berkeley Springs, West Virginia, stands out most in my mind as a young child. A small town with a population of about seven hundred people, it is located about twelve miles northwest of Big Springs, West Virginia.

Berkeley Springs, West Virginia, was established in 1776 under the name of "Bath," which is still its official name. Soldiers from Virginia regiments were taken there for treatment and rest during the Revolutionary War. President George Washington and his wife, Martha, owned land there. The water in Berkeley Springs, which maintains a uniform temperature of 74 degrees Fahrenheit, flows from five main sources in the springs.

I would enjoy taking my mother, Cesarina, and her lady friends to bathe in the mineral springs that were located there. Bathhouses were set up with individual stalls for privacy. Heat treatments and massages were also available. I especially enjoyed swimming in the beautiful pool there. The water was always crystal clear and ever so refreshing. The drinking water acts as a natural laxative. It has a sulfur-like taste. The water also has seventeen known minerals that make it very healthy.

In addition to the summer activities, Berkeley Springs, West Virginia, offered ten weeks of special events during the winter festivals of the waters, beginning in early January. One of my favorite events to attend was the apple butter festival that was held on Columbus Day weekend. Giant kettles of fresh apple butter were cooked over open fires delighting those lucky enough to attend with the sweet aroma of cinnamon and cloves filling the air.

Artisans would exhibit their crafts and musicians would perform concerts throughout the day. It was a memorable time and one of great happiness for me. I could never resist coming home with at least a jar or two of apple butter that we would spread on hot buttered toast for breakfast or an afternoon snack.

Another favorite childhood memory occurred when all of the children of the village would alternate gathering at different neighbors' houses to tell stories and play games. We were usually treated to homemade lemonade and freshly baked cookies. We would spend hours talking about our own experiences and learning a great deal from listening to the experiences of those around us. Some of the older children would tell us tales of the Old West and they would also describe for us what it was like for them to work in the mines. After storytelling, we would play hide and seek, jacks, checkers, and marbles.

The game of marbles was one of my personal favorites. I had accumulated a large bag full of marbles. We would draw a huge circle and place marbles in the center. The object was to knock the marbles out of the circle. I enjoyed the game so much that I would play it often, even in the cold weather. Consequently, my knuckles became very sore and bruised. Nevertheless, I did not allow that to stop me from playing my favorite game. When my hands became too raw and battered, I would place a pad under my knuckles to cushion them so that I could still continue to play. I still have a scar on my right hand knuckles as a reminder of my fondness for playing marbles. The experience was worth all of the pain, however, because I really enjoyed the game of marbles.

Growing up in a large family meant that there were many chores to do. Each child was given a specific chore that was expected to be done without question. One of my favorite chores was taking the two cows that we owned out to pasture during the warm weather months for several hours a day.

I was especially lucky because I had the best helper in the world, my collie dog, Rex. Rex was an extremely intelligent dog. He would remain with me until I was ready to return the cows to the barn. Once I was ready to do so, I would signal to Rex and point in the direction of the barn. Rex would immediately begin to round up the cows and lead them home, while making certain that they did not stray from him. Once the cows were in the barn, I would feed and milk them. I also made sure that they were brushed daily. Rex was rewarded with his favorite treat—a warm glass of cow's milk that I squirted into his mouth right from the cow.

Rex remained my faithful companion up until the time he died at ten years of age after being hit by a truck. I was devastated when Rex died for I felt as though I had lost my closest and most loyal friend. I never did own another dog after Rex died since we were forced to sell the cows, and I joined the U.S. Navy shortly thereafter.

CHAPTER ELEVEN

MARTINSBURG HIGH SCHOOL

While many of us were fortunate enough to have had an opportunity to attend Baker's Grammar School and to partake of the excellent education offered there, many other students were unable to do so. Because of a decrease in enrollment, it was necessary to close Baker's Grammar School. The remaining students were relocated to Martinsburg, West Virginia, much to their sadness and disappointment. The once quaint Baker's Grammar School was demolished around 1941, thus ending an era of education that could never again be recaptured.

Courtesy of Martinsburg High School

Once we had completed our grammar school education, we were bussed to Martinsburg High School,

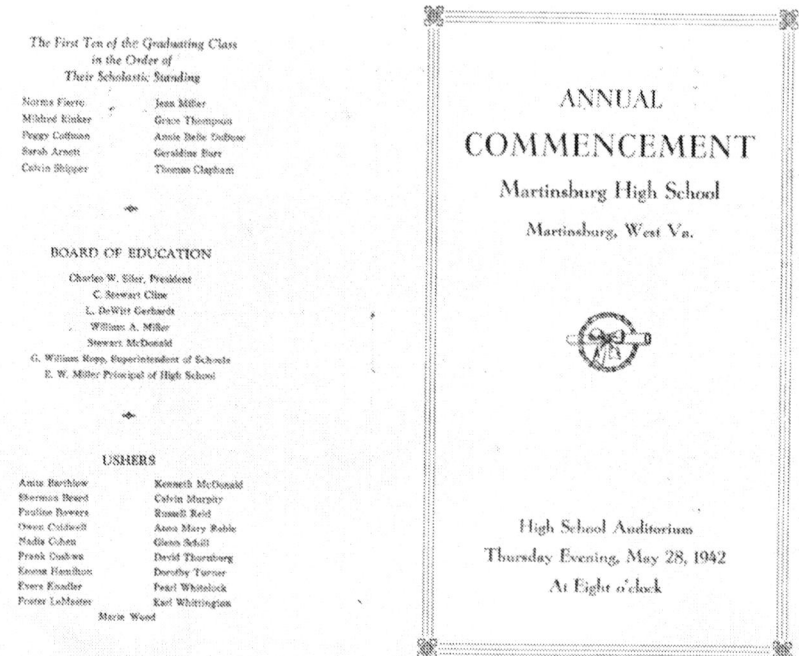

which was located at the southern tip of Martinsburg, West Virginia. I can vividly recall my first day at Martinsburg High School. To put it mildly, I was completely terrified. The city students were much more advanced, and I found it difficult at first to keep pace with them. Having been educated in the country, we had very few books in our home and the main newspaper was written in Italian.

In order to make the most of this new educational opportunity, I would stay after school everyday and seek extra help with my studies. After school, I would go to work in a tailor shop where I was an apprentice to a master tailor and designer by the name of John S. Ferro.

My father would constantly give me encouragement and praise. He would tell me over and over again how important it was for me to learn as much as I possibly could in school so that I could advance myself in life either in a trade or through higher education. I respected my father and treasured his sound advice. He remained a true source of pride and inspiration for me throughout my life.

Because of my tight schedule, I did not have any spare time to become involved with extra-curricular activities at the school. Instead, I put all of my energies into my studies. Still, I yearned to play baseball and firmly believed that I would have made the team if only I had the time to participate.

...PROGRAMME...

E. W. Miller, *presiding*

Priests' March—from "Athalia" .... Mendelssohn

Invocation .... Rev. John I. Byler

Dear Land of Home .... Finlandia - Jean Sibelius
Kashmiri Song .... Finden - Howorth
Song of Farewell .... Richard Kountz
Advanced Girls' Glee Club

Commencement Address .... Dr. Lyle Hance
Editor and Author

Clarinet Solo .... Thomas Clapham
Auld Lang Syne (Air Varie) .... G. E. Holmes
Audrey Clendening, piano accompanist

Presentation of Diplomas .... Charles W. Siler
President of Board of Education

Presentation of Citizenship Awards .... E. W. Miller

Benediction .... Rev. John I. Byler

Recessional

(Audience will please be seated after the benediction and remain seated until the class retires from the auditorium.)

Class Roll

Sarah Louise Arnett	Anna Mae Foster	Myron Lipsic	Evelyn Mae Slonaker
Catherine Lorraine Ashton	Marie Hoffman Fulk	Wanda June Locke	Neva Virginia Slonaker
Marguerite Angle	Rebecca Funk	Clarence Willard Long	Dennis Small
Joyce Barbour	Naomi Jane Gageby	Elsie Jane McDonald	Lena Pearl Smeltzer
Fay Barney	Richard Frederick Gambino	Betty Fae McDaniel	Elsie Geraldine Snyder
Geraldine Elouise Barr	Charles Wade Gantt, Jr.	Elva Louise Miles	Lucy Somers
Charles Calvin Bayer	Jean Gates	Ann Elizabeth Miller	Clifford Sperrow
Daisy Louise Bayer	Dorothy Marie Gerbrick	Helen Maxine Miller	Irene C. Stelmack
James Wallace Biedler	Mildred Anne Gore	Jean Irene Miller	Jane Ann Stelmack
Norman Birnbach	Velva Lee Gray	Robert Franklin Miller	Mary Almeda Steryous
Jean Kyner Blue	Harold Franklin Gregory	Lee Richard Moore	Mary Elizabeth Stewart
Geneva Virginia Boyles	Charles William Grubb	Donald Holliday Myers, Jr.	Betty Lee Stokes
Alma Lee Braithwaite	Margie Ellen Haines	Robert Lee Noll	Oneta Irene Stotelmyer
Kenneth Lee Brown	Jean Marie Hicks	Tito Joseph Orsini	Dorothy Stotler
Phyllis Marie Burnette	Eileen Elizabeth Hines	Marvin Earl Otto	Chloe Studwell
Carrie Lee Busey	Naomi Catherine Holliday	Calvin Earl Parkinson	Robert E. Tabler
Todd Wayne Butler	Barbara Ann Hollis	Joseph Frederick Payne	Catherine Elizabeth Thompson
Irving M. Byers	Helen Elizabeth Hollis	Joseph Blaine Pence	Grace Pauline Thompson
Garnett Samuel Canby	James LeRoy Hollis, Jr.	Anna Elizabeth Penn	June Louise Thompson
Harold Castleman	Carrie Lee Hovermale	Gardner William Pierce, Jr.	Hilda Geraldine Thorpe
William Catrow	Henry C. Howard	Izetta Virginia Poland	Belle Marie Thurston
Thomas Miller Clapham	Carl William Hull	Ruth Arlene Powell	Wayne Tucker
Donald Eugene Clark	Lillian Virginia Hutzler	Frederick S. Rankin	Anibelo Vailese
Helen Margaret Clark	Frances Lee James	Dorothy Powell Reid	Milton Tabler VanMetre
Betty Lee Cline	William Harry Jenkins	Milton Braden Ridenour	Vivian Janet Wall
Margaret Ann Coffman	Earle Lewis Johnson, Jr.	Mildred Evelyn Rinker	Mary Jane Webster
Jane Ann Collins	Alice Jane Johnson	Wanda Marie Rodgers	Betty Pearl Weller
Lottie Belle Cook	Renus Artenus Kackley	Amelia Virginia Ropp	Garnetta Ruth West
Anna Lee DeHaven	Emilie Elizabeth Kerlin	**Vincent R. Saladini**	Vivian May Whitelock
Phyllis Larue Dickens	Donald Hugh Keller	Harriet Kathleen Sapp	Elsie Lorraine Widmeyer
Bernadine Louise Dinteman	Mary Maxine Kettering	Robert Allen Sencindiver	William Norman Widmeyer, Jr.
Vernon S. Dodson	Elizabeth Margaret Koncer	Laura Catherine Shackelford	Paul Frederic Willis
C. Bruce Dorsey	Helen Margaret Kramerage	Reva Elizabeth Shackelford	Joseph Ellsworth Wilson
Nancy Lee Downey	William David Krause	Glenville Ships	Evelyn Wilson
Annie Belle Elizabeth DuBose	Joseph Fenton Lacount	John Calvin Shipper	Ellen Pauline Wintermoyer
Virginia Elizabeth Estep	Stewart William Laidlow	Victor Wendell Shrader	Meade Kennedy Wolford
Hilda Evans	Ella Mae Lamp	Mona Jean Sibert	Janet Marie Wright
Bessie Mae Fellers	Gertrude Elizabeth Landis	Eileen Deloris Silver	Bruce Lincoln Young
Norma Lee Fierro	Archie LeRoy LeMaster	Flora Lee Silver	Margaret Elizabeth Young
Robert Dorsey Flagg	Evelyn Mary Lewis	Derwood Guy Slonaker	Thomas Robert Youtz
Harry Lee Folk			

CLASS COLORS: BLUE AND GOLD

I can recall my classmates' talking about all the fun they would have attending parties, school dances, and other social events. However, I continued to follow my father's advice and made education my number one priority.

Although my father lacked a formal education, he, like many of the other men in the village, was extremely knowledgeable and highly skilled in many areas. For example, he was proficient in plumbing, stone cutting, masonry work, carpentry, shoemaking, and barbering.

John Ferro measuring Kenny Steryous for a suit at his tailor shop at Martinsburg West Virginia 1938

Because he lacked a formal education, my father was prevented from advancing on the job and was denied the opportunity to earn the monies that he should have earned for the work that he performed. I was determined to follow my father's advice by receiving a formal education; I wanted to avoid being placed in the same unfortunate position as my father due to his lack of a formal education. Through sheer determination and endless hours of hard work, I was able to graduate from high school at the age of eighteen. I can still recall the look of joy and pride on my parents' faces as I reached out and took hold of my high school diploma. I have never seen my parents look happier as they did on that proud day. Because my parents had so very little money, I could not afford to buy my high school yearbook or pay the required fee to have my photograph placed in the yearbook for our class picture. While this was one luxury that I so yearned for, I never let my parents know how deeply saddened I was that I could not buy my yearbook. I did not ever want to upset them or make them feel inadequate. Instead, I accepted the fact that it was not to be.

My sister, Minnie, was kind enough to pay for my high school class ring. She also bought my brother

Angelo's class ring as well as my sister Lucy's class ring. Were it not for Minnie's love and generosity, we would not have been able to have our class rings. I shall always be grateful to Minnie for her selflessness and caring.

Because I had to work so many hours and monies were scarce, I could not afford to attend our class prom. I consoled myself with the thought that despite our financial hardships, I shared a love and sense of closeness with my family that no amount of money could buy. In spite of the many financial hardships that we endured, I never lost faith in my family, nor did I ever lose faith in my ability to succeed in life. With love and determination, all things are possible.

One of my dreams came true recently when I wrote to the principal of Martinsburg High School and asked if any 1942 yearbooks were still available. He referred me to a gentleman named Dale Hicks, an English teacher at the high school. As it so happened, his sister, Jean, was a classmate of mine. I had actually met Dale Hicks at one of our school reunions.

I am happy to report that Dale Hicks contacted me with the exciting news that he had located a 1942 yearbook for me at a local book dealer's shop and if I wanted it, he would purchase it for me. I was so excited to hear from him that I immediately sent him a check for $35.00 to reimburse him for the purchase.

I cannot even begin to describe the feelings of joy and excitement that I felt when I actually received my yearbook in the mail. Dale Hicks not only sent me the yearbook, but also, he was kind enough to include various maps of West Virginia as well as a 1942 graduation commencement program. Even though I could not afford to have my picture in the yearbook, just holding the yearbook in my hands after so many years brought back many fond memories.

From the bottom of my heart, I shall be forever grateful to Dale Hicks for his kindness and assistance in making this one special dream come true for me. Every time that I browse through my yearbook, I relive my high school days all over again, and I am reunited with a part of my past that I never thought I could recapture again.

Upon my graduation from high school, I knew that it was impossible for me to attend college. My family had barely enough money to make ends meet, and we still had many young children at home who needed food and clothing. I never gave up hope that one day I would attend college and receive my college degree. With college having to take a back seat for the moment, I concentrated on continuing my work at the tailor shop and I soon began to master the art of custom tailoring and design. It was very uncommon in those days for a young boy to follow the vocation of tailoring and design. Instead, most of the young boys went to work in the mines.

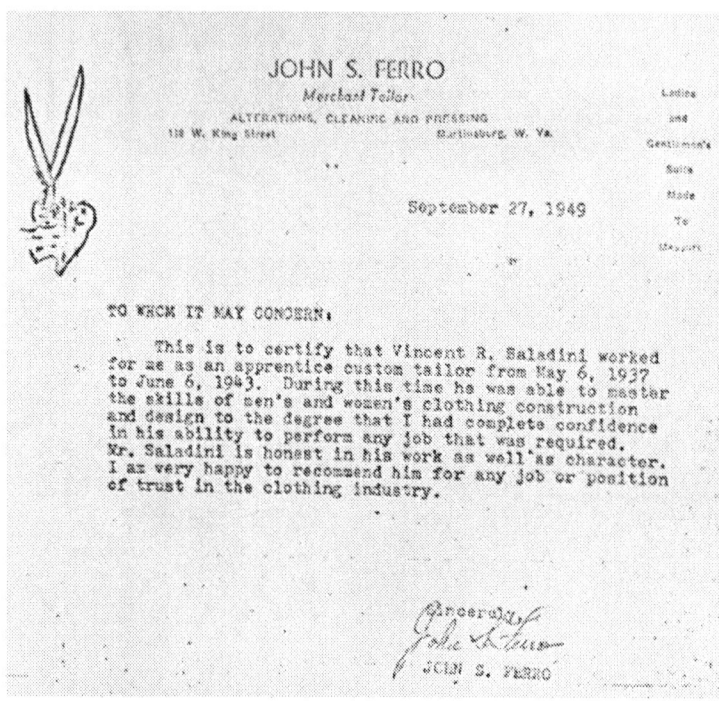

I enjoyed tailoring and the challenge that it presented to me. I marveled at my ability to turn a plain piece of cloth into a useful garment that was admired by others and worn with pride. As my skills increased, so did my earnings. I began to gain more confidence and satisfaction from my work. John S. Ferro, the master tailor, was so pleased with my work that he began to give me more responsibility and even greater challenges. My family and friends offered me endless encouragement.

Before long, I earned a reputation as an outstanding custom tailor and designer. I had always had the ambition of going into business for myself in the future. More importantly, I dreamed of earning enough money so that my father could retire from the mines and work with me in my own tailor shop.

I was grateful to have had the opportunity to acquire a saleable skill that enabled me to earn a living, especially during the time of the depression when job opportunities were scarce. Moreover, my skills allowed me to be able to contribute to the support of my family and ease the financial burden that my father bore alone up until that time. I cannot even begin to describe the feeling of satisfaction and pride that I felt being in a position to help my father and my family and to repay my father for all the years of unselfish love and emotional support that he had given to me and my brothers and sisters. At last my hard work and self-sacrifice had paid off, and I was able to enjoy the fruits of my labor.

Berkeley County Schools

Martinsburg   West Virginia

Martinsburg High School

This Certifies That

Vincent R. Saladini

has completed the Course of Study prescribed by the Department of High Schools and is hereby awarded this

DIPLOMA

Given at Martinsburg, West Virginia, this 28th day of May, 1942

111

CHAPTER TWELVE

WORLD WAR II

The great exodus from the village of Big Springs, West Virginia, came during World War II. All of the able-bodied young men went into the various branches of the service. In 1943, I volunteered for the United States Navy. My brother, Angelo, took my advice and also joined the United States Navy. My brother, Carlo, a six-foot tall handsome man with reddish colored hair, had already joined the United States Navy in 1942. He was stationed at the naval base in Roanoke, Virginia.

Tragically, my brother, Carlo, was killed in a bus accident on his way home from the base. Apparently, two buses collided on a foggy highway in Virginia. Carlo was sitting in the back of the bus. He was only ten minutes away from his destination when he decided to move his seat to the front side of the bus. As fate would have it, no sooner had he settled into his new seat then the two buses collided and struck in the very area where he had just sat down. The only victim of the collision, he was killed instantly. The news of Carlo's death was devastating to all of us, especially since we knew how much he loved the Navy and longed for a career in the service. Carlo's death brought home to us the reality and horror of war and made us truly appreciate the strong bond of love and support that we shared as a family.

Louie Rossi, my cousin Patsy Saladini, and Elio Bigiarelli joined the United States Air Force. Italo

Bigiarelli, Sammy Piccolomini, John Piccolomini, Louie DeStefano, Orlando DeStefano, and Tom Smith joined the United States Army. Tito Orsini and Chris Piccolomini joined the United States Navy. Fortunately, all of the men returned home safely after the war.

The older group of men, my brother Joe, my cousins Angelo and Ralph Saladini, Chris Angelo, and Louie Angelo were all deferred from the draft because they were needed to work in an area that was vital to the war effort.

SERVING ABOARD U.S.S. JASON (ARHI)

MY LOG AND DIARY

For week ending JULY 20, 19 44

At or
SUNDAY en route from SAN PEDRO, CALIF To PEARL HARBOR

Remarks: ARRIVED AT PEARL HARBOR JULY 26, 1944

At or
MONDAY en route from PEARL HARBOR To PURVIS BAY, W. Solomon ISLAND

Remarks: LEFT PEARL HARBOR AUGUST 6, 1944
ARRIVED IN PURVIS BAY AUGUST 17, 1944

At or
TUESDAY en route from PURVIS BAY To FINSCH LAFEN, NEW GUINEA

Remarks: LEFT PURVIS BAY SEPTEMBER 11, 1944
ARRIVED IN FINSCH LAFEN, NEW GUINEA SEPTEMBER 13, 1944

At or
WEDNESDAY en route from FINSCH LAFEN, NEW GUINEA To MANUS ISLAND

Remarks: LEFT FINSCHLAFEN SEPTEMBER 15, 1944
ARRIVED IN MANUS ISLAND SEPTEMBER 19, 1944

At or
THURSDAY en route from MANUS ISLAND To ULITHI (CAROLINE ISLAND)

Remarks: LEFT MANUS ISLAND OCTOBER 25, 1944
ARRIVED IN ULITHI November 2, 1944

At or
FRIDAY en route from ULITHI To LEYTE (PHILLIPINES)

Remarks: LEFT ULITHI JUNE 4, 1945
ARRIVED IN LEYTE JULY 6, 1945

At or
SATURDAY en route from LEYTE To OKINAWA

Remarks: LEFT LEYTE AUGUST 30, 1945
ARRIVED AT OKINAWA SEPTEMBER 3, 1945

CRUISING RECORD

WEIGHED ANCHOR		DROPPED ANCHOR			DISTANCE FOR N.D.
DATE	PLACE	DATE	PLACE	TIME OF TRIP	

TOTAL MILES
AT SEA TO DATE

MY LOG AND DIARY

For week ending SEPTEMBER 5 1945

At or
SUNDAY en route from OKINAWA   To JENSEN, KOREA

Remarks: LEFT OKINAWA SEPTEMBER 6, 1945
ARRIVED IN JENSEN, KOREA SEPTEMBER 9, 1945

At or
MONDAY en route from   To

Remarks:

SERVING ABOARD U.S.S. SIBLEY (APA 206)

At or
TUESDAY en route from SAN FRANCISCO   To PEARL HARBOR

Remarks: LEFT SAN FRANCISCO JANUARY 15, 1946
ARRIVED AT PEARL HARBOR JANUARY 21, 1946

At or
WEDNESDAY en route from   To

Remarks: LEFT PEARL HARBOR FEBRUARY 3, 1946
ARRIVED IN SAN FRANCISCO FEBRUARY 8, 1946

At or
THURSDAY en route from   To

Remarks: LEFT SAN FRANCISCO MARCH 1, 1946 BY
TRAIN. ARRIVED AT MARTINSBURG WEST VIRGINIA
MARCH 5, 1946. AFTER A SHORT LEAVE, I

At or
FRIDAY en route from REPORTED TO USN PERSONNEL SEPARATION

Remarks: CENTER APRIL 10th 1946. BAINBRIDGE, MD,
HONORABLY DISCHARGED APRIL 14, 1946!

At or
SATURDAY en route from   To

Remarks:

CRUISING RECORD

WEIGHED ANCHOR		DROPPED ANCHOR		DISTANCE FOR S.S.
DATE	PLACE	DATE	PLACE	TIME OF TRIP

TOTAL MILES
AT SEA TO DATE

115

U.S.S Jason (ARH1)
7/20/44 - 9/8/45

Vincent Saladini

West Virginia men serving aboard U.S.S Jason (ARH1)
1944

I will never forget the day that I left home for the United States Navy. My father came down to the train station with me. I could sense that he was extremely upset. When I kissed him good-bye the tears began to flow uncontrollably. I quickly boarded the train and tried my hardest not to look back. I simply could not bear to see the pain and anguish in my father's eyes.

Vincent Saladini
January 1, 1946
Big Springs, West Virginia

Vincent Saladini 1943

At the same time, I could not bear the thought of never seeing my father again, and so I forced myself to catch one last glimpse of him as the train slowly pulled away from the station. He was sobbing and wiping his eyes. His tears were matched only by my own, which now flowed freely as I saw my father for what was to be the last time. I would have to say that of all the pain I have ever experienced in my life, saying good-bye to my father was the most excruciating pain of all. I have never felt such an emptiness and longing as I did that day.

That night as I fell asleep after many hours of tossing and turning, I relived the pain of saying good-bye to my father over and over in my head. Suddenly a melody and lyrics entered my mind. When I awoke the next morning, I wrote down the words and the music on a crumpled piece of paper that I had in my duffle bag. I called my song, "Our Last Good-bye," and I dedicated it to my father, the sole source of my inspiration. This song will serve as an eternal dedication to my father for all of the love and support that he gave me throughout my life. I copyrighted my song in March 1970 and renewed my copyright again in March 1998. Sadly, my father never got to hear the special song that I wrote for him because he died while I was away at sea. By the time I was able to receive clearance to leave, my father had already been laid to rest. I will forever remember that painful part of my life, and I shall always consider "Our Last Good-bye" as one of my greatest and most cherished accomplishments in my life.

When I departed for the United States Navy, I was assigned to the Great Lakes Naval Base in Illinois. Because of my tailoring and design background, I was offered a job inspecting clothing for the Navy at the base. I was advised that it was an excellent assignment and that I would not have to serve overseas. I was also promised a promotion after a relatively short period of time. While the offer may have been tempting to some, I immediately refused the offer because I would have felt more like a civilian than a sailor. Instead, I requested to be assigned aboard a ship. The officers in charge could not believe that I would refuse such an offer, especially since many sailors were begging to receive such an assignment.

After reviewing my records, the officers decided to assign me to the Mare Island Shipyards to be trained as a sheet metal worker. I was assigned there for one year of training. I found this assignment to be extremely boring because I did not enjoy working with metals. Although I preferred to work with cloth, I made the best of this

Vincent Saladini
U.S.S. Sibley (APA206)
February 22, 1946

assignment and performed my duties most competently. Still, I was thoroughly convinced that after I left the service, I would continue to work as a custom tailor and designer if I did not become a professional baseball player.

After leaving the Mare Island Shipyards, I was assigned to the USS Jason (ARH1), a repair ship. We were assigned to join Admiral Halsey's third fleet in the Pacific. The ship was assigned to repair damaged ships on water. By actually repairing the ships at sea, a great deal of valuable time was saved because repairs did not then have to be made at Pearl Harbor. Our assignments were comparable to the Sea Bees, only we carried out our duties at sea.

Vincent Saladini
U.S.S. Sibley (APA206)
February 20, 1946

After surviving the hardships of living at Big Springs, West Virginia, with its lack of central heating, lack of inside plumbing and lack of inside bathrooms, life in the Navy was heavenly for me. I can recall speaking to several friends while at sea who were complaining about how difficult life was aboard ship. I listened patiently and then burst out laughing. One of the men asked me what was so funny. I candidly replied that life aboard ship for me was like a picnic compared to what I was accustomed to while growing up in Big Springs, West Virginia.

I likened the conditions aboard ship to that of a country club. The men could only gaze at me in disbelief. I had sparked their interest, and they began to ask me question after question about my life's experiences growing up in Big Springs, West Virginia. Most of my friends in the Navy had come from the New York City area and did not realize how people elsewhere were living.

Joseph Spero   William Sodeck   Vincent Saladini
U.S.S. Sibley (APA206)
February 20, 1946

After I shared my experiences with them, they all shook my hand and thanked me for making them aware of the difficult living conditions which existed in other parts of the country. They had developed an even greater respect for me and marveled at how I was able to endure such hardships and still emerge so unscathed from the experience.

The USS Jason (ARH1) left San Piedro, California, on July 20, 1944, and arrived at Pearl Harbor on July 26, 1944. While anchored at Pearl Harbor, we were able to enjoy the beautiful beaches and mild climate. Anyone who chose to could fish over the side of the ship. We also had an opportunity to visit some of the beautiful sites in the area. The people were very friendly and pleasant to us and enjoyed conversing with us at every opportunity. After an eleven- day stay at Pearl Harbor, we left on August 6, 1944. We arrived in Purvis Bay, West Solomon Island on August 17, 1944.

Vincent Saladini   William McDonald
U.S.S Sibley (APA206)
February 24, 1946

It was customary for all sailors who were crossing the Equator for the first time to be initiated. This was a Navy tradition. I will never forget this experience. The veteran sailors who had previously crossed the Equator were very busy making plans for the big event. On August 12, 1944, the fateful day had arrived. With fear and trepidation, we took our place in line up on the deck of the ship at which time we were also instructed to open our mouths. As we walked by the waiting veteran sailors, we were slapped on the backside with a wet towel while a mixture of hot pepper, salt, and vinegar was squirted into our mouths.

Needless to say, no one desired dinner that night. Fortunately, however, we all survived the initiation without any serious after effects, and before long, it was business as usual. At the end of the ceremony, the veteran sailors greeted us with a handshake and formally welcomed us into the "Domain of Neptune Rex," at which time they awarded each of us with a formal certificate.

After twenty-five days of being anchored at Purvis Bay and performing repairs on damaged ships, we left on September 11, 1944. We then arrived in Finschlafen, New Guinea, on September 13, 1944. We did not remain there for very long, however. In fact, we left the same day and then arrived in Manus Island on September 14, 1944, where we remained for the next forty-one days. While there, we had an opportunity to leave the ship and go ashore.

We were kept quite busy repairing damaged ships during our stay. The USS Jason (ARH1) received many commendations for the services performed for the third fleet. I can recall a cruiser's having its guns replaced. That was a job that ordinarily required that the ship go to Pearl Harbor for such repairs. The crew of the USS Jason was made up of very highly trained technicians, who had the knowledge and skills necessary to perform whatever repairs were required.

Arc-welding aboard
U.S.S. Sibley (APA206)
February 20, 1946

We left Manus Island on October 25, 1944, and arrived in Ulithi, on November 2, 1944. Ulithi was a small atoll that was used as a resting area for servicemen. We were anchored at Ulithi from November 2, 1944, until June 4, 1945. During that time, we were able to service many ships that were damaged. This was supposed to be a safe area to repair damaged ships; however, such was not the case. Japanese suicide planes attacked us on several occasions. During one particular attack, a suicide plane dove right for our ship and missed the ship by only seven feet. Unfortunately, an aircraft carrier that was anchored nearby was not as fortunate as we were. It was hit so hard that the aft end of the ship was ripped away, thus resulting in heavy damage to the vessel and the loss of many innocent lives.

After remaining at Ulithi for approximately eight months, we finally sailed for Leyte in the Philippines and arrived there on July 1, 1945. It was a big change for all of us. I enjoyed the thirty-six day stay, especially since we were able to visit the neighboring cities and towns.

We left Leyte on August 30, 1945, and arrived at Okinawa on September 3, 1945, but we only remained there for several days. During that time, we experienced severe weather conditions. It was typhoon season and the ocean was extremely rough. Fortunately, our ship successfully weathered the storm. Although a few smaller ships sank as a result of the high waves, the men aboard were safely rescued. I can vividly recall being

Helping to tie up the U.S.S. Sibley (APA206) February 20, 1945

in the center of the rough seas with water surrounding us on all sides. I was stationed as a lookout at the bow of the ship. That position afforded me the unenviable experience of feeling the ship rock "fore and aft" as it made its way through the choppy waters. Whenever we would hit a wave, the water would actually pour over the bow of the ship like a river. Fortunately, I was strapped to a seat that prevented me from being washed overboard; however, it did not do anything to ease the queasy feeling that I felt in my stomach with each passing wave.

I was constantly drenched from the high waves. I could actually feel the ship buckling beneath me as it made crackling sounds against the rough waters. The ship would actually drop approximately twenty-five to thirty feet at the bow after each passing wave. After this grueling experience, I gained a greater respect for the forces and powers of Mother Nature.

On September 6, 1945, we sailed to Jensen, Korea. We arrived on September 9, 1945. While stationed there, we were able to visit nearby cities such as Inchon and Seoul. The visits proved to be very interesting as well as educational because I was exposed to new cultures and new ways of life that I could only have imagined.

While serving aboard ship in the China Sea area in 1945, a terrible tragedy struck my family. My father, Pasquale, was killed in an accident at the mines. From all accounts, my father had fallen off of a twenty-foot ladder into a pile of rock. He consulted with the company doctor, who informed him that everything appeared to be normal and that he could go back to work. My father did not feel well, however, and he constantly complained of chest pains. The company doctor again examined him and again told him that everything was normal.

The doctor relayed his findings to the mining company. After forty years of loyal and faithful service, my father was informed by the company that he would lose his job and be evicted from his home if he did not return to work. In spite of the terrible pains in his chest, my father reported to work because he feared the loss of his job and his home. As he proceeded to lift a heavy jackhammer, he clutched his chest in agony and fell flat on his face against the jagged rocks. He was carried home where he died shortly thereafter on October 2, 1945, at the age of fifty-seven.

The night before my father's death, I had a terrible nightmare. I dreamed that a very heavy metal plate was falling on me and I was helpless to save myself. I began screaming out at the top of my lungs while shaking and trembling the entire time. My shipmates awakened me and tried their best to calm me down, but I could not shake the nagging terror inside of me that something was terribly wrong back home.

The very next day I received a telegram from the Red Cross informing me of my father's tragic death. I was terribly upset because I knew that it would be impossible for me to arrive home before the funeral. My father had already been laid to rest for three months before I was able to return home to assist my family at which time I was given a thirty-day leave to help settle his affairs. As devastating as my father's death was to me, it was even more devastating to my mother and family whose grief seemed unending. Calling upon the love and strength that we had always come to rely on, my family and I remained strong and carried on as we knew my father would have wanted and expected from us. It was difficult, but we made it through this tragedy.

At the end of my thirty- day leave, I was directed to report to the Philadelphia Navy Yard for further assignment. Upon my arrival, I had met the Chief Petty Officer in charge. Since he was in a hurry to catch a train home, he refused to check me in, as he was required to do.

He repeatedly told me to get lost and do whatever I wanted. Being the conscientious man that I had always been, and not wanting to disobey my instructions, I remained and insisted on being checked in as directed. Since I did not want to be considered AWOL, it was imperative for me to be checked in by the officer. At that point, he told me not to unpack because he was going to put me on a troop train that was destined for the West Coast the following morning.

I could not believe what I was hearing. My worst nightmare had come true. The very next day I was boarded on the troop train and shipped out to the West Coast. When the names aboard were called, my name was missing. The officer in charge advised me that I did not belong there, but that it was too late to let me off the train. I did not even have a bunk assigned to me. Instead, I was directed to share a bunk with another sailor.

By now, I had become extremely upset. All of my records were still in Philadelphia and so I was unable to receive my wages. When the sailors aboard heard about my plight, they decided to take up a collection so that I would have enough money to spend when we arrived in San Diego, California. I will never forget the sense of care, concern, and camaraderie that these men exhibited towards me.

We arrived in San Diego at 8:00 p.m. in the evening after a three- day run. Once again, I was informed by the officers in charge that they did not have any of my records. As fate would have it, they were in the process of assigning men to the APA206SIBLEY, an attack ship. The officers in charge informed me that they needed someone with my rank of metal smith, 2nd Class Petty Officer. I was instructed not to unpack my bags because I was going to be assigned to that ship.

The ship was assigned to Okinawa and Japan. Their mission was to pick up a load of Marines who were heading back to the United States. What made this situation even more bizarre was the fact that I was originally scheduled to be discharged in one month. These plans were canceled, however, since the ship would be gone for several months or more. The officers on the ship were very understanding as well as surprised that I was re-assigned to overseas duty after a short stay in the states.

Unfortunately, I was powerless at this point to change my fate and instead resigned myself to trying to make the best of this nightmarish situation. In time, I did adjust to my assignment. The officer in charge was very pleased with my

Vincent R. Saladini Sr.
U.S.S. Sibley AP206
San Francisco Harbor
April 1946

skills and the manner in which I conducted myself. He asked me if I would consider re-enlisting for a six year term during which time I would be promoted to the rank of Chief Petty Officer. I thought about the offer, but then advised him that I did not want to make the Navy my career. I thanked him for his confidence in me at which time he shook my hand and told me that he fully understood my decision.

CHAPTER THIRTEEN

EXODUS FROM MARTINSBURG

When I returned home from the service on April 16, 1946, I discovered that the village of Big Springs, West Virginia, had remained relatively the same. I had high hopes of becoming a professional baseball player. I was considered to be an excellent catcher with a promising future as a professional player. I decided to try out for the Hagerstown Owls, a class "B" team. I jumped at the chance to play and seized the opportunity when I learned that I was accepted on the team. My joy was short-lived when I sustained a serious knee injury, which ended my once promising career. I decided then and there that I would pursue a career in the field of fashion and fulfill my dream of becoming a fashion designer.

Vincent Saladini
May 24, 1946   Hagerstown, Maryland

In order to get started in my career, I visited Mr. Lipsic, an old friend of mine from Martinsburg, West Virginia, who owned a large and successful clothing store. His son, Sonny Lipsic, was a high school classmate of mine. When I asked Mr. Lipsic about his son, Sonny, he began to cry. After he calmed down, he informed me that Sonny was killed in an airplane crash after leaving the service. He was heartbroken and deeply saddened by the loss of his son whom he loved very much. Sonny, too, had high aspirations of taking over the family business, a dream that would tragically never come true.

Mr. Lipsic asked me if I would be interested in taking over the business. He said that he would assist me financially and he would also help me to learn how to manage the business. I gave his kind and most generous offer a great deal of thought, however, I decided that I would not be happy living in Martinsburg, West Virginia, because I wanted to fulfill my dream of attending a fashion design school in order to pursue a career in fashion design. Although Mr. Lipsic was disappointed with my decision, he understood my hopes, dreams, and aspirations of becoming a fashion designer. I shall be forever grateful to him for his generosity towards me and for the faith and confidence that he had in my abilities to take over his family business.

I finally made the decision to pack up and leave for the city of Baltimore, Maryland, where I had hoped to use my GI Bill to further my education in fashion design. Baltimore is one of the leading fashion centers in the world, along with New York and Chicago.

1946 home of Clementine Lattimore
Place where I roomed
708 N. Collington Ave, Baltimore, Maryland

131

I arrived in Baltimore, Maryland, on August 16, 1946, with $50.00 to my name and one suitcase. My salary, which was $300.00, was used for the income taxes that I had to pay before I entered the service. I went directly to the YMCA where I found a room for the night. The following day I decided to look for a permanent place to stay. The YMCA carried a list of families who took in boarders. As I searched through the list, I came across a woman by the name of Mrs. Clementine Lattimore. Since her unusual name stood out from the rest, I decided to visit her home. That day was particularly hot and sweltering, with temperatures approaching 95 degrees. I walked the two miles from the YMCA to her home. When I arrived, I knocked on her door. A woman, who had been visiting the family, answered the door. Her unruly appearance and manner of dress caused me to walk away. Just then, I heard a voice coming from inside the house from a woman who had apparently just undergone an operation. She was calling out for me to return. I finally returned and spoke to Mrs. Lattimore, the owner.

She was immediately impressed with me and asked me to consider renting a room from her. She went on to explain that she was a widow with two grown daughters. She advised me that the rent was $5.00 per week and that I could basically have the run of the house. I found her to be a godsend since I needed a good place to stay and could not afford much more than $5.00 per week for rent.

I graciously accepted her offer and enjoyed my stay with the Lattimore family. They treated me just like a son, and I, in turn, helped their family whenever possible. We had a pleasant relationship that made life more bearable at a time when I was just making my way in the world.

My next obstacle was to find employment. I was so desperate to earn money that I was willing to accept just about any job just to get on my feet once again. I went to apply for an usher's job at the local theater. They were willing to accept me, but they did not have a jacket that fitted me. At that time, I had a 48" chest and a 36" waist. I had acquired them through weightlifting techniques that I had learned in the service under the guidance of Gene Stanley, the world-renowned professional wrestler and weightlifter. Gene Stanley served with me on the USS Jason (ARH1). Deeply disappointed that I did not get the usher's job, I decided to place an ad in the newspaper for a custom tailor's position. I indicated that I was an all-around custom tailor and a very trustworthy, conscientious, reliable worker.

I had gone to church that Sunday morning and prayed that I would soon find a job, for my money was running low. My situation grew so desperate that I had to call my brother, Angelo, for some money. God bless him, he immediately sent me enough money to carry me over until I could find a job.

When I returned home from church, Mrs. Lattimore informed me that I had gotten a call from Mr. Lew Hess of Essex, Maryland, a small town about fourteen miles from Baltimore. He saw my ad and was very impressed with my credentials. I immediately returned his call and set up an appointment to meet with him. The interview went extremely well, and I was offered the position of custom tailor in charge with a salary of $80.00 per week. I was ecstatic since I had never earned that much money before in my life.

Vincent Rocco Saladini, Sr.

Along with working, I also enrolled in a cloth-cutting class that was offered in the evening division in Baltimore. I enjoyed the class very much. Mr. Diel, my teacher, was a highly professional cloth cutter who was able to impart to me valuable knowledge. I took advantage of his skills and put in extra time whenever possible so that I could learn as much as I possibly could from him. Fortunately, the GI bill paid the tuition for this course or else I would not have been able to go to school.

I found working for Mr. Hess to be very enjoyable. He was extremely pleased with my work and praised and commended me for doing such an excellent job. In addition to custom tailoring, Mr. Hess taught me techniques in effective window displays and sales. I gained a great deal of valuable experience that came in handy in the future. However, after one year of working for Mr. Hess, I began to grow restless. More than anything, I wanted to attend a fashion design school in New York City. Still, all the while that I was working in Baltimore and planning my future career in fashion design, I kept in close touch with my family back home in West Virginia.

I was informed that during the war, my brother, Angelo, was assigned tugboat duty at Staten Island. He trained to be a yeoman aboard ship. During this training, he gained valuable experience that prepared him for his future job working with the Navy Department in Washington, D.C. His commanding officer highly recommended him for the position of clerk for the Navy. My brother, Angelo, greatly enjoyed his work and was highly skilled in his field. In spite of the fact that Angelo never had a formal college education, he worked hard and managed to advance himself from stockroom clerk to an administrative position buying parts for the Navy, an extremely responsible position.

During his employment with the Navy Department, Angelo won much praise for his many useful suggestions on saving money through efficiency at the work place. Angelo retired after thirty-five years of service. He is presently residing in Washington, D.C., with his family. He has a wife, Louise, a son, Angelo, Jr., who himself has two sons, and a daughter, Jenny, both of whom reside in Virginia. After many years of dedicated service to his country, Angelo is enjoying his retirement and welcomes the opportunity to spend time with his family.

In addition, my brother, Joe, excelled in high school. He always had a sharp, keen mind for solving complicated mechanical problems. He was knowledgeable about the entire operation of the mines and was often called upon whenever problems arose in the mines that no one else could handle. Joe was a true professional when it came to solving problems. For example, one time the miners were having a severe problem with water that was accumulating in a certain part of the mine. The mining company had called in several expert mining engineers who tried unsuccessfully to solve the water problem.

Joe was then called in to see if he could solve the water problem. He informed them that the problem could be solved if they would follow his instructions. He indicated that a hole would have to be dug from the top of the mines and a pump would have to be inserted to pull the water. Amazingly, Joe was able to calculate exactly where they would have to dig the hole on the outside of the mine to correspond with the precise location of the water hole inside the mine. Joe carried out his plan of action with the utmost skill and success, and when he had concluded his operation, the water problem was solved.

The outside hole that was drilled came directly over the water hole inside the mines. Joe had won high praise not only from his fellow workers, but also, from the top management for his ability to solve such a perplexing problem.

My brother, Joe, has long since retired from the mines. Up until his death on November 3, 2001, he resided in Martinsburg, West Virginia, with his wife, Enase, his son, Tommy Joe, and our sister, Teodolinda. Joe's daughter, Mary Jo, lives nearby so that the family has the opportunity to see each other often and spend time together relaxing and enjoying life. Joe had indicated to me many times that he truly enjoyed his retirement years, although at times, he did miss the hustle and bustle of working in the mines. He earned a rest, however, after the many strenuous years that he worked in the mines, and he fully made the most of his retirement years.

CHAPTER FOURTEEN

ARRIVAL IN NEW JERSEY

A friend of mine, who was taking the cloth-cutting class with me in Baltimore, Maryland, informed me that a custom tailoring school was soon to be opening in Newark, New Jersey. He asked me if I would be interested in applying. I immediately expressed my keen interest in attending such a school. It seemed that I was one step closer to my dream of fashion design.

I met with Mr. Hess, my employer, and told him of my dreams and hopes for the future. While he wanted me to pursue my plans and fulfill my hopes and desires, he was deeply saddened with the prospect that he would be losing me as an employee, especially since I was one of his most trusted and talented employees. Still, he understood and wished me well. I gave Mr. Hess two weeks' notice so that he could find a replacement for me. Although I was sorry to be leaving Mr. Hess, I was eager and excited beyond words to pursue my dream at last.

On October 8, 1947, my friend and I headed for Newark, New Jersey, in an old 1937 Model A Ford. We arrived in Newark about 11:00 p.m. that night. We immediately sought a place to stay. After searching for about one hour, we found a room on Walnut Street in Newark. The very next day, we enrolled at the Camp School of Tailoring. We began taking classes on October 9, 1947.

The Camp School of Tailoring had an excellent and highly skilled teaching staff. All of the teachers had many years of experience in the field of custom tailoring and design. I learned a great deal in the class and became even more highly skilled in the field. I completed the course with high honors and was awarded a certificate in March 1949.

I was able to secure full-time employment after finishing and receiving my certificate in custom tailoring at Camp School of Tailoring in Newark, New Jersey. It was not difficult for me to find a job because I was considered a journeyman custom tailor and designer for men's and women's clothing. In addition, I received excellent recommendations from my teachers. I also had the drive and determination to succeed, and I had tremendous confidence in my ability to perform my work successfully.

My first job was working for J. Schneider, a custom tailor for men's and women's clothing. I began my new position in February 1948 and worked through March 1949. Mr. Schneider was an excellent craftsman and a very astute businessman. He had such complete confidence in my skills and abilities to be successful that he would always give me his most difficult jobs to do. I was given the opportunity to become involved with the entire process in garment construction. I would take the client's measurements, cut out a pattern from those measurements, and then complete the entire garment, including the finishing.

Camp School of Tailoring, Inc.
26 CAMP STREET
NEWARK 2, N. J.

September 23, 1949

To Whom It May Concern:

The bearer, Vincent SaMdini, was a former student of the Camp School of Tailoring, Inc., 26 Camp Street, Newark, New Jersey, pursuing a course in Men's Custom Tailoring. He has attained excellent progress in his work, has been conscientious and it is felt he will be an asset to the Needle Trades Industry. He has assisted his instructor in many phases of the work relating to the cirriculum at this school.

We wholeheartedly recommend Mr. SaMdini for a job in the Needle Trades Industry.

Very truly yours,

[signature]
John T. Doe,
Director
CAMP SCHOOL OF TAILORING, INC.

By: LAWRENCE A. LEVIN,
Ed. Director

LAL:bls

I considered myself to be very fortunate to have had the opportunity to work with such a truly talented and skilled craftsman as Mr. Schneider. He was a patient man who always took the time from his busy schedule to offer me advice and tips in the fine art of custom tailoring and design. I welcomed this opportunity to learn as much as I

141

possibly could since I was able to refine my skills and become even better at my craft.

During these years, life was no longer all work and no play as it had been in the earlier years. I spent my after work hours from Monday through Thursday at the public library where I would read every book on fashion design that I could find until the library closed for the night. On Fridays, Saturdays, and Sundays, I would attend the social dances at the Continental and Terrace Ballrooms in Newark, New Jersey. I enjoyed dancing very much. I was also beginning to make many new friends. The people who attended these dances were always cordial and friendly. Soon I got to know all of the regulars who attended and we became like one big, happy family.

Vincent R. Saladini
Lincoln Park, Newark, NJ
May 2, 1948

Although I was finally settling in, I missed my family and friends in Big Springs, West Virginia. Newark, New Jersey, seemed like a whole world away, and many times the overwhelming feeling of emptiness and sadness would be all consuming. I found it difficult to adjust to life in the city after having been raised in the open hills of West Virginia. I constantly had the burning desire to return to my hometown, but something inside of me kept telling me to stay and pursue my dream of a career in fashion design.

Deep down inside I knew that this was where the opportunities were, not back in my old hometown. Still, I felt like a lonely, empty soul in a huge metropolitan city. While I longed for the safety and comfort of my family and friends back in Big Springs, West Virginia, I knew that I could never return there again. I made up my mind then and there that I would have to endure this tremendous sacrifice if

Vincent R. Saladini Sr.
at pressing machine
School #93 Baltimore Maryland
May 17, 1947

I ever hoped to realize my dreams. I would stay and make a future for myself. I vowed to be true to my dreams and I never looked back again.

CHAPTER FIFTEEN

MY FUTURE WIFE

Always seeking to better myself, I decided to head out to Hollywood, California, with two of my friends. We planned to open up a custom tailoring business to the stars.

My two friends immediately flew out to California and began looking for a suitable place so that we could start our business. I had made arrangements to arrive in California the following week. With our game plan already set in motion, I decided to attend the last Saturday night dance at the Terrace Ballroom in Newark, New Jersey, before leaving for California the following week. Little did I know at the time that this last Saturday night dance would change my whole life forever.

When I arrived at the Terrace Ballroom, I could hear music playing softly in the background. The dance hall was crowded, yet I felt strangely alone. I almost decided to head back home when my eyes were drawn, as if by magic, to a breathtaking young woman standing in the distance near the edge of the dance floor. I strained my eyes to make sure that I was really seeing her. She was strikingly beautiful, with flowing auburn hair cascading across her shoulders. I was immediately attracted to her and felt compelled to meet her. Nervously, I walked through the crowd of people oblivious to everyone around me. All I could think about was reaching this beautiful woman before she disappeared from my sight. As I approached her, our eyes met and she smiled at me. I introduced myself to her and she softly whispered to me that her name was Viola Russo. As soon as we began chatting, I felt as though I had known her all of my life. I asked her for a dance, and she accepted.

While we were dancing the jitterbug, her high- heeled shoe flew off of her foot. We both began to laugh as I scrambled through the crowd of dancers to find her missing shoe. I retrieved the shoe and gently placed it back on her foot. I could feel my heart beating wildly in my chest as she placed her hand upon my shoulder. Although we had only just met, we both felt so comfortable together.

John Russo   Antionette Russo

Viola Saladini's Parents

At the end of the evening I asked Viola if I could see her again. Happily, she said yes. I then made arrangements to see her again the following Tuesday at her home. When I arrived at Viola's home, her entire family was there to greet me and we all felt very much at ease with each other. When I met Viola's family, I could immediately sense that she shared a bond of love and closeness with her family that paralleled the kind of love and closeness that I shared with my own family. They were kind and attentive. They had prepared a delicious meal for us that resembled the feasts my mother would serve.

As we sat around the kitchen table and talked, Viola's father remarked that fate seemed to have brought us together. He went on to say that Viola had not wanted to attend the dance that Saturday night. She was tired from having worked a long day and just wanted to stay home and rest. Her father had told her to get out and enjoy herself because she was always sitting at home.

He also said that when Viola came home that Saturday night after having met me, she was bubbling with excitement. All she could talk about was how much she was attracted to me and how she felt in her heart that I was that special someone who would forever share her life. I felt the same way about Viola. From the moment that I first saw her, I knew in my heart that she would one day be my wife.

At this point, I had serious reservations about moving out to California. I could not bear the thought of leaving Viola for I was deeply in love with her and wanted to spend the rest of my life with her. As our relationship blossomed, I knew that I had found my special soul mate in Viola. She was intelligent, gentle, kind, and deeply compassionate. Having come from similar family backgrounds, we discovered that we had many things in common and felt completely comfortable with each other. We also shared similar dreams and hopes for the future. From that moment on, we began a courtship and shared a love and bond of trust that would endure for a lifetime.

I immediately wrote to my friends in California and told them of my change in plans. Although they were disappointed, they completely understood my feelings and wished me much luck and happiness for the future. They remained in California and opened up their own custom tailoring business. I knew in my heart that I had made the right decision, and I never looked back.

Prior to marrying Viola, I decided to attend American Gentlemen School of Men's and Women's Designing and Grading in New York City. I had finally realized my lifelong dream of attending such a school. I will never forget my arrival in New York and my first introduction to the big city. I arrived in New York City around 10:00 p.m. one cold, dark evening. I was completely terrified. I had no idea where I would sleep that night and I did not know a soul there. I decided to walk down 34th Street to look for a room. I arrived at 34th Street and 8th Avenue where I noticed a huge sign that advertised rooms for rent at reasonable rates. I decided to enter and rent a room for the night.

Much to my surprise, a woman who was intoxicated and who appeared not to have taken a bath in a week greeted me. When she saw me she blurted out, "What's a nice clean-cut man like you doing here?" I was taken aback and could only stare at her in disbelief. She indicated to me that the rent for the night would be fifty cents and that if I were interested, I should follow her. I was so tired and desperate for a room that I decided to spend the night there. She led me up to the third floor. The building was terribly run-down, and the hallways had a sickening stench.

As I looked around at this run-down hovel, it suddenly dawned on me that I had just entered a flophouse. Most of the occupants were bums and homeless people from the bowels of the city. Disheveled men and women were lying out in the open hallways, some still clinging desperately to their empty booze bottles. While my first inclination was to run for the door as fast as I could, I was so exhausted from traveling that I could not go any further. Against my better judgment, I decided to take the room for the night and paid my fifty-cent rent. I vowed, however, that I would keep one eye open at all times.

As I entered my room I was extremely disgusted by its run-down condition. The stench of the room was so foul that it smelled like death. The sink was so encrusted with filth that I could not even tell what color it actually was. The water barely poured from the faucets, and there were dead roaches all over the floor. The sheets and covers on the bed were so soiled and stained that they looked like they had never been changed.

Wearily, I sank down in a chair, afraid to touch anything in the room. Finally, after sitting in the chair for several hours and trying to rest as best as possible under the circumstances, I could no longer tolerate such deplorable conditions. At 3:00 a.m., I decided to turn in my key at the desk and leave. I quietly exited, making certain not to wake anyone, and stepped out into the darkness. The stinging chill of the morning breeze felt surprisingly refreshing after having breathed the stale stench of the flophouse all night.

Alone and scared, I decided to walk the streets to see if I could find a better place to stay for the night before my classes started in April 1949 at the American Gentlemen School of Design. As I walked to 21st Street and 5th Avenue, I noticed a sign in the window advertising rooms for rent at the rate of $5.00 per week. The building was directly across from the school. For a moment, my heart raced. Could my luck finally be changing for the better I wondered?

I sat in front of the apartment house for the remainder of the night waiting for the renting office to open the next morning at 8:00 a.m. As soon as the office opened, I immediately went in and asked about renting a room. A very sweet and kind woman greeted me with a big smile and a cheery hello. She was surprised that I had come so early to the office. When I explained my predicament to her and told her what had happened to me the night before, she was deeply sympathetic. After answering some routine questions for her, she offered to rent me the room, and I eagerly accepted.

While the room itself was anything but a choice location since it faced a huge office building without any view at all, I felt fortunate to have found a decent place to live for the time being. Besides, I knew that I would not be spending much time in the room other than to sleep. When I first saw the bed I could not believe my eyes. It had to have been made for a midget for when I stretched across it, my legs extended out over the edge by at least a foot.

I decided to make the best of the situation and tolerate the inconvenience. After all, I was young and healthy, and more than accustomed to adjusting to the most difficult of living conditions after all that I had been through in the past.

As time passed, I began to feel a bit more at home in the city. My uncle, Emidio Saladini, who lived in the Bronx, New York, would come to visit me often. I always looked forward to his visits and delighted in spending time with him and his family at their home.

My weekends were reserved strictly for the love of my life, my girlfriend, Viola Russo, however. I missed her terribly and felt a constant aching longing whenever we were apart. Viola was always so happy to see me when I went to visit her. She treated me like a king and I treated her like a queen. I would surprise her with beautiful wool suits that I made for her. I even made her a coat that I specially trimmed in black velvet. We really looked forward to our time together and dreaded every minute that we were apart. We agreed, however, that we would endure this sacrifice now so that we would be able to share our lives together and fulfill our dreams and goals.

Whenever I would visit her, Viola would make me all of my favorite, delicious home-cooked meals. She always made sure to cook extra food so that I would have plenty of food to take back with me for the week. All the way home I would savor the aroma of her spaghetti and meatballs and her chicken parmigiana. Her father would always be sure to pack fresh loaves of Italian bread in the bag so that I could enjoy them with my meals. The only thing that kept me going during the long, lonely weeks was the thought of being with Viola on the weekends. She was my ray of sunshine, the embodiment of all of my hopes and dreams, and the one and only true love of my life. She was all I ever really wanted, and I could not get her out of my mind.

I began classes at the American School of Designing and Grading in April 1949 under the GI Bill. Were it not for the GI Bill, I could not have afforded to attend this school. During this time, I had also enrolled in a correspondence course at the Master School of Design in Chicago, Illinois. Although I maintained an extremely busy schedule, I was determined to make every precious minute count.

I felt blessed and fortunate to have been afforded the opportunity to be able to attend the American Gentlemen School of Design and Grading. The school was considered to be one of the best in this field. Not only were all of the teachers of the highest caliber in the industry, but also, they took a special interest in the students that was unsurpassed. The members of the staff were highly respected for their talents as well as their knowledge of design concepts and procedures. Students came from all over the world to attend this prestigious school because of its reputation for excellence.

I gained invaluable experience while attending American Gentlemen School of Design and Grading. During my time there, I made every minute count, and I spent countless extra hours above and beyond those required by the courses, perfecting my skills and mastering my craft. The hard work and determination paid off, and I graduated in September 1949 with high honors and glowing recommendations and commendations. At the same time, I also graduated from the Master School of Design (correspondence course), and received my diploma from there in September 1949.

Graduation day was one of the happiest moments of my life. At last my dreams were coming true and I felt as though I had the whole world at my feet.

Shortly after my graduation, I proposed marriage to Viola and she happily accepted. Al Mehana, my future brother-in-law, who was familiar with the jewelry trade, purchased the engagement ring for us. Arrangements were made and we were married on October 23, 1949, at St. Francis Church in Newark, New Jersey. We had a double-wedding ceremony with her sister, Lillian, who was also getting married on that same day.

Vincent Saladini   Viola Saladini
10/23/49 Newark, NJ

I would have to say that my wedding day was one of the happiest days of my life. Viola was stunningly beautiful in a snow-white, flowing wedding gown, and a lace veil that draped across her face. We were both so excited that we could barely say our vows.

After the wedding, we headed off to Niagara Falls for our honeymoon. We also traveled to Big Springs, West Virginia, so that Viola could meet my family.

Viola Saladini
10/23/49 Newark, NJ

Having been raised in the city, Viola was unaccustomed to the dark county roads and the rolling back hills of West Virginia. At first, she found it difficult to adjust to the unstirring quiet stillness of the country nights and the sense of loneliness that they can sometimes evoke. After awhile, she looked forward to long, peaceful walks along the country trails and delighted in the quiet rides in the open countryside.

My family loved Viola from the moment they first met her, and she was equally at home with them. We all had a wonderful time reminiscing about the past and sharing our dreams for the future. After several days, Viola and I said our tearful good-byes to my family and we headed off to begin our lives together. We vowed that we would always love each other, be there for each other, and never allow anything to keep us apart again.

When we returned home from our honeymoon, Viola and I moved into a quaint little apartment in Newark, New Jersey, that was owned by Viola's father John Russo. He was a kind and gentle man who reminded me very much of my own father. He told us that we could stay in the apartment for as long as we desired.

Vincent Saladini Viola Saladini
1949 Newark, NJ

CHAPTER SIXTEEN

EARLY TEACHING EXPERIENCE

Upon my graduation from American Gentlemen School of Design and Grading, I was fortunate enough to secure a teaching position. A friend of mine informed me that very soon, the New York Technical Institute of Technology was planning to open a custom tailoring school in New York City. Since I possessed all of the necessary skills and training, he felt that I was highly qualified for the position and encouraged me to apply.

I immediately submitted my application to the school and anxiously awaited a response. Shortly thereafter, I was interviewed by the owner, Mr. Williams, who was so impressed with me, that he offered me the position. On September 6, 1949, I began my teaching assignment at a salary of $180.00 per week. I could not believe that I was earning that much money. I kept wondering if it was all a dream from which I would soon awaken.

I derived a great deal of pleasure out of teaching at the New York Technical Institute. I had the added pleasure of working with an excellent staff whose goals for the students matched those of my own. All of the staff members were highly trained individuals, who were extremely knowledgeable in the area of fashion. We worked together well in an atmosphere of harmony that allowed us to share our ideas and suggestions on how to improve our teaching skills.

157

Equally satisfying for me was the opportunity to work with the students, who were always so eager to learn. They reminded me very much of myself when I was a student. I enjoyed being in a position to share my skills and knowledge of fashion with them so that they could also acquire all that was necessary to one day enjoy success in the field of fashion design and custom tailoring.

In addition to my regular teaching assignment, I would put in several extra hours each day preparing the teaching materials necessary for the staff. In order to do so, I would utilize the round and straight blade cutting machines. These particular machines permitted me to cut many layers of fabric in one cutting thus saving time and eliminating the need to have to do so by hand. I received extra compensation for this additional assignment, which came in handy now that I was married and my expenses were greater.

Mr. Williams would sponsor a picnic during the summer so that all of the staff members and their families could get together and become better acquainted. I always looked forward to these events. We would play horseshoes and then a game of softball. Everyone worked together to make the day special and we always had an enjoyable time. Mr. Williams was a highly trusted and respected man who was admired and revered by his staff. He treated everyone with the utmost respect and sense of professionalism.

I remained at New York Technical Institute until the school eventually closed on August 1, 1952. This was one of the saddest days of my life for I truly looked forward to teaching there each day and working with the staff and students. We worked so well as a team that losing them was like losing members of my family.

I next applied for a job at LeRoy Botnick Clothier in Newark, New Jersey. After a brief interview with Mr. Botnick, he accepted me for the position of head tailor in charge of the entire tailoring division. In August 1952, I began my new position. Although it was one of tremendous responsibility, I enjoyed the challenge and achieved a great deal of success in performing my duties there. Mr. Botnick was very pleased with my work and commended me for my success in dealing with the clients as well as with my fellow workers.

New York Institute of Technology Staff and Family Party
May 1950   Mayer's Parkway Restaurant
613 E. 233 St. in the Bronx, NY

CHAPTER SEVENTEEN

MARRIED LIFE

For the first several years of our marriage, my wife, Viola, continued to work at the RCA Plant in Harrison, New Jersey, where she would make radio tubes for the men in service. At the time, she was earning forty-two cents an hour, which was considered a good income at that time. The hours were long and grueling and the work was stressful and often tedious. Still, Viola wanted to do her part and contribute to our expenses despite the sacrifices that she had to make. We were a team, and we were determined to realize our dreams together. Her working was a tremendous help for me. We were able to save her salary and live off of my salary.

Viola Saladini
1950

Viola maintained her grueling schedule without ever complaining. Even to this day, I still marvel at her uncanny ability to have worked full time while taking care of our home during those early years. In our spare time, we still enjoyed attending the social dances at the Terrace Ballroom and Continental Ballroom. We loved dancing very much and had become quite good. Dancing also gave us an opportunity to meet new friends and to relax after having worked hard all week long.

After three years of marriage, our first daughter, Denise, was born, on October 10, 1952, at the Presbyterian Hospital in Newark, New Jersey. Doctor Edwin Ciccone, our family doctor and long time friend, delivered Denise.

My wife and I decided that she would quit her job and remain at home so that she could fulfill her lifelong desire to be a full-time mother and to devote all of her time to raising our child. Viola was and still is an excellent, loving mother. She managed to make time to take care of Denise, run the household, and still be the best wife that any man could ever hope to find. Viola and I worked very hard to instill solid, lasting values in Denise and to raise her to respect others. She was the joy of our lives. We devoted ourselves to her and showered her with constant love and affection.

A loving and devoted mother, Viola would spend part of her day taking Denise for long walks in Branch Brook Park in Newark. When the weather permitted, they would spend several hours there each day enjoying the fresh air and sunshine. Viola had a chance to meet with other parents who were also visiting the park with their children. They enjoyed being out in the fresh air and looked forward to their daily visits.

Branch Brook Park is a beautiful park to visit, especially when the Japanese Cherry Blossom trees are all in bloom. The fragrance is breathtaking and the rows and rows of pink and white and blossoms are a sight to behold. People would travel from neighboring towns and afar just to catch a glimpse of the cherry blossoms when they were in bloom. Viola and I would take a drive through the park with Denise and delight in her excitement as she watched the blossoms cascade to the ground with each gust of wind that passed through the branches.

Now that we had a child and our expenses had increased, I decided to change jobs. I applied for a position at Charles W. Elbow Custom Clothier in Paterson, New Jersey. Mr. Elbow required an interview as well as a handwriting analysis as part of the hiring process.

Mr. Elbow was an expert in analyzing handwriting. He asked me to write out my name and along with it, a short statement as to why I should be hired for the job. I eagerly set forth my reasons for desiring the position and presented my statement to Mr. Elbow. After he reviewed my statement, Mr. Elbow smiled at me and told me that he was extremely impressed with my credentials and the results of my handwriting analysis. After a brief interview, Mr. Elbow accepted me for the position of head tailor in charge. I started my new position in April 1954.

With this new position came an increase in salary and a greater challenge, which I was eager to undertake. Mr. Elbow had a well-established business, which he had started over seventy years ago when he was a very young man. Mr. Elbow had become so successful that he purchased the entire three-story building on Main Street and Market Street in Paterson, New Jersey. It was appropriately named "The Elbow Building."

Mr. Elbow was a highly respected, honest businessman. He carried top of the line clothing and specialized in both ready-to-wear and fine custom clothing. I enjoyed my job there and had performed so successfully, that Mr. Elbow gave me the full responsibility of running the entire clothing department.

I felt fortunate to have been able to work with Mr. Elbow and his staff of highly trained professional custom tailors. They all excelled in their field. One tailor in particular, Salvador Cassetti, had worked at Elbow's for over fifty years. The average length of service for the group of tailors was thirty years, a true testament to the respect and loyalty shown to them by Mr. Elbow.

Mr. Elbow's business was based primarily on referrals from other satisfied customers. Three generations of customers have shopped there. Mr. Elbow was a true icon. I would have to say that he was one of the most honest people I have ever met. He would always tell me to satisfy the customer regardless of how long it took to achieve an excellent fitting garment for that customer. Mr. Elbow truly practiced what he preached. He always made certain to hire only top notch personnel who were highly skilled in their craft. Even his sales staff was of the highest caliber. His secretary, Ms. Sanders, had been with him for over forty years. She was always courteous and professional to everyone. She would consistently go out of her way to be helpful and pleasant to the staff as well as to the customers. She was well loved and respected by those around her.

After saving our money, my wife and I decided to have another child. Our second daughter, Deborah, was born on August 23, 1955, at the Presbyterian Hospital in Newark, New Jersey. Like our first daughter, Denise, she was also delivered by our family physician, Dr. Edwin Ciccone. As usual, my wife was a devoted, caring, and loving mother to Deborah. Although taking care of both the house and the children was often difficult work, she never complained. Viola took great pride and joy in being a wife and mother, and her love enriched our lives a hundredfold.

I strongly believe that the early years of a child's life are very crucial. The child must be loved, nurtured, and made to feel wanted and important. A child needs a strong sense of belonging, and must always be treated with kindness and compassion. He must be gently guided, yet given the freedom to grow and experience life and gain his own perspectives on the world around him.

Although the role of the mother is of utmost importance, the father's role also has an important effect on

Vincent Saladini
(holding Deborah Saladini)

Branch Brook Park, Newark, NJ
May 5, 1957
Denise Saladini   Cherry Blossom Trees in background

the total development of the child. One aspect of the child's development is that of having appropriate male and female role models. The absentee father cannot adequately be a male role model if he is not functioning as a part of that child's life. To a young child, both male and female, the father is viewed as the supreme authority figure on everything objective and factual. He is the protector, the one who has the power to make everything right, to keep them safe and to give them a sense of security. Children will usually turn to their mothers, however, on subjective matters and the fine subtleties of social relationships.

In our own role as parents, my wife and I have tried to raise our children in an atmosphere of love and security where we each share an equal parental responsibility. We have always viewed ourselves as equals and that feeling has carried through to our children. We have also endeavored to create a bond between our children and ourselves. Such a bond would allow them to feel comfortable talking to either of us about any subject at all without fear of rejection or lack of understanding.

May 5, 1957
Branch Brook Park, Newark N.J.
Cherry Blossom Trees in background

Viola Saladini   Deborah Saladini

Raising a child is no easy task. In fact, I would have to say that it is one of the most difficult jobs that one could ever undertake, but undoubtedly one of the most rewarding jobs of all. Being a good parent requires a tremendous amount of love, patience, and understanding as well as a genuine desire to understand the needs and desires of the child. The development of a child and the emergence of his individuality as displayed through his behavior begin at an early age. As such, the parent must strike a delicate balance between giving freely to the child and not over-indulging the child so that his sense of values becomes askew.

Denise Saladini

Vincent Saladini
(holding Deborah Saladini)

Branch Brook Park
Newark, NJ
May 5, 1957
Cherry Blossom Trees in background

My wife and I have always believed

that a child must be given love, respect, and consideration if the child is to be expected to give the same in return. Since we firmly believe that children learn by example, we have strived to teach our children solid values by providing them with positive parental role models to emulate as opposed to providing them with mere lip service. Even today, we have maintained the same open and loving relationship with our children that had been fostered in them since birth.

On March 18, 1958, we were blessed with the birth of our third child, our son, Vincent Rocco Saladini, Jr., who, like our two daughters, was delivered by Dr. Edwin Ciccone at the Presbyterian Hospital in Newark, New Jersey. Weighing in at 10 pounds six ounces, Vincent was fortunately born a healthy, happy child. Once again, we were blessed to have Dr. Ciccone present because he always went out of his way to provide us with excellent medical care. We considered him to be a conscientious and skilled doctor as well as a friend, who genuinely delighted in the births of each of our children.

To show our appreciation to the devoted hospital staff, Viola and I arranged for the delivery of fresh baked pizzas for them to enjoy. They were so grateful for our gesture of kindness and we in turn appreciated the care and genuine concern that they gave to us each time.

After the birth of our third child, Viola and I realized that we could no longer remain in our Newark apartment, where we had lived for ten years, because we needed more room to accommodate our growing family. Thus began our long and arduous search for a single- family house in the suburbs. We were living the American dream and it was about to get even better.

One bright, sunny morning in September 1958 while riding down Grove Street in Clifton, New Jersey, on my way to work, I noticed a man on a bulldozer excavating sections of open farmland. This particular area was famous for its cabbage farms. For some compelling reason I was drawn to this land and vowed to find out why this land was being excavated. On my way home from work that evening, I stopped by the spot where I had been earlier that morning. As fate would have it, the building contractor, Mr. Poydeniecz was standing nearby, and I asked him what was planned for this excavated tract of land.

Mr. Poydeniecz informed me that he intended to build fifty single- family homes with varying price ranges

depending on the style of home being built. I asked him if he intended to build any ranch-style homes since Viola and I wanted our home to be on one level because Viola had injured her leg and could not climb stairs. I was delighted to learn from Mr. Poydeniecz that he would be able to build us a ranch home to our specifications if we so desired. He also advised me that if we wanted our home built there, we should not wait too long to make a decision since it was choice property and the lots were selling quickly.

When I arrived home that night, I was bubbling over with excitement, and I could hardly wait to share the good news with Viola. She was equally thrilled, and we spent the next several hours discussing plans for our dream home. We decided that we would visit the building site together

168

before we made our final decision. When we arrived, there were several other people looking at the building site.

Viola immediately fell in love with the area and expressed her desire to raise our children there. We were fortunate to have excellent schools nearby as well as an area that was clean and open.

Left to Right:
Deborah Saladini, Viola Saladini
(holding Vincent Saladini Jr.), Denise Saladini
October 12, 1958 11 Pilgrim Drive, Clifton, NJ
(home under construction)

As soon as we decided to build, we did not waste any time with our plans. I had brought along my checkbook just in case we decided to buy. Within hours, we had secured our building lot, and we anxiously looked forward to watching our dream home become a reality.

After going through all of the necessary steps to acquire a mortgage and after all of the legal issues of purchasing a home had been concluded, the contractor immediately began to build our home. I shall never forget the tremendous sense of relief I felt when the Montclair Savings Bank called me and told me that my mortgage had cleared. Mortgage rates back then were 5% and real estate taxes were approximately $200.00 per year. Since I was earning a decent salary, I did not have any difficulty meeting my mortgage payment.

Everyday on my way to work, I would stop by the building site and check on the progress of our home. Then I would excitedly call Viola to tell her how everything was coming along. Little by little our dream home was taking shape. On the weekends, we would drive by the site together with the children and watch the progress. On one particular day, it had rained heavily the night before, and there were huge mud puddles everywhere.

Deborah had gotten out of the car with my wife to walk around to the back area of the house. About an hour later we left and returned to our apartment in Newark. As we entered the apartment, Deborah began to cry uncontrollably. Within minutes Viola and I realized that she had lost her favorite teddy bear that she took with her everywhere she went.

We immediately climbed back into the car and drove all the way back to Clifton to find her teddy bear. As we were driving up to the house, we saw some boys playing football. When they saw us approach, they ran out of sight. It did not take long for me to figure out what they had been using for their football—Deborah's favorite teddy bear! By now, it was tattered and torn and caked with mud.

When Deborah saw her teddy bear all ripped and muddy, she became inconsolable. Viola, ever the loving mother, gently cradled Deborah in her arms and told her not to worry. She promised Deborah that she would "help make Teddy all better," and she did. Viola

Vincent Saladini Sr. (holding Vincent Saladini Jr.)
Deborah Saladini at side
11 Pilgrim Drive, Clifton, NJ
October 1958
(home under construction)

washed and repaired Teddy and even made him a new outfit to wear. No one would ever be the wiser. Deborah was delighted and Teddy continued to be her constant companion for years to come.

Our home was completed around January 1959. We were fortunate in that we were able to move into our dream home on January 16, 1959. Deborah was so excited that she ran through all of the empty rooms mesmerized by the sight of her new home. She and Denise could not wait to show us their new bedroom that had been painted in their favorite shade of pink.

Viola and I worked long into the night to make sure that the girls' bedroom would be all ready for them when they went to sleep that night. Viola searched for the iron in the pile of boxes that had been stacked everywhere. She carefully pressed the white and pink curtains that the girls had selected, and then lovingly hung the curtains while the girls remained right at her side.

As I gazed into the girls' completed bedroom with the frilly pink bedspreads and crisp white sheets and watched them fall asleep for the first time in their new home, I could feel my heart melting. Viola and I embraced each other and counted our blessings. Our dreams were coming true, and we could not be happier.

Left to Right
Deborah Saladini, Denise Saladini
Viola Saladini (holding Vincent Saladini Jr.)
11 Pilgrim Drive, Clifton, NJ
October 12, 1958 (home under contruction)

In the weeks ahead, Viola and I worked very hard to put the house together. It seemed as though we would never reach the end of the pile of boxes. Eventually though, we had unpacked everything and our dream home was beginning to take shape. Although still very young, Deborah and Denise were a tremendous help to us during that time. Deborah especially loved to help take care of her baby brother, Vincent, Jr. In fact, they were inseparable during those early years, having developed a bond of love and caring that remains as strong today as it was then. Deborah was just like a second little mother to

Denise Saladini Deborah Saladini
11 Pilgrim Drive, Clifton, NJ
October 25, 1959

Vincent, Jr. She would help my wife feed him and put him down for his nap. Once Vincent, Jr., was asleep, she and Denise would play quietly in the living room so that they would not disturb him.

Fortunately, our home was situated on a large piece of property that was approximately 100' by 70'. It provided plenty of room for the children to play as well as a place for me to plant the garden that I had always dreamed of having. The following spring, I set out to landscape the property. Since landscaping was one of my favorite hobbies, I looked forward to the challenge and could not wait to get started. I had worked out specific plans as to the type of landscaping that Viola and I wanted.

I started the project in early spring so that I would have plenty of time to organize what specific shrubs we would have and where they would be positioned around the property. In the front of the house, I planted a wide variety of miniature shrubs and all types of perennial flowers in between. Along the sides of the property, I planted several different varieties of colorful ground flowers, tulips, and daffodils. In the back yard, I reserved a huge section for my vegetable garden where I planted tomatoes, peas, peppers, corn, and squash. Flowering trees were also planted throughout the property.

11 Pilgrim Drive
Clifton, NJ
Saladini Residence

One thing that I made certain to do was to buy only the highest quality of shrubs and plants available. I did most of my purchasing at that time from Richfield Farms and Plochs, two of the finest nurseries around. The owners of the nurseries were always willing to assist and to offer suggestions on planting techniques, design strategies, and plant care. While my landscaping project involved a great deal of time and work, I thoroughly enjoyed being outside and working close to nature. The true reward came the following year when the fruits of my labor yielded a bounty of beauty that was unsurpassed.

In my spare time, I would tend to my gardens and trim the shrubs. I had also managed to develop a beautiful rich green lawn, which soon became the talk of the neighborhood. As time passed, many of my neighbors asked me to help them with their own gardens and I readily accepted the challenge.

In time, I also planted a patch of sunflowers, which the children just adored. Because of the rich compost that I had prepared, we were able to grow sunflowers that towered above the roof of the house. Deborah, Denise, and Vincent, Jr. would gather the heads of the sunflowers once they had dried, and they would set them out on the picnic table for the birds and squirrels to enjoy. Every now and then a hungry rabbit would stop by to nibble the edges of the sunflowers. We all delighted in watching the animals scurry about. Viola and I enjoyed spending time with the children outdoors in the gardens. By working with the earth, the children learned to love and appreciate nature and to respect all forms of life.

Viola and I knew right away that we had made the right choice in moving to Clifton, and especially to our particular neighborhood. All of the couples in our area were approximately the same age as we were and they had children that were close in age to our own. The children bonded well and established close friendships that still remain today.

Vincent Saladini
11 Pilgrim Drive
Clifton, NJ
"backyard"

Viola and I have always enjoyed living in Clifton. In fact, we still live in the same home that we first purchased in 1959. Clifton has successfully served the needs of its people for years. The municipality has maintained a fine police department, which has strived over the years to keep crime to a minimum. Our streets are clean and the quality of life is excellent.

I can honestly say that our particular neighborhood has not changed much throughout the years. In fact, many of the same neighbors, who moved in around the time that we did, have remained in their homes during their retirement years. In some cases, the children of those neighbors have taken over their parents' home and started their own families there, thus beginning a new generation of Cliftonites.

The homes in our neighborhood have always been very well maintained. The families have taken pride in beautifying their homes and helping each other whenever possible. In all these years, there has never been a battle between the neighbors to compete with one another. Instead, I have always found our neighbors to be loyal and respectful people who took pleasure in being there for each other without asking for anything in return. In fact, my neighbors in Clifton reminded me very much of my friends and neighbors in West Virginia when I was growing up. Everyone tried to help one another and look out for one another. We shared our experiences together, and instilled in our children similar values and beliefs.

11 Pilgrim Drive
Clifton, NJ
Pine tree Vincent Saladini planted at age 5: 1963

One of my most precious memories of my home in Clifton took place when our son, Vincent, Jr., was just five years old. On one particular spring day, he came to me with a pinecone tightly clutched in his tiny hand and asked me if we could plant it in the front yard. Together we dug a hole and gently placed the pinecone into the ground. In time, much to our surprise, the pinecone sprouted a branch that grew several inches that year in 1963. The following year, Vincent, Jr., and I transplanted the tree to its present permanent location at the northwest corner of the house. As the tree took root and continued to grow with each passing year, I could see the look of happiness and excitement on Vincent's face. I explained to him that it would take many years before the tree would reach maturity and that in the interim, we would need to feed the tree, water it, and give it constant nurturing. Vincent, Jr., eagerly took on this responsibility, and for the next twenty-five years, he continued to tend to his tree with a love and devotion that has always made me proud. Over the years, the tree has grown over twenty feet tall, and it still stands proudly today in the very spot where Vincent, Jr., and I had planted it over thirty-five years ago.

Even today as I gaze out upon our tree, my mind races back to that earlier time years ago when Vincent, Jr., was just a young child and the world held magic and wonder for him. If I close my eyes, I can see him once again reaching out to me with the pinecone clutched tightly in his hand, and for a moment, we are one again.

Towering Pine Tree
Clifton, NJ
Planted by Vincent R. Saladini Jr. at age 5 in 1963

CHAPTER EIGHTEEN

CHILDREN SET GOALS

I did not have an opportunity to attend college upon graduating from high school because of my family's financial situation. I did not want the same fate for my children. My children were always encouraged to value an education. They knew that my wife and I would make the necessary sacrifices to insure that each of them would receive a college education if they so desired. We never forced our wishes on our children because we wanted them to attend college of their own volition, without any prodding on our part. A person must have a strong desire to attend college for it entails a great deal of work, and a tremendous amount of dedication and sacrifice.

DENISE SALADINI CEURVELS

On October 10, 1952, my wife and I were blessed with the birth of our first child, a beautiful daughter, Denise Ann Saladini.

My daughter, Denise, always had aspirations of becoming a language teacher. She excelled as a student at Clifton High School and graduated in the top two percent of her class. When she applied to Montclair State College, now known as Montclair State University, she was readily accepted. Denise majored in Spanish and English and received her Bachelor of Arts degree in these areas. She later earned her Master of Arts degree from the same college in 1984. Throughout her college years, she was a conscientious and dedicated student whose hard work resulted in her graduating Summa Cum Laude. As a result, she was accepted into the National Honor Society and remained a member throughout her college career.

During her junior year at Montclair State College, Denise expressed a strong desire to participate in a student exchange program in Madrid, Spain. My wife and I encouraged Denise to pursue her goals and made the necessary financial sacrifices in order for her to attend the program. By living abroad, Denise was afforded a golden opportunity to hone her language skills and experience the Spanish culture firsthand while attending the University of Madrid and traveling throughout Spain.

Upon graduation from Montclair State College in 1974, Denise received a position as a teacher of English as a Second Language in Passaic, New Jersey. Although it involved a tremendous amount of preparation and hard work, Denise found the teaching profession to be rewarding. She took her work seriously and taught with pride, secure in the knowledge that she was playing a vital role in her students' lives.

While attending a training seminar at Montclair State College, Denise met a fine young man named Warren

Ceurvels. At that time, Warren was employed by the college as an administrator at the Adult Education Resource Center and an adjunct professor in its evening division. After a short courtship, they were married on November 7, 1981.

On October 1, 1990, Denise and Warren were blessed with a son, Matthew James Ceurvels. Our first grandchild, he is the absolute joy of our lives. Matthew is already demonstrating his love of education and his dedication to learning. He is a straight-A student and has a constant thirst for knowledge. Just like his older brother, Frank, who is Warren's son from a prior marriage, Matthew enjoys skiing and karate. Denise and Warren are devoted to Matthew, and strive to instill in him the same strong values of family and education that were instilled in them as they were growing up. Denise and Warren are extremely proud of Matthew and always encourage him to do his best and to take pride in his work.

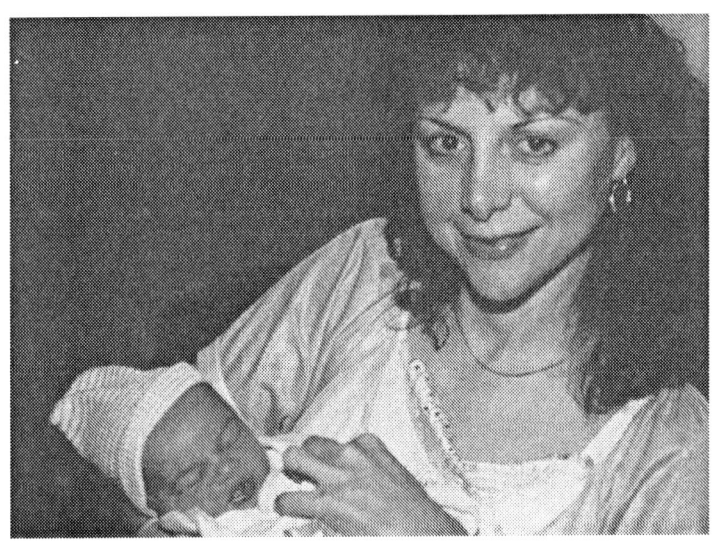

My daughter and her family reside in Vernon, New Jersey. Their beautiful home is nestled in a lovely, rustic, country setting. Denise, Warren, and Matthew enjoy the peaceful serenity that comes with living in the country. We always look forward to celebrating family events at their home because it exudes peace and warmth. We look forward to spending many more years of happiness together.

Denise is still employed as a teacher of English as a Second Language at Passaic High School in Passaic, N.J. She continues to enjoy the teaching profession and finds her work to be both challenging and rewarding. She hopes to teach for many years to come. I have no doubt that she will.

2. DEBORAH JEAN SALADINI

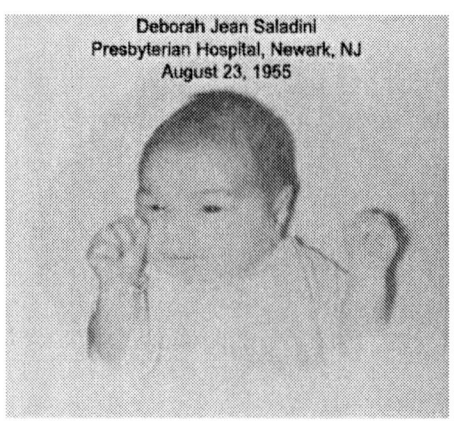

Deborah Jean Saladini
Presbyterian Hospital, Newark, NJ
August 23, 1955

On August 23, 1955, we were blessed with the birth of our second child, a beautiful daughter, Deborah Jean Saladini. Always a happy and loving child, Deborah delighted in helping others whenever possible. She especially enjoyed helping my wife around the house with cooking, cleaning and decorating. Like Denise, Deborah also excelled in school, and remained an "A" student throughout her educational career. Deborah also developed a love for education at an early age and always knew that she wanted to become a teacher. In fact, one of my fondest memories of Deborah took place when she would come home from school, go down to the den, and line up her stuffed animals in front of the blackboard that we had bought for her. She would proceed to "teach" her toys all of the new things that she had learned in school that day.

Even as a young child in grammar school, Deborah would stay after school several days each week tutoring the other students in their subjects. It pleased Deborah to no end to be able to help the other students work through their difficulties and enable them to understand what they were being taught by their teachers. She continued to tutor throughout junior high school and high school, all the while gaining the respect and admiration of her classmates as well as her teachers.

One of Deborah's passions is her deep love for animals. Even as a young child, Deborah had nearly every pet imaginable. Over the years, she has raised hamsters, guinea pigs, chickens, and rabbits. I can honestly say that there was never a time in Deborah's life that she was without a pet, and there will probably never be a time in her life when she will not have one. In fact, Deborah loved animals so much, that on the weekends, we would visit local farms where she would help care for the animals. Deborah always had an uncanny ability to relate to all types of animals, and they always took so naturally to her, never showing fear in her presence and always allowing her to cuddle them and hold them close to her. Deborah's deep love for animals remains an important part of her life even as an adult. She is presently "Mom" to an adorable Bassett Hound named Scooter, alias "Luigi," and a precious Yellow Labrador Retriever named Boomer, alias "Twinkie." They are truly the joy of her life and a constant source of comfort and unconditional love to her and to all of us.

Upon graduation from Clifton High School in 1973, Deborah applied to Montclair State University where she was accepted into the English and Spanish programs. In 1977, Deborah graduated Summa Cum Laude with a 4.0

average and received a Bachelor of Arts Degree in English and Spanish. In 1979, she went on to receive her Master of Arts Degree in English and graduated Summa Cum Laude once again. Deborah also obtained additional concentrations in Guidance, Counseling and Human Services, and Administration and Supervision. She received her Principal/Supervisor Certificate in 1983.

Deborah's love of learning and her natural ability to instruct and help others enabled her to enjoy a very successful teaching career. Deborah taught various courses in poetry, writing, research, and American and Afro-American writing at Montclair State University. She also taught English and poetry classes at the middle school and high school levels.

Deborah J. Saladini
(holding Boomer - 3 months old)
Clifton, NJ, 1991

Deborah's insatiable desire to help others eventually resulted in her obtaining her Juris Doctor Degree from The West Virginia University College of Law in 1988. While attending law school, Deborah participated in Law Review during which time she served as Student Work's Editor. Her article on prison reform was selected for publication.

Upon her graduation from law school in 1988, Deborah returned to New Jersey to practice law. As soon as she learned that she passed the New Jersey bar, Deborah immediately opened her own private practice. While she is licensed to practice in the Courts in West Virginia as well as in the Courts in New Jersey, Deborah prefers to devote her time to her New Jersey private practice. She enjoys a very successful private practice where she concentrates in the areas of matrimonial, criminal and municipal law. She has also taken on a number of cases defending animals' rights, which allows her to continue her deep passion for animals.

Most recently, Deborah has become involved in divorce mediation, an area that allows her skills as an attorney as well as her prior background in counseling to effectively assist her clients. Despite the long hours and often -grueling work schedule, Deborah enjoys the practice of law and the freedom that

Paul A. Massaro, Deborah Jean Saladini Stewart Inn in NJ.

it allows her to help others.

Over the years, she has mastered the fine art of maintaining a balance between effective counseling and compassion for her clients. She is certainly a formidable adversary who works hard for her clients and who makes herself available to them whenever they need her. She has gained the respect and admiration of those around her for her "never say die" attitude even in the most pressing of circumstances. Deborah plans to continue to practice law for many years to come.

In her spare time, Deborah enjoys quiet walks in the country with the love of her life, her boyfriend, Paul A. Massaro, who is also an attorney. Deborah and Paul also share a passion for gardening, and on any given day, they can be found planting and re-arranging their perennial gardens. They also enjoy hiking, traveling to different bed and breakfast inns and taking long, quiet walks by the ocean near Deborah's Harvey Cedars shore house. Deborah and Paul also delight in taking long drives in the country, especially on small unknown roads that have rarely been traveled upon. They enjoy the challenge of the unknown, and the thrill of discovering new and different small towns throughout New Jersey. We are truly grateful for the love and joy that Paul has brought to our lives, especially Deborah's life, and we look forward to many more years of enjoyment together.

"TO MY PARENTS WITH LOVE"

By Deborah J. Saladini

You were always there
when I needed a friend.
You gave me strength,
made me care enough
to go on living.
You were my port in the storm,
my rainbow of love
shining through all uncertainties.
You reached out when I was lost
and guided me to safety.
You calmed my fears,
held me close,
kissed away the tears
of doubt and insecurity.
And when I reached the end
you gave me hope,
helped me face the world again
with courage and dignity
and you never stopped believing in me.
Your love remained constant
through all my joys and sorrows
yet you asked for nothing in return.
You understood and accepted
my need to be me

Viola E. Saladini, Vincent R.
Saladini Sr., Deborah J. Saladini
Christmas 1993

You gave me life
showered me with love,
then gave me the freedom to grow
and realize my dreams.
And though we've said it to each other
a million times before
I'll say it again—
I love you Mom and Dad
Need anyone ever ask why?

3. VINCENT ROCCO SALADINI, JR.

On March 18, 1958, we were blessed with the birth of our third and last child, a beautiful son, Vincent Rocco Saladini, Jr. Vincent weighed in at 10 lbs. 14 ozs. The nurses at the Presbyterian Hospital in Newark, New Jersey, nicknamed him "Two Ton Tony Galento," after the famous heavyweight boxer. We were thrilled to add a son to our family.

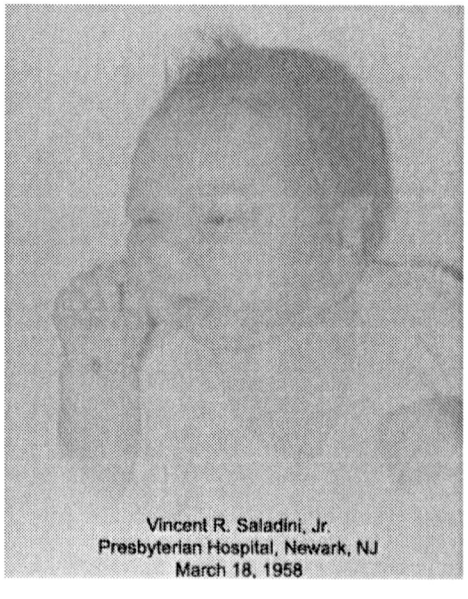

Vincent R. Saladini, Jr.
Presbyterian Hospital, Newark, NJ
March 18, 1958

When Vincent was nine months old, we had a new ranch home built in Clifton, New Jersey. Vincent delighted in playing in the backyard with his two sisters. He especially enjoyed watching me landscape, plant the garden and tend to all of our beautiful rose bushes and other shrubbery.

When Vincent was five years old, he picked up a pinecone from the nearby woodshed and placed it in a flowerpot. He would watch the pot each day. One particular day, Vincent noticed a green shoot bursting through the soil, and excitedly ran to show me his discovery. Over the next several months, Vincent's plant continued to grow until it ultimately became a towering pine tree, over thirty feet tall. It continues to this day to grace our front yard, standing proud and tall, having served as a calm and peaceful resting place for many animals and birds over the years. In fact, I was so inspired by Vincent's pine tree that I was moved to write the following dedication to his "discovery." **"When I look upward at the towering pine that graces our front lawn at 11 Pilgrim Drive, Clifton, New Jersey, I am reminded of the Spring of 1963, when my son, Vincent Rocco Saladini, Jr., at the tender age of five, planted a lonely pinecone, and thus began the many years of nurturing, patience and tender loving care. It grew straight, tall and strong because it grew slowly and well."**

Over the years, Vincent, Jr., has always conducted himself in a manner that has made us proud to call him our son. He was always helpful around the house and delighted in gardening with me. A dedicated and conscientious student, Vincent, Jr., excelled in his studies throughout his school years, and remained a straight-A student even during the strenuous years of study at Columbia University and Columbia Medical School in New York City.

Vincent graduated from Clifton High School in 1976 having achieved many honors and awards for his academic excellence. Following his graduation from Clifton High School, Vincent attended Columbia University in New York City from 1976-1980, where he graduated Magna Cum Laude and was a member of Phi Beta Kappa.

Vincent, Jr., next attended Columbia University Medical School from 1980-1984, where, after many years of hard work and dedication, he graduated with honors and received an internship in its Anesthesiology Department from 1984-1985. In 1984, he was awarded the prestigious Medal of the Alumni Association. He also completed his residency there from 1985-1988. After completing his internship and residency at Columbia University, Vincent accepted a position at Hackensack University Medical Center in Hackensack, New Jersey, where he continues to this day to administer to the needs of his patients with the utmost level of professionalism, dedication, and care.

While at Hackensack University Medical Center, Vincent met a beautiful young and talented doctor, Dr. Linda Barra, who shared his dreams and goals and whose dedication to her patients equaled that of his own. They were married on June 22, 1996, and made their home in Saddle River, New Jersey.

In 2001, during our annual Christmas Eve gathering at the home of Mr. and Mrs. Joseph Barra, we were pleasantly surprised when our son Vincent, Jr., announced that Linda was expecting their first child in July. We were all delighted to hear the good news.

The big day arrived on July 15, 2002, at exactly 10:02 a.m., when Linda gave birth to a beautiful baby boy at Valley Hospital in Ridgewood, New Jersey. He was proudly named Harrison Cole Saladini. We were all overjoyed to hear the good news and welcomed our newest addition to the Saladini family with open arms.

Linda Victoria Saladini
holding Harrison Cole Saladini
Vincent R. Saladini Jr.
Christening reception   October 19, 2002

CHAPTER NINETEEN

CHANGE OF CAREERS

In 1966, after approximately twenty years in the fashion industry, I was soon to experience something that would change my whole career as well as my life. One evening, I received a telephone call from a former co-worker, Carlo Mongrandi, with whom I had worked at New York Technical Institute of Technology. I had not seen him for fifteen years, and hearing from him was a pleasant surprise. He informed me that a teacher of custom tailoring was needed in the evening division at the High School of Fashion Industries in New York City. Carlo Mongrandi had knowledge of my intensive background in fashion design. He was also aware of my dream of teaching at that high school.

As fate would have it, I was in the process of looking for another job anyway since Mr. Charles Elbow had passed away. His son, Bill had told all of the employees that he planned to retire and close down the business. We were all devastated and saddened by the death of Mr. Elbow for with his passing went an era that would never come to pass again. I immediately called Carlo Mongrandi and told him that I was very interested in the teaching position at the High School of Fashion Industries. He gave me an excellent recommendation. With that, I arranged for an interview with the Chairman, Mrs. Theresa Fanelli. The interview went extremely well, and I was offered the teaching position. The date of September 26, 1966, launched the start of my teaching career, a career that would span the next two decades. I enjoyed teaching so much that I began making preparations to take courses to qualify for the teaching profession. In the spring of 1966, I began taking courses in the area of vocational technical education at New York State Industrial Teacher Training in New York City.

Vincent Rocco Saladini, Sr.

Charles W. Elbow
CORRECT DRESS FOR MEN
280 MAIN STREET
PATERSON, N. J.

January 26, 1968

TO WHOM IT MAY CONCERN:

 This is to attest to the fact that Vincent R. Saladini
has been in our steady employ from April 27, 1954 to April
17, 1967. His duties have included complete management of
our Custom tailoring shop, fitter in our Clothing Department,
and throughout the whole period has performed and/or super-
vised every type of alteration that has been required. His
skill in analyzing the requirements of an alteration to achieve
a perfect fit is of a high order, based as it is on a very
thorough knowledge of the techniques of pattern design.

 Throughout this period we have always found Mr. Saladini
to be an extremely diligent and interested member of our
organization, speedy in his work with no sacrifice in quality.
One of his outstanding virtues has been his friendly and
interested manner when dealing with customers in his capacity
of fitter with the result that our customers have complete
faith in his judgment.

 He is a man of wide range in interests beyond those
relating to his field of daily work; a man with an enquiring
mind which results in an urge to explore in a serious way
subject matter in the area of human relations and natural
resources.

 We recommend him to your attention with both confidence
and pride.

Respectfully,

Charles W. Elbow.

194

From spring 1966 until spring 1969, I earned a total of forth-five credits. I also received a diploma on May 22, 1969, from Manhattan Community College of the City University of New York Vocational-Technical Teacher Education in Men's Clothing Manufacturing. In addition, during the fall of 1968, I began to take courses at Fashion Institute of Technology in New York City. I earned thirty-six credits from fall 1968 to spring 1971. Although my schedule was grueling, I was determined to achieve my lifelong dream of obtaining a college degree.

During these trying times, my wife, Viola, was the glue that held our family together. She was extremely supportive, and she remained a constant source of encouragement and inspiration to me. Because I had to spend so many hours away from home commuting back and forth to take classes, Viola was left to assume most of the day- to- day chores and responsibilities around the house. I would leave at 5:30 a.m. each morning, and I would not return home until 11:00 p.m. each night. By the end of the night, I was physically exhausted.

The only thing that kept me going was the thought of returning home to Viola and the children each night and feeling their love and warmth all around me. Without their constant love and support, I would never have been able to achieve my dream of obtaining a college education. My family would always encourage me to strive to do my best, and they were always eager to assist me in any way possible to realize my dream.

On January 17, 1967, a full-time position became available at the High School of Fashion Industries day division. I immediately applied for the position. I studied hard for the written and practical examinations that I would have to take in order to be considered for the position. After what seemed like endless hours of studying, I took the test and was elated with the exciting news that I had passed

and was accepted for the new position. I was given a permanent appointment on April 17, 1967.

To further qualify for the necessary education needed in order to maintain such a permanent position, I decided to enroll at the New York State University at Oswego, New York Vocational Technical Education, to earn a Bachelor of Science Degree. I was accepted into the program at the age of forty-five. I was anxiously looking forward to pursuing my dream of earning a college degree. I began to take courses during the summer of 1969. I then continued taking correspondence courses throughout the fall and spring semesters.

During my summer semesters at Oswego, my wife and our three children accompanied me. We were delighted to have the chance to spend the entire summer together in Oswego. I shall never forget our first trip to Oswego. Because we would be away for the whole summer, we tried to anticipate what we would need to take with us. Space was limited since we were going to travel in our only means of transportation, our 1955 Chevy. We all woke up very early in the morning, too excited to sleep.

Despite our best efforts to get an "early" start, it was well after 10:00 a.m. before we actually pulled out of Clifton, New Jersey, and headed for Oswego, New York. We were certainly a sight to behold. Our little two- door Chevy was packed to the gills with pillows, suitcases,

guitars, electric frying pans and every other amenity imaginable. There was barely any room for us once we were fully packed; however, no one seemed to mind at all. We were too thrilled about the summer of excitement that lay ahead.

When we finally arrived at Oswego, New York, we were given wonderful accommodations right on the campus itself. We had an entire dorm suite all to ourselves for the whole summer with three bedrooms, a living room, kitchen and full bath. Once we unpacked, we toured the campus and met many other families who would also be spending the summer there.

One of the most memorable moments was when my family and I took a pleasant walk along the banks of Lake Ontario just as the sun was setting for the day. The brilliant colors of pink, orange, yellow and crimson were breathtaking. Each night whenever possible, we would renew our pleasure by gazing out over the lake and feeling the cool summer breezes tickling our faces.

Vincent R. Saladini Sr.
Graduation from
Oswego St. University
Oswego, New York
August 1971

During the day while I was in classes, my family would volunteer their time around the campus. They especially enjoyed assisting with the summer theater group. On any given day, my wife and children could be found working on theater sets and props, and organizing the costumes for the musical plays that were produced by the theater group during the summer. I would join them in my spare time since fashion design and costume making were my areas of specialization.

My family and I greatly enjoyed our work with the theater group as we found it to be challenging as well as rewarding. We also welcomed the opportunity to spend our time together on such a useful project. During our first summer, the theater group produced the delightful musical, *Carousel.* The crew actual constructed a working carousel for the musical with painted horses and colored carriages.

We saw the production rehearsals so often that by the time the actual musical took place, we had memorized everyone's lines and were able to sing along with the cast members. At the conclusion of each summer, a huge cast party was held for everyone who had participated in the production. We all had a wonderful time meeting the actors and actresses who had taken part in the musicals.

In the subsequent summers that we were at Oswego, the theater group produced *Once Upon a Mattress* and *Man of La Mancha*. When *Man of La Mancha* ended its final run of the summer, I was presented for my work on the musical, with the stone shield that had been created especially for the show. Despite its size and weight, my family and I managed to find a spot for the shield in our Chevy when we headed back to Clifton at the end of that summer.

My older daughter, Denise, who was seventeen years of age at the time, decided to take a course in chemistry at Oswego to earn college credits prior to attending Montclair State College (now Montclair State University) in Montclair, New Jersey, in the fall of 1970. I was taking the same chemistry course.

If I needed any help in chemistry, Denise would tutor me. Indeed, I was grateful for Denise's assistance since I had graduated from high school in 1942, and had little recollection of what I had learned in science so many years ago. Having graduated from Clifton High School in 1970 with high honors, Denise was familiar with the sciences, and she had a knack for making difficult scientific concepts easier to comprehend. With Denise's help, I passed my chemistry course with flying colors.

After many hours of grueling coursework, tests, reports, and countless projects, I was awarded a Bachelor of Science Degree in Vocational Technical Education from

Oswego State University in August 1971. Graduation day was one of the proudest moments of my life. I had finally achieved a dream that at one time in my life I had thought was impossible. Were it not for the constant love, support, and encouragement of my family, especially my wife, Viola, I would never have been able to realize such a dream.

Viola and our three children were all in attendance the day I was presented with my diploma. As I reached for my diploma, I could see the tears in Viola's eyes. I knew how proud she was of what I had achieved. Deborah, Denise and Vincent, Jr., all showered me with hugs and kisses as we made our way through the crowd of well-wishers. Seeing the love in my family's eyes, and knowing how proud they were of me made all of the hard work and the endless hours of sacrifice worthwhile. I was the only one of all of my brothers and sisters who had the opportunity and honor to achieve a college degree.

Having earned my college degree further enabled me to excel as a teacher at the High School of Fashion Industries. In 1973, I wrote the handbook entitled *Guidance for High School of Fashion Industries Student Handbook* for the High School of Fashion Industries which became the central guidebook for all of the students who attended classes there. In addition to my regular assignments, I also volunteered for the following:

1. Vocational Department Social Committee—1972-1976
2. United Federation of Teachers Consultative Committee—1976-1978

3. United Federation of Teachers Delegate—1978-1980
My duties included attending meetings and reporting
back to the teachers via written and verbal reports.

I greatly enjoyed performing these extra duties as
they allowed me to gain invaluable experience in the
educational process, and they further enabled me to share
my knowledge with my colleagues for the common good of
both the educators and the students. Both the teachers and
the chairman commended me for my work as a delegate.

Ever seeking to better myself and to gain as much
knowledge and information as possible, I next sought to
obtain a Master of Arts Degree in Student Personnel
Services. I enrolled at Montclair State College (now
Montclair State University). During the fall of 1971, my
daughter, Denise, was also a student at the same college
where she was pursuing a degree in Spanish and English as
a Second Language with the goal of entering into the
teaching profession.

My schedule at this point was especially grueling
since I was teaching full-time at the High School of Fashion
Industries in New York City and carrying a full college
course load at night. I found the courses that I was taking to
be interesting as well as challenging. Every day was a new
adventure that I was eager to experience and enjoy to the
fullest.

Most of the courses that I took required a great deal
of reading and research. The professors for the most part
were knowledgeable and motivating, and they tried to make
the courses as interesting as possible. I always looked
forward to attending classes and learning as much as I
could. In fact, throughout my entire college career, I never

missed a day of classes and graduated with a perfect attendance record.

My dreams finally came true when, in the summer of 1973, I completed my Master of Arts Degree in Student Personnel Services. What made this momentous occasion even more special was the fact that my daughter, Denise, and I both participated in the same graduation ceremony the following year. As I received my Master of Arts Degree, my daughter received her Bachelor of Arts Degree.

Our pride in ourselves and in each other for our accomplishments was evident as we were handed our diplomas. My wife, Viola, and our other children, Deborah and Vincent, Jr., all expressed to us how proud they were of

Denise and me. We celebrated with a quiet family dinner during which time we reflected on the years of hard work and the boundless love that had brought us to that special moment. Without my family, I would never have been able to accomplish all that I had, nor would the joy have been as great, if at all.

With my Master of Arts Degree behind me, I set my sights on continuing my education even further. In the summer of 1973, I enrolled in a Post-Masters Certification Program in Supervision at Montclair State College (now Montclair State University). The course work for this program included a great deal of research and home assignments and projects. Once again, I eagerly accepted the challenge and worked hard to achieve my goals.

Although I was the oldest student in the class, I had the distinct advantage of being able to draw upon my life's experiences to assist me in solving the many problems that were posed to us for a resolution in these classes. I was able to contribute to the class discussions and share what I had learned with the other students, who were eager to learn from my experiences.

In 1975, I was assigned to work in the guidance office at the High School of Fashion Industries as a part-time counselor. I would teach two periods a day and spend the remainder of the school day working in the guidance department. The administration felt that I had the background, ability, and personality to do an excellent job, especially since I had developed a good rapport with the students and staff alike.

Although I found guidance work to be very challenging and rewarding, I also enjoyed being in the classroom and imparting knowledge to the students. One of the highlights of my teaching career at the High School of Fashion Industries was my being able to convince the administration to admit females to my production techniques class. Prior to 1975, the class was only open to male students. I was assigned to teach that class for the 1975 fall term with all male students. Several of the female students, who were in my pattern-making class, asked me if I would accept them into my production techniques class as they were very interested in that area of study.

The female students were confident that I would do my very best to admit them into the class so that they would be afforded the same educational opportunity as were the male students. I spoke with my Chairman, Ms. Clementine Mantegari, regarding changing the requirements to admit female students. At first she questioned whether or not the female students could meet the challenge of the course and perform the duties required such as lifting heavy bolts of fabric and working with the heavy equipment. I assured her that during World War II, women were able to perform all of the jobs previously performed only by men and that they were successful in doing so.

My sisters worked at an aircraft factory and were able to perform duties far more strenuous than the types of skills and duties required for the Production Techniques course. Ms. Clementine Montegari advised me that she would speak to the Principal, Mr. Michael Katzoff, and secure his permission to allow females to enroll in the course.

Mr. Katzoff summoned me to his office to discuss the pros and cons of admitting females to the course, and after much convincing on my part, he finally agreed to give it a try. In fall of 1975, we admitted three females to the course.

In addition to performing all of the work required, the female students excelled over many of the male students in some of their skills. As word spread throughout the school as to our successful admission of females to the course, more and more women signed up for the course in subsequent semesters.

The course had become so popular, that we had to open up a second class to accommodate all of the students who had registered for the course. I am proud to have been a part of this historical moment in the history of the High School of Fashion Industries and consider it to be one of my greatest achievements in life. My program, which is the only program of its type in the United States, is still presently being used and continues to remain popular with the students.

Once I had completed my education, I decided to apply for a position as an Adjunct Professor of Men's and Women's Fashion Design at the Fashion Institute of Technology in New York City. I submitted my application, which included a recitation of my experiences and background in the field of fashion. Professor Edmund B. Roberts, the Chairman, interviewed me. He was very impressed by my credentials, and offered me a position that I eagerly accepted. In September of 1975, I was hired as an Adjunct Professor in the evening division for Men's and Women's Fashion Design. Fashion Institute of Technology is part of the New York State University system. With its excellent reputation, the Fashion Institute of Technology is recognized and respected worldwide.

With this added responsibility, my daily schedule was especially grueling and exhausting. I would go directly from my daytime position at the High School of Fashion Industries to the Fashion Institute of Technology Evening Division. I did not mind the hectic schedule, however, since I enjoyed both of my jobs very much. I was also fortunate in that the two schools were only two blocks apart, so I did not have to be too concerned about the time involved in traveling between jobs.

I found college teaching to be challenging and rewarding since the students were enrolled there not because they had to be, but rather, because they wanted to be. The students came from all parts of the world and brought excellent skills, boundless talent, and interesting new ideas and challenges. My classes were always well attended and filled to capacity each semester.

The students would take part in producing a school fashion show from the garments that they had produced in the classroom. The shows were always a huge success. Many people from the fashion industry would attend these fashion shows because of the vast pool of talent, and potential designers for hire after graduation.

In the summer of 1976, I realized another lifelong dream. I had earned thirty credits and was qualified to receive a Post-Master Certification in Supervision. With my educational accomplishments and qualifications, I set out to pursue the various licenses in a variety of other areas. In addition, I satisfactorily completed a pilot professional seminar for first level supervision sponsored by the New York City Board of Education. During the summer of 1976, I was awarded a certificate. To date, I have achieved the following licenses:

1. The University of the State of New York—5/9/50—Permanent- Private Trade School Teacher's License

2. New York City—2/16/66—Permanent- Teacher of Men's Clothing Manufacturing, Public School

3. The State of New York—2/1/71—Permanent- Tailoring As A Trade Shop Subject, Public Schools

4. The State of New Jersey—3/74—Permanent- Student Personnel Services, Public Schools

5. The State of New York—9/1/75—Permanent- Guidance, Public Schools

6. The State of New Jersey—10/76—Permanent- Supervisor, Public Schools

7. The State of New Jersey—1/77—Permanent- Principal, Public Schools

8. The State of New York—2/1/78—Permanent- School Administrator and Supervisor, Public Schools

9. Fashion Institute of Technology, New York City— 10/18/82- Certified as an Adjunct Professor of Men's and Women's Fashion Design

10. The City School District of New York—8/18/83— Permanent- Guidance Counselor, Secondary Schools

The following is the statement of my educational philosophy that I was required to submit in order to obtain my licenses in the areas of Assistant Principal of Guidance and Assistant Principal of Needle Trades.

My decision to pursue a license as Assistant Principal of Guidance and Assistant Principal of Needle Trades has not been a hasty one. In a sense, it started at the age of twelve when I began my career as an apprentice custom tailor. I was very fortunate to have a master craftsman as my teacher, who, through his example, instilled in me a positive attitude, which has helped shape the educational philosophy I hold today. I

was encouraged to take pride in what I was doing, and to work to my fullest potential. The environment that prevailed was one of respect, understanding, and sensitivity to the needs of others. I was encouraged to be open and honest not only with my employer, but also, with my fellow workers.

I strongly feel that the prevailing climate in our schools today requires an individual with a broad knowledge not only in the area that he/she is supervising, but also, in the areas of individual and group dynamics. My past experiences have been broad and highly diversified. I started out as an apprentice custom tailor, and gradually progressed through a variety of jobs requiring responsibility and skill. I served in the United States Navy aboard naval ships. This required working closely with others for long periods of time.

My academic and technical education includes a Bachelor of Science Degree in Vocational-Technical Education, a Master of Arts Degree in Student Personnel Services, and Advanced Certification in Educational Administration Services, and an Advanced Certification in Educational Administration and Supervision. I also hold a diploma and four certificates from technical schools related to the fashion industry.

My teaching experience includes private, secondary, adult continuing education and college levels. I also served seven years in the guidance department at the High School of Fashion Industries in all phases of guidance services. My experiences include work in the admissions office, the cooperative education program, as grade advisor and coordinator for the ninth, tenth, eleventh and twelfth year grade levels and three years as a college advisor.

My union experiences include ten years as an Executive Board member of Journeyman Tailors Union, Local 195, where I was involved in negotiating contracts.

All of my aforementioned experiences have made me more fully aware of the many complex problems facing the various disciplines. I feel that with my broad diversified background, I will be in an excellent position to better cope with the problems and decisions that must constantly be made.

I strongly believe that a supervisor should, by example, create a climate in the school where ideas and suggestions can be freely exchanged between teachers and administrators and constructive criticism is encouraged.

In conclusion, I am confident that my qualifications and past, diversified experiences in the areas of industry, business, labor education, and the military have given me the necessary foundation for making a positive contribution in my role as an Assistant Principal of Guidance or as an Assistant Principal of Needle Trades.

I successfully received a permanent license and certificate in both of the above areas listed in New York State, New York City and New Jersey in February 1978.

In 1980, my chairman, Professor Hilda Jaffee, requested that I write a new program of study for the Ladies' Custom Tailoring Division at the Fashion Institute of Technology. I enthusiastically accepted the assignment, and set out to pursue my goal. First, I did extensive research. I also relied on my technical writing skills and knowledge of the clothing trade. The assignment was time-consuming since the material had to be thorough and accurate.

In 1981, I accomplished my goal, having successfully produced an excellent program that was accepted by my chairman, Hilda Jaffee. She commended me on my worthy accomplishments and excitedly put the program into effect. I had produced a four term level course of study from the very basic skills to the more advanced skills of coat making. I am proud to say that I was awarded a copyright in April 1982 for my work entitled *Four-Term Ladies' Tailoring Program.* The program has been well received by the administration as well as the teaching staff and students.

At the High School of Fashion Industries, I continued to work in the guidance office part- time until the guidance test opened up for permanent counselors in 1981. Our chairman, Emanuel Alpert, was very pleased with my work in guidance, and I had received a number of excellent observations and reports as to my work with the students. I immediately applied for the guidance test and began the long preparation process to sit for the examination.

In order to adequately prepare myself to sit for the guidance examination, I read every possible book that I could find in the library. I also reviewed all of my notes and papers from all of the courses that I had taken in the area of guidance when I was studying for my Master of Arts Degree in Student Personnel at Montclair State College (now Montclair State University).

The guidance test, which consisted of six hours of written and oral material, was extremely difficult. Of the one thousand students who sat for the examination, I was one of only two hundred students who actually passed the test.

In June of 1983, Mr. Emanuel Alpert retired after many years of exemplary service at the High School of Fashion Industries. He was always available to offer assistance to those around him when needed. I shall be forever grateful to him for helping me to develop professionally as a guidance counselor.

In September of 1983, I was permanently appointed to a position of full- time guidance counselor at the High School of Fashion Industries. This day was indeed memorable for me and for my family since I had always hoped to become a full-time counselor.

I have long been deeply interested in the social sciences and humanities. I was confident that with my early training, occupational background, my love for working with people, and the training that I had received pursuing a Masters Degree, I would be able to make a positive contribution to the Guidance Department. I was finally able to realize my dreams as a full-time guidance counselor.

I was fortunate in that I had the opportunity to work with an excellent staff of dedicated, caring counselors who took pride in their work with the students. Martin Block, Assistant Principal of the Guidance Department, was always available to lend a helping hand. His support and assistance were invaluable.

In the early years as a full-time guidance counselor, I was assigned to the freshman class where I gained a great deal of valuable experience. I had the added pleasure of being able to follow the class throughout their four years at the school, which enabled me to take an active part in helping them to plan a course of action that would best enable them to shape their futures.

My dedication and outstanding work with the senior students gained so much recognition that Mr. Block requested that I work with the senior class on a permanent basis, which was a challenge I was eager to accept. Working with the senior class required a great deal more work. Since they would be graduating, more attention was needed with respect to the classes and credits that they were taking.

One of my most pleasurable and rewarding tasks in working with the senior class was being asked by the seniors to write letters of recommendations on their behalf to prospective schools and colleges that they hoped to attend upon graduation. I was also responsible for making certain that the seniors had taken all of the necessary courses that they needed in order to graduate, and that they had met all of the other graduation requirements. I am proud to say that one of my counselees, Jenny Hwang, became a full- time counselor at the High School of Fashion Industries.

As a full-time guidance counselor for the senior class, I also had a number of other duties, one of which included conducting career days for the students. I would organize a college fair day where I would invite college representatives from all over the United States to visit our school and offer information about their colleges' programs. Such an event enabled the students to be in touch with a variety of schools and to be in a unique position to ask questions to determine if any one particular school best suited their individual needs.

If one school happened to peak their interest, the students could request copies of literature for that school directly from the representative, and then review it at their leisure. At any given college fair, we would have between fifty to seventy colleges in attendance for the benefit of the students. The fairs were always a huge success.

As a member of the Guidance Department in my capacity as Grade Coordinator and College Advisor, I would work closely with the staff, parents, students, businessmen, social agencies, and other such types of organizations. I would also inform parents of their child's educational progress, college information, scholarships, job opportunities and other information required. I also worked closely with such outside agencies as the Bureau of Guidance, Youth Services, and other social agencies.

Part of my job included working closely with Mr. Block, Assistant Principal of Guidance, coordinating various activities such as grade meetings, and organizing and implementing field trips to different industries and colleges. My goal was to expose the students to as broad a spectrum of experience as possible so that they would best be able to select a course of action that would most benefit them in the future.

As previously mentioned, in 1973, I wrote a student handbook to further assist the students, for which I was highly commended not only by the students and parents, but also, by Mr. Alpert, Assistant Principal of Guidance. I derived a tremendous amount of joy and satisfaction from working with the students, especially the seniors, and from being in a position to assist them in planning their futures. We were fortunate in that we had access to a computer that listed all of the colleges in the United States. The students would use the computer quite frequently to obtain valuable printouts of the different colleges and the programs of study that they offered.

Not only would the printout list the types of programs offered at any given school, but also, it would inform the students as to the entrance requirements for each school. Knowing what was required of a particular school enabled the students to determine what coursework they needed if they intended to apply to that particular school.

I found my work as a guidance counselor to be extremely rewarding for it gave me the unique opportunity to assist students in planning their future and achieving their goals. I also discovered from working with students that they respected the sound advice, honesty, and sincerity that I offered to them during the counseling process.

The students respected the fact that even though I would give them the bad news along with the good, I always tempered the bad news with a positive outlook towards the future. It is easy for students to become discouraged when they receive a rejection letter from a college of their choice, for with that rejection comes a certain feeling of self-loathing and profound disappointment.

As such, I always made certain to encourage the students to continue to strive for their goals, and to not allow anyone or anything to hinder their hopes and dreams. I also encouraged them to do their best and to believe in their abilities.

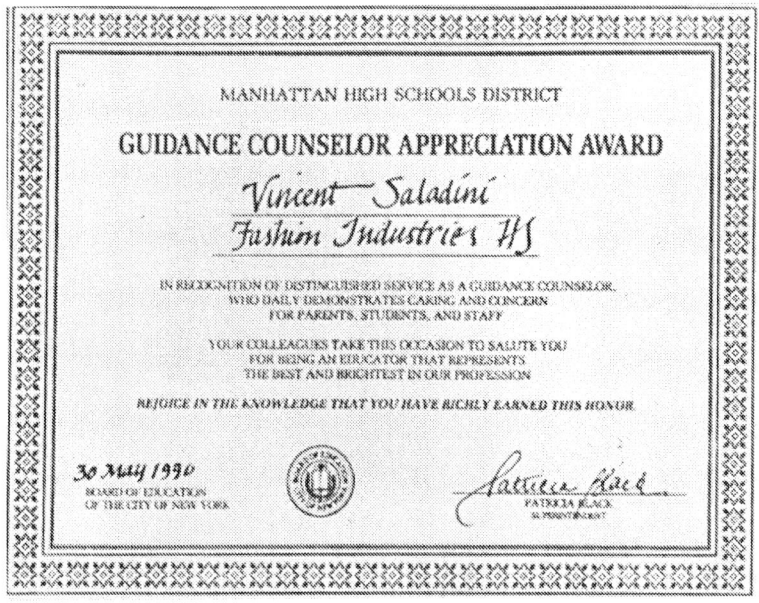

Vincent Rocco Saladini, Sr.

Board of Education
The City of New York

High School of Fashion Industries

225 West 24th Street, New York, N. Y. 10011

Charles Bonnici Principal I.A.   ALgonquin 5-1235

```
Person Observed-Vince Saladini, Counselor    Obs.     5/20/91
Observer-Martin Bloch, A.P. P.P.S.           Conf.    5/21/91
Type-Individual Interview                     Report   5/23/91
```

Dear Vince:

This is an observation report of a meeting you conducted
with Tanya, a 12th grade student and her mother. The meeting
was requested by the parent after she received a letter from
you informing her that Tanya had failed two subjects and that
her graduation was endangered if she did not pass her classes
at the end of the term.

You opened the session by asking the parent what she wanted
to discuss. The parent asked for an explanation of the
letter (enclosed). You explained that Tanya failed her
English and physical education classes the second marking
period and that both are required for graduation. If Tanya
does not pass the classes she will not be eligible to attend
graduation ceremonies and will have to attend summer school.
You asked Tanya why she was failing the classes.

Tanya said that she had not turned in several assignments in
her English class and that she had cut physical education or
was unprepared too many times. You asked if the student had
spoken to her teachers to see how she could make up the work
she did not do. The student said she hadn't. The mother
asked why not? The student did not respond.

You made the parent and student aware that teachers are
required to give students the opportunity to make up missed
work. You suggested that the assignments in English could be
done between now and the end of the term and that she could
make up the physical education classes by attending during
lunch periods or after her last class of the day, since Tanya
leaves school at the end of seventh period. Tanya agreed to
speak with the teachers about making up the work.

Tanya's mother asked how not graduating in June would affect
her daughter's admission to college. You told her that as
long as she received her diploma no later than August (summer
school) she could begin college in September.

216

You reviewed the students record and pointed out that she passed all her RCT's and needed only to pass her classes and her trade exam to qualify for the Fashion Industries endorsement. You ended the interview by saying that you hoped you would see both of them at graduation in June.

Discussion

You presented Tanya's record in a clear and succinct manner. The parent appeared to understand what you were saying and had all her questions answered. You presented practical and viable strategies for Tanya to use in her effort to pass her classes and graduate. You also pointed to the student's strengths by reviewing her record with the parent and showing that she can qualify for the school endorsement. The interview ended on a positive note.

As a follow up to the interview and the intervention strategies you presented, we discussed you calling the student next week to see what the results of the her efforts with her teachers were.

Thank you for the opportunity to observe this interview. Since this may be the last observation report I write for you before you retire, I want to commend you for all your efforts over the years to help seniors negotiate their last year of school. I am particularly grateful that I could count on you to run the college office, Metroguide and still counsel students. It is a herculean task that not many can do successfully or would even undertake. To know that you were doing the job was to know that a competent, caring person was available to students and parents as they experienced the pressures and anxieties of leaving high school for the next stage of their lives. Its been a pleasure to know you and work with you. You will not be easliy replaced.

Sincerely,

Martin Bloch

I have read this observation report and understand a copy will be placed in my personnel file.

Vince Saladini   5/24/91
Vince Saladini   date

Vincent Rocco Saladini, Sr.

I am proud to say that during my years as a guidance counselor, I received many commendations for my work from my colleagues as well as from my counselees. In fact, even to this day, I still hear from some of my students who have long since graduated and have gone on to pursue their hopes and dreams in the fashion industry.

I was pleasantly surprised to one day receive a newspaper article from a town in Pennsylvania which discussed two students whom I had formerly counseled at the High School of Fashion Industries. In the article the students explained the advice that I had given them regarding the possible opportunities awaiting them in the clothing industry.

It seems that the majority of the students were only interested in learning the designing aspect of the trade. I would advise the students, however, that they should first learn the technical aspects of the trade because that would best prepare them for learning other important aspects of the trade. These two particular students profiled in the article had followed my advice and explained how fortunate they felt for having done so. Interestingly enough, they became husband and wife, and opened up a very successful clothing manufacturing plant. I find such success stories to be most gratifying for they demonstrate my philosophy that anyone can realize his/her dreams if the desire is there and if he/she is willing to put forth the drive and determination to follow those dreams and make them a reality.

One of the highlights of my career while teaching at the Fashion Institute of Technology in New York City was being recommended by my chairman, Professor Edmund B. Roberts, to appear on a television program, *Financial News*

Network, "Money Talks," to represent the college. I agreed to appear gratis on the college's behalf as I felt it an honor to be selected for such an occasion.

On November 28, 1988, I appeared at the studio and proceeded to cover the topic entitled **"You can get the most value for your money if you use a little care in selecting your wardrobe."** The feedback that I received was very positive. In fact, I received many calls from former students and personal acquaintances who called to commend me for having given an excellent presentation. I found this experience to be most challenging and educational.

Another highlight of my teaching career while at the Fashion Institute of Technology was being selected by my chairman, Professor Edmund B. Roberts, and my colleagues, to render expert information in the field of men's and women's fashion designs and garment construction and to assist with that information in helping to write several articles for *Consumer Report Magazine.*

Approximately twenty leading clothing manufacturers were selected throughout the United States of America to submit women and men's garments. To prevent any possibility of bias based upon brand names, all labels were removed from the garments prior to our having conducted an evaluation, analysis and comparison based on quality of construction, materials, price ranges and design.

Amazingly, I discovered that the higher-priced garments were not necessarily the best buys. On the contrary, the true value depended upon who designed the garments, and where they were manufactured and sold. This assignment proved to be educational, interesting as well as challenging.

Throughout my teaching and guidance careers, I always felt truly honored to have been given the unique and rewarding opportunity to assist others in planning their futures and realizing their dreams. After over twenty-five years in the field of education, I finally decided to retire in June of 1991.

I must admit that my decision to retire was not an easy one for me for I truly loved what I did, and I enjoyed the one on one contact with the students and my colleagues. Even to this day, I reflect upon the many moments of happiness that I derived from my profession, and I remember my students and colleagues with fondness and joy. I am proud to have been able to make a difference in the lives of those around me. I am proud to report that many of my former students have gone on to become very successful in the field of fashion, and I still hear from many even to this day.

One particular student who stands out in my mind was a young man, approximately twenty years of age, who applied to my Custom Tailoring Class at Fashion Institute of Technology, New York City. From the first moment that I observed him at work performing his assignment, I knew that he had a tremendous natural talent for the field of fashion. Apparently his parents left Cuba to seek a better life in America. His father was a famous architect in Cuba and he had hoped that his son would follow in his footsteps. His son, however, had other ambitions. He aspired to become a clothing designer. Since he was so artistic and creative, I felt certain that he would enjoy a successful career in the fashion field.

His father was devastated and disappointed when he learned that his son did not share his same love of architecture, however, the young man had made up his mind and was determined that he would not allow his dreams and hopes of a career in fashion design to be dashed. He would spend all of his time at the college learning as much as he possibly could so that he would be able to pursue his dream.

He was able to quickly grasp the many difficult concepts and techniques of fashion design. Instead of producing only one or two garments as required, he would produce three original designs, each of them equally outstanding.

At the end of the semester, he submitted his garments to the Fashion Show Committee. Not only were his garments readily accepted for the fashion show, but also, he was given an award for the most creative garment in the show. I was truly proud of him and all that he had accomplished through hard work, determination, and perseverance. Upon graduation, he went on to study and work in Paris, France, where he remained for several years to refine and perfect his skills.

He eventually returned to the United States where he secured a position as a head designer in one of the most famous and prestigious fashion houses in New York City. This is truly a remarkable success story that fills me with great pride for I never had any doubts that he would realize his dreams of a successful and challenging career in the field of fashion.

CHAPTER TWENTY

VISIT TO MARTINSBURG

One of my most memorable visits to Martinsburg, West Virginia, was in 1965. I was anxious to make the pilgrimage home to see what the village of Big Springs, West Virginia, looked like after having been away from my birthplace for so many years. With some trepidation and feelings of uncertainty, I made my way home.

When I arrived, my brother Joe and I drove up to the area where fourteen active families once lived. We were greeted by a "No Trespassing" sign at the entrance of the road leading to the village. Since my brother was still employed by the Standard Lime and Stone Company as a foreman, he had access to the area.

Nervously I made my way beyond the "No Trespassing" sign only to have my worst fears realized. Heartbroken and dismayed, I stared in silence at the horror before me. The houses that once held laughing children and hopes for the future were no more. All that remained were empty foundations and debris from days long gone.

As I painstakingly made my way through the debris, I came upon the spot where my childhood home once stood proud and tall. Flowers were still growing in the garden that my parents had planted so many years ago. I knelt down to touch them in a desperate attempt to somehow recapture my past. Their fragrance was as sweet as ever, the only reminder of a childhood lost in time. My eyes welled with tears as I tightly closed them, trying to forget the aching pain that I felt deep inside.

As I drank in the flowers' sweet aroma, my mind drifted back to an earlier time, a happier time when it seemed as though my childhood innocence would last forever. For one brief, fleeting and timeless moment, I was a little boy again, running through the fields and charging through the front door for one of my mom's home-baked cookies. Suddenly, my brother's tap upon my shoulder sent me reeling, and I returned to reality once again. It was truly one of the saddest days of my life.

As we continued to walk through the surrounding meadows, the sight of overgrown weeds and shrubs devastated me. I could not help but remember the fertile lands and the neatly planted crops that once graced the countryside as well as the caring friends and relatives who toiled endlessly in the fields to give their families a better life. They were now gone but not forgotten, as I shall never forget the many fond memories of carefree childhood days playing with my friends and never worrying about tomorrow. No one can ever take away my memories for with the passing of time, they only become richer and more indelible in my mind. In spite of all the hardships that we had to endure, I still feel a deep and abiding sense of pride in having been a part of this truly remarkable community.

Amelia Caparotti   Adam Caparotti Sr.

The old swimming hole was barely recognizable under the heavy overgrowth of weeds and trees. The delicious water that once ran crystal clear and quenched our thirst on a sweltering summer day was now muddied and polluted. The creek had in some strange way become our solace and source of comfort during our many trying times. To see what it had become was heart wrenching and most unbearable. A rotted sign nearby warned everyone to stay away from a once cherished childhood delight.

I can remember as a young child, filling huge wooden buckets with this "nectar of the Gods" and rushing home to share such a priceless treasure with my family and friends. The section of the creek where watercress was once grown for sale in the local markets no longer existed. Instead, the overwhelming stench of stagnation filled the air as I strained to remember the crystal waters of long ago. Sadly, our childhood haven had succumbed to the ravages of time, as had so many of our other natural resources over the years.

My brother Joe and I sat in quiet reflection by the edge of the creek and began to reminisce about the past. One of the saddest times in my life was when Umberto Bigiarelli and his son, Adolph, decided to visit relatives in Italy. Their visit was filled with happiness and enjoyment until Adolph contracted a serious illness. More than anything, he pleaded to return to Big Springs, West Virginia. Sadly, Adolph died shortly after returning home.

Adolph loved the water and the sense of renewal and rebirth that it offered. He worked as a tailor in Martinsburg, West Virginia, where his talents and creativity were widely recognized. His brother, Italo Bigiarelli, who was trained as a shoemaker, had worked at his trade for many years and had become quite successful. After leaving the service in 1946, Italo Bigiarelli decided to seek employment at the Standard Lime and Stone Company where he remained until he retired. His brother, Elio Bigiarelli, upon leaving the service, applied for a job at the United States Post Office where he worked for many years as a mail carrier. He was also a member of the Army Reserve until his retirement. Elio was a talented man who had a keen mechanical mind as did so many of the other men of Big Springs, West Virginia.

My brother, Joe, married Umberto Bigiarelli's daughter, Enase, in 1947. They have two children, Tommy and Mary Jo Saladini. My nephew, Tommy, followed in his father's footsteps and has worked in the mines since he graduated from college. I have been told that Tommy is the last descendant of the original miners to be employed at the mines. All of the other descendants have opted for other careers.

Today, the mining operation has changed. A new company, Merriott Stone Company, purchased the mines over twenty years ago. As a result, working conditions have greatly improved. Today, the workers receive better wages, medical benefits, and retirement plans. Also, very little mining is done underground as had been the practice in the past. Instead, most of the stone is produced from the outside. Even to this day, Merriott still produces some of the best quality cement products in the country.

Joe and I glanced around one last time at the creek before heading back. They say that you can never go home again. Perhaps they are right, but I am not so sure. Home is in your heart, in your waking moments, and in your quiet times of reflection. I choose to believe that you can go home again, if only in your dreams, for they last forever.

CHAPTER TWENTY-ONE

SALADINI FAMILY REUNIONS

In 1983, my sister, Amelia Saladini Capriotti, of Charlestown, West Virginia, who has since passed on, decided to bring all of the families together. She arranged to hold the family reunion in Martinsburg, West Virginia. She obtained permission from the Park Division in Martinsburg, West Virginia, for us to hold our reunion at Military Park.

Our first reunion after not having seen each other for many years was exciting to say the least. Relatives traveled from far and near to join in the festivities. Each family was to bring a covered dish of favorite food to share with the others. Tables were set up under a huge canopy in the center of the park.

When we arrived, my brother Joe, his wife, Enase, my niece, Mary Jo, and my nephew, Tommy, greeted us. After many tears and warm hugs, we made our way through the crowd, eager to see everyone and to catch up on all of the "lost" years in between.

Festive tablecloths adorned the tables and the air was filled with the scent of delicious foods and other delicacies. We could not have asked for a more perfect day. The weather was beautiful with warm breezes and bright sunshine. My wife and I brought one of our favorite meals to share—chicken omelettes, a tasty recipe that my daughter, Deborah, created for us many years ago. Since desserts are one of Deborah's specialties, we also brought along a rich and luscious double fudge chocolate cake, homemade cherry cheesecake, chocolate chip cheesecake, and a variety of homemade cookies and pies.

Soon the tables were filled with hot, piping trays of homemade lasagna, ravioli, meatballs, sausage and peppers, home-baked breads and rolls, baked polenta, prosciutto, homemade salads, and dozens of other succulent delicacies. Homemade wine and beer were also available along with iced tea, lemonade, and other cool drinks.

That first year, over one hundred relatives joined in the celebration representing four generations of family members. We spent the day reminiscing about the past and looking forward to our future reunions together. Some of the old-timers went off to play bocce, a favorite pastime of long ago, not unlike that of modern-day croquette where wooden balls are hit through hoops with a large wooden mallet. Hearing their laughter in the distance reminded me of days long gone when my father and his friends would go out into the open fields and play bocce for hours on end until the daylight turned into a misty haze and evening beckoned them homeward once again.

Most of our relatives lived in the Maryland, New Jersey, Pennsylvania, and Virginia areas. My sister, Lucy Cutrone, who has since passed on, would travel by bus all the way from Rosedale, New York. My Aunt Alba and her children, Sammy, Noemi, and Virginia also came with their families all the way from Somerset, New Jersey. We spent the day remembering the "good old days" and catching up on all of the experiences that we shared over the years with our own families.

Everyone exchanged cherished family photographs while the younger children splashed in the nearby creek, bringing back many fond memories for me. Our family reunion soon took on a life of its own and we found ourselves already eagerly planning for the next one.

Whenever we attended our family reunions, we would stay at my sister, Minnie's house in Hagerstown, Maryland. She would always welcome my family with open arms. Being with Minnie was truly like being home. Minnie has a special knack for making everyone feel comfortable and totally at ease. Her home is adorned with an assortment of homemade dolls and other beautiful crafts that she makes herself and shares with others. Her bedrooms are reminiscent of a country toy store with beautiful dolls and soft, fluffy quilts gracing the beds. Deborah and Vincent, Jr., especially loved the large, stuffed clowns that Minnie had sitting so regally in their own rocking chair by the lace curtain windows.

Minnie's kitchen is the favorite gathering place when we visit for it is always filled with the tantalizing aroma of freshly baked cakes and pies. No visit with Minnie would be complete without her famous Sunday turkey dinner. My wife, Viola, and Deborah would help Minnie begin all of the preparations the night before. The vegetables would be cut and the turkey broth would be simmering on the stove while they prepared the best part of all—the stuffing!

Soon the entire house was filled with the delectable aroma of a feast fit for a king. Minnie would slow bake the turkey all night long so that when we awoke on Sunday morning, we were greeted by the most incredible scent imaginable. Minnie, Viola, and Deborah would then prepare the sweet potatoes and mashed potatoes along with a variety of fresh vegetable dishes. Minnie would prepare her famous broccoli, cheese, and rice casserole. She would always be sure to make my son, Vincent, Jr.'s, favorite dessert. It was an éclair icebox cake laden with rich creamy pudding and gooey chocolate fudge topping.

Around noontime, my niece, Rosemary, (Minnie's daughter), and her daughter, Sharon, (Minnie's granddaughter), along with my nephew, Bobby, (Minnie's son), and his family would gather at Minnie's house to join in the feast. My nephew, Jimmy, Minnie's other son, lives in Georgia with his family. Although he is not able to physically join us, he is always with us in spirit during such festive occasions.

My sister Rosie and her husband Jim, who has since passed on, would also stop by for dinner with their three sons, Stanley, Joseph, and Steven. Unfortunately, not long ago, Joseph died at the age of forty from natural causes. His death was a tragic loss to all who knew him and loved him.

Rosie was always sure to bring along her famous rum cake, another of Vincent, Jr.'s, favorite desserts. We would set up tables and chairs in every nook and cranny imaginable and somehow, we always managed to find room for everyone. No meal would be complete without having Minnie prepare a tray with "all the fixings" for some of her neighbors who did not have families of their own. Deborah enjoyed helping Minnie prepare the trays which would then be brought to Minnie's neighbors. They were always grateful and delighted with such a bountiful feast.

Saying good-bye to Minnie, Rosie, and their families was always so difficult for us for we truly loved being with them and sharing in these special times. Minnie would pack us a lunch of cold turkey sandwiches with home-baked rolls and extra stuffing on the side. She would be sure to include a healthy helping of Vincent's rum cake and an éclair icebox cake "for the road" as she would always say.

During the yearly reunions we also had a chance to visit with my sister Amelia and her four children, Adam Jr., Gene, Cesarina, and Linda, now deceased, the rest of whom all still live in the Charlestown, West Virginia, area. I have the utmost respect for my sister, Amelia, for were it not for her love and unselfish act of raising us after our mother died, we would not have been able to stay together. She showered us with love and was always there to listen to all of our troubles along the way. Amelia, an artistic and talented woman, is also an excellent seamstress who often made clothes for us when we could not afford to purchase them.

At the age of seventy-eight, Amelia was given an award for her artwork in Charlestown, West Virginia. A sincere and kind woman, Amelia befriends those around her and is always willing to lend a helping hand to those less fortunate. Even though we have different mothers, I regard Amelia as my true sister. Sadly, Amelia has since died.

Amelia was married to Adam Capriotti, Sr., for many happy years until he passed away twenty years ago. Although Adam did not have a formal education, he had the ability to perform all types of construction work. He personally built two beautiful houses for his family in Harpers Ferry, West Virginia. He also raised the finest wine grapes in the area and harvested the most succulent apples, peaches, and plums imaginable.

The grapes that he grew on his property were pressed into delicious wines that he made himself. Everyone would pitch in to gather the grapes and pour them into vats to be pressed into wine. The people that participated in Adam's adventures in making wine always had a wonderful time.

There is also a special place in my heart for my twin sisters, Minnie and Rosie. Throughout my life, they have always treated me with the utmost love and respect. Minnie would prepare sumptuous feasts for us whenever Viola and our children would visit her and she made us feel as though we belonged. When she told us "my house is your house," Minnie meant every word.

Even when we would visit Rosie and Jim, they would go out of their way to make our visits special and memorable. Rosie and Jim would cook for days, happily preparing all of our favorite foods to surprise us when we arrived at their house. Being with them was truly like being home once again.

Both Rosie and Minnie are immensely talented and artistic women who create all types of crafts, quilts, blankets, and other country delights. Not a holiday passes that we do not receive some of their delightful crafts from crocheted hearts for Valentine's Day, to knitted shamrocks for Saint Patrick's Day, to magnet Easter bunnies for Easter, to snowmen for Christmas. Deborah treasures each craft and proudly displays each one throughout her home and office for all to share.

I am blessed to have such a warm and loving family, and I shall always cherish the times that my sisters, brothers, and I spent together as children and later as adults. Their love has helped to shape my life and fulfill my dreams.

Vincent Rocco Saladini, Sr.

Vincent Rocco Saladini, Sr.

234

Left to Right
Lucy Saladini Cutrone, Rose Saladini Crabtree, Teodolinda Saladini,
Joseph Saladini, Minnie Saladini Manspeaker, Enase Saladini
June 1999   Martinsburg, West Virginia

Left to Right
Lucy Saladini Cutrone, Brian Smith, Bobby Smith, Rita Smith,
Rose Crabtree, Minnie Saladini Manspeaker
Saladini Family Reunion, Martinsburg, West Virginia
June 1999

235

CHAPTER TWENTY-TWO

1942 CLASS REUNIONS

Throughout the years, I have always tried to maintain contact with my former classmates so as not to lose touch with my past and all that I had experienced. I looked forward with eager anticipation to attending the yearly class reunions held in Martinsburg, West Virginia. We would hold the reunions at the Knights of Columbus Hall in Martinsburg, West Virginia, and then later make the trek to our old alma mater, Martinsburg High School, where we would relive the past, and relish all of our yesterdays when life seemed far more innocent and less complicated.

One dear friend who made each yearly reunion a special treat was Glenvile Shipe. I have always had the utmost respect for Glenvile's friendship. I can recall my first day of school at Martinsburg, West Virginia, and the sheer terror that I felt being in such an unfamiliar environment. Having always attended a one-room school, I was especially apprehensive about now attending such a large school as Martinsburg High, and fitting in with the other students. I did not know what to expect, or how the other students would treat me since my background was so different from theirs.

Administration

The ideals and aims of a club are the result of fine executive ability of its president. Good organization of a corporation is the result of the leadership of its highest executive. Likewise the high standard of any school is due in great measures to the character of its principal. We look to Principal Edwin Miller for guidance and inspiration. Our teachers in classes feel that they are our advisers for the year that we have under their guidance. Our principal is responsible for us for our entire four high school years. Any work which we attempt in later years will show the development of the four years we have spent under the guidance of Principal E. W. Miller.

Principal Edwin W. Miller   **Courtesy of Martinsburg High School's yearbook, The Triangle**

Faculty

JAMES ANDREWS
FRANK ARNETT
MARGARET BAKER
VANNETTA CHAMBERS
JOHN COBOURN
RUTH DARBY

HUGH BEALL
BERKELEY BARNEY, Sec'y.
VIRGINIA BYRER
MARY DEAN
VIRGIL FILES
NEVA FUSS

Vincent Rocco Saladini, Sr.

1942 Martinsburg High School Faculty

Catherine Chamberlin
Ann Cattell
Susan Hammer
Louise Jones Ambrose
John Knipe

Roderick Linger
Charles Lord
Irene Lough
Harry Luria
Elizabeth Miller

Frederick Miller
David Mudge
Nell M. Phillips
Minnie Rauch
Lena Reed

Kenneth Rentch
Guy Reynolds
Elanor Rogers
Katharyne Sompsell
Golan Studley

Virginia Schleun
Iren Shreve
Oren Smith
Mabel Swope
Paul W. Swope

George Whitehair

**Courtesy of Martinsburg High
School's yearbook,
The Triangle**

As I walked down the looming hallway, Glenvile Shipe approached me and introduced himself. I shall never forget how kind and cordial he was to me. He told me that he was there for me if I needed him and if I had any problems. He assured me that everything would turn out fine, and that I would soon adapt to my new environment. He went on to tell me that I would have no problem competing with the other students and achieving success. His words of encouragement boosted my confidence and self-esteem and enabled me to forge ahead with a renewed feeling of inner peace. He gave me a sense of belonging that I have never forgotten. I shall be forever grateful to this fine friend.

Another former classmate I shall never forget is Robert Sencindiver. Like Glenvile, Robert also introduced himself and made me feel right at home. He encouraged me to do my best and to always believe in myself. Somehow he sensed that I was in need of a friend and that my new school experience was overwhelming. He offered me hope and reminded me that I was not alone in my feelings, since many other students had felt the same apprehension when they first arrived at a new school.

Courtesy of The Triangle

Robert was especially understanding of my feelings since he, too, came from a small school in Pikeville, West Virginia. I can remember his telling me that he needed my friendship as much as I needed his, and that together, we would get through and succeed. Since we were in the same classes, our friendship continued to grow. During one of our yearly class reunions, we reminisced about our early days at Martinsburg High School, and smiled when we remembered how young and frightened we were back then and how far we had come since then.

I shall always cherish the many friends that I made in school and remember them with the same kindness and compassion that they offered to me. In spite of my difficult beginning, I enjoyed my years at Martinsburg High School, and shall always be grateful for having had such a meaningful experience.

During one of our reunions, particularly our May 23, 1987, reunion, we met at the Knights of Columbus in Martinsburg, West Virginia, where a beautiful photograph was taken of all of us who attended that year. I was so moved by the entire experience of seeing my old classmates and of being able to participate in the photograph that I am including it in my book as a reminder of so many pleasant memories of the past.

During one of our yearly reunions, some of my former classmates reminisced with me about a presentation I had given which involved an Italian ham known as "prosciutto." At that time, my biology teacher had instructed each student to produce a project for "show and tell," which we would then have to present before the class. I thought long and hard as to what my project would be, when suddenly, an idea came to me. I decided to give a class presentation on the process of how we cured meats.

Excitedly, I went home that day and spoke to my parents about my idea. I asked their permission to bring in a "prosciutto" (ham) to class so that I could explain how the hams were cured. My parents happily gave me their permission to do so. I was very excited about explaining the curing process to my classmates.

When my big day finally arrived, I packed a large prosciutto and several loaves of freshly baked Italian bread, and proceeded to carry them to school. I started my presentation by placing the prosciutto and bread on the table. The enticing aroma of the freshly baked bread and the prosciutto was mouth-watering.

I proceeded to explain to the class how we butchered hogs and how we prepared the prosciutto for curing. The bone, called the plate, was removed. The ham was then heavily salted and peppered before being placed between a press for curing. From time to time, we used a vice-like handle along with the press that allowed us to squeeze all of the juices from the ham. After several months of undergoing this process of extracting the juices, the ham was finally cured and ready to eat.

Prior to eating the prosciutto, the salt and pepper were removed. This rendered the ham ready for slicing. I asked the teacher if we could slice the prosciutto that I had brought. He went to the school cafeteria for a sharp carving knife. I then proceeded to thinly slice the prosciutto. The thinner the slice, the more appetizing it was. I also sliced the loaves of Italian bread and proceeded to place the prosciutto on top of the bread.

The aroma was incredible. I could tell by the reaction of the students that they were greatly enjoying my presentation for with it came the added bonus of a free sample of a true Italian prosciutto sandwich. My classmates insisted that I take the first bite since it was my presentation. No sooner had I done so, the rest of the students as well as my teacher also began to dig into their special treat. They were mildly surprised at the excellent flavor and aroma of the sandwich. Very few of them had ever eaten this type of food before.

I explained that prosciutto and bread were staple foods for the Italians and were generally eaten on a regular basis in Italian households. Needless to say, my presentation was a huge success with many students clamoring for the recipe that I was only too happy to share with them. My presentation not only allowed me to share a special treat with my classmates, but also, it gave them a true sense of what people from other cultures experienced. They remarked to me that they were grateful for having been given the opportunity to gain a greater understanding, respect, and appreciation for others, as well as what they had to offer to each other.

Even after so many years later, they remarked that they could still smell the enticing aroma of the prosciutto and freshly baked Italian bread as though it were yesterday. One of my former classmates told me that he was so impressed with my presentation that he decided to try the curing process at his own farm; he also learned to bake the Italian bread to serve with the prosciutto. His success made me extremely happy. He expressed deep gratitude to me for having shown him how to become successful. It gave me a warm feeling inside just knowing that I had accomplished something useful and was able to help a friend.

CHAPTER TWENTY-THREE

UNFORGETTABLE INCIDENTS

One of the most vivid incidents that stand out in my mind was the time that Mrs. Octavia Piccolomini, a neighbor from Big Springs, West Virginia, was fatally injured in an accident while she was attempting to feed the hogs. The hog pen was located about one hundred yards from the back of the house that was positioned on a steep slope.

One early November morning around 10:00 a.m., I was shaken to the bone by a loud shrill coming from the area of the Piccolimini home. Apparently, Mrs. Piccolomini was in the process of carrying two large buckets of feed to the pigsty when she lost her footing on a patch of ice on the ground and tumbled head first down the bottom of the hill.

Running as fast as I could, I made my way to the area of the pigsty when I noticed Mrs. Piccolomini was lying on the ground writhing and screaming in pain. I shall never forget the look of agony and terror on her face as she screamed and screamed for someone to help her. The bone from her shin was protruding, and she was bleeding profusely.

I raced to the house and called out for her sons Johnny and Chris who happened to be home. I explained to them what had happened and all three of us rushed to the bottom of the hill. Carefully, we carried Mrs. Piccolomini back to the house. At this point, she was hallucinating and going into shock due to the loss of blood from her leg wound.

Because we did not have any phones in our houses, we had to run down to the nearest store about one mile away in order to call for a doctor. Mrs. Piccolomini was delirious by now. Drifting in and out of consciousness, she kept repeating that she knew she was going to die. She begged us to make sure that her children were cared for and loved. She did not want them to ever be alone.

During one of her moments of lucidity, she pleaded with us not to call the same doctor who was present when she gave birth to her children because she had had a very bad experience with him. We assured her that we would try to find another doctor if possible but that we did not have much of a choice since there were so few available doctors in the town of Martinsburg, West Virginia.

In desperation, we were finally able to locate Dr. Power who came immediately when we told him what had happened. We watched as he tried in vain to administer medical care to Mrs. Piccolomini. He voiced his concerns as to the likelihood of her recovery because she had lost a tremendous amount of blood, and she was in deep shock from the trauma and extent of her injuries.

Despite having done all that he could to save her, Dr. Power was deeply saddened when Mrs. Piccolomini died several days later from her injuries. We were all terribly devastated by her untimely death. We all loved her and respected her, and she was often thought of as a second mother to many of the children in the village.

I can remember how kind and compassionate she was to me when I once got hit over the eyebrow with a bat while serving as catcher during a baseball game that we were playing. It seems that I was catching when I somehow got too close to the batter, who, coincidently, was her own son, Sammy Piccolomini. The pitcher, Elio Bigiarelli, threw the ball, and when I went to reach for it, I came too close. The bat came back and landed over my right eyebrow, splitting it wide-open and splattering blood everywhere.

I was really scared to go home because I did not know how my father would react. I decided, instead, to go to Mrs. Piccolomini's house since it was nearby and I felt comfortable with her. When I explained to her what had happened and that I was afraid for my father to see me when I was bleeding so profusely, she took me in her arms and held me close. All the while she comforted me and told me not to worry because she would explain everything to my father.

In the meantime, she took a clean cloth and squeezed the open cut for about an hour to stop the bleeding. She then gave me warm tea and crackers. After my father came home from work, Mrs. Piccolomini took me to him and gently explained what had happened. My father looked at me with a twinkle in his eye and a slight smile on his face and asked me "Well, did you break the bat?" With that he held me in his arms and told me how much he loved me. I knew then that I would not be reprimanded and I was greatly relieved. My father told me that he knew how much I loved baseball and that accidents will happen. My father delighted in calling me "Babe Ruth" since I was an excellent baseball player.

I shall never forget Mrs. Piccolomini and the love that she gave to all those around her. When she died so tragically and unexpectedly, everyone in the village felt her deep loss. She would never be forgotten by the many villagers whose lives she touched.

Another incident that will always stand out in my mind concerned the untimely death of Richard Qualini. It seems like young Richard's father was soon to celebrate his birthday and young Richard volunteered along with his friend, Louis Rossi, to go to the store and buy a birthday cake and birthday candles. The store was located about two miles from Big Springs, West Virginia.

It was already starting to grow dark around 6:30 p.m., when young Richard and Louis Rossi set out on foot to the store. They finally reached their destination and purchased the items that they needed. As they were heading back, tragedy struck. About a mile from home, a car suddenly veered off of the road striking young Richard who had been walking on the inside curb of the highway. The impact was so severe that young Richard was thrown about fifteen feet down the highway and was killed instantly. Louis Rossi escaped serious injury.

When the two boys failed to return home after several hours, their parents became deeply worried. They decided to search for the boys. About a mile up the highway, they noticed an ambulance and two police cars. As they approached the scene, they could hear Louis Rossi sobbing uncontrollably on the side of the road. When they asked him what had happened, he told them that Richard was gone. Richard's parents became hysterical and inconsolable as the horror of what had occurred began to sink in, and they realized that they would never see their son alive again.

Richard's parents were never quite the same again. They were so overcome with grief at the death of their son that they lost their will to live. As a parent myself, I realize now more than ever how devastating it is to lose a child, especially one as young as Richard. In my mind, Richard will always be that carefree, handsome young boy who ran with us through the fields and delighted in the simple joys of playing baseball and skipping stones in the river. Upon his passing, we all felt his loss deeply and we all missed him dearly.

Another unforgettable incident happened to me when I was around twelve years old. It seemed that I had gotten a bad cold accompanied by a high fever. I had also complained of a severe pain in my right side above my kidneys.

My parents, who by now had become deeply concerned, summoned Dr. Power, our family physician, who immediately came to our house to examine me. By the time he arrived, I had developed a severe swelling in the lower right side of my back that felt like a solid mass. Dr. Power looked solemnly at me as he proceeded to tap with his fingers in the area where I had the severe swelling and pain. I could see the expression on his face as he tapped along my back and with each tap came a sickening thud.

Dr. Power shook his head and told my father that he was very concerned about my condition. He said that he would return the next day, and that if I did not show any sign of improvement, I would have to be hospitalized. At that point, I grew frightened and extremely worried. I did not know what to expect, but I imagined the worst. All I knew was that the swelling had increased and the pain had become unbearable.

That night, I cried myself to sleep and prayed to the Lord that I would not have a serious illness. I asked God to heal me and to allow me to recover quickly. During the middle of the night, I was awakened by what seemed like a swishing sound. I opened my eyes and to my surprise, there appeared to be a vision of the Sacred Heart of Jesus at the foot of my bed. As I stared at the vision, I was suddenly overcome by an intense feeling of calmness and serenity. I was not afraid. Neither one of us spoke; however, a warm glow emanated from the vision. I then fell back into a deep sleep.

To my surprise, when I awoke the next morning, the pain and swelling in my back area were completely gone. I could hardly believe my eyes. I no longer had any pain, and my fever had broken. When Dr. Power returned to examine me later that day, he stared at me in disbelief. He told my parents that inexplicably, I was now fine, although he could offer no medical or scientific reason for my remarkable recovery.

I knew deep inside that the Lord had answered my prayers and healed me. I prayed to the Sacred Heart of Jesus once again, and gave him thanks for healing me. I made a promise to him to be a decent human being throughout my life, and I have always strived to honor that promise. To this day, I have only shared my miraculous vision of the Sacred Heart of Jesus with my wife and one or two other close people. I firmly believe that there is a greater power watching over all of us who guides us and comforts us in our hour of need. If one believes in the Lord, good things will come.

Another event that remains vivid in my mind centered on my military experience. When I entered the United States Navy in 1943, I was assigned to Great Lakes Navy Base, Illinois, for my basic training. I can recall my first visit to the dentist's office for a check up. I had never been to a dentist before I entered the Navy. As a young child, I had heard many horror stories about going to a dentist, and I was understandably nervous and apprehensive about my anticipated first visit.

When that fateful day finally came, I arrived at the dentist's office fifteen minutes before my appointed time. The waiting room was filled with sailors standing in line, each looking equally nervous. I took my position in line and waited anxiously to be called. After standing in line for about on hour, my name was finally announced. I could feel my body go numb as I made my way to the door of the office. I truly did not know what to expect.

As I sat down in the chair, I felt a cold chill run up and down my spine. The dentist proceeded to examine my teeth. Then he took a complete x-ray of my mouth. He told me that I had a cavity that needed to be filled. The next fifteen minutes were a complete blur. I could hear the shrill sound of the drill as the dentist began to drill my tooth. I felt an excruciating pain in the back of my head and I could hear myself screaming in agony. I later learned that the dentist was using an old-fashioned drill, and did not give me any Novocain to deaden the pain.

The more I cried out in pain, the harder he drilled. At one point he told me that if I did not stop screaming, he would clamp my jaws open. A wave of nausea came over me, and I could feel the room spinning. Finally the drilling stopped, and I felt my body go limp in the chair. Although my terrible ordeal was over, this painful experience left an emotional scar on me that took a long time to heal. I never did go back for another dental appointment.

Another incident that I experienced while in the Navy occurred during basic training at Great Lakes Navy Base, Illinois. Volunteers were needed to test blister gas on the skin. We were told that if we volunteered, we would receive a special weekend pass, a letter of commendation, and a special meal. Being young and naive, I was willing to volunteer for just about anything.

Along with ten other men, I volunteered for this experiment. The experiment consisted of inserting our left arms in a slot with the gas's being directed to the under part of our arms by means of a tube. We had to remain in that position for one hour while the gas bombarded our arm.

After we were finished with the procedure, we were taken to a room that was about one hundred degrees. They required us to exercise for one hour without a break. After we were through exercising and the experiment had ended, we asked about the promise made to us to give us a special weekend pass, a letter of commendation, and special meal.

We were abruptly told to go back to our barracks, and that we were not going to receive anything. Disillusioned and upset, we returned to our barracks, realizing at that moment that we had been misled into volunteering. I developed a huge blister on my left arm that left a scar I still carry today.

Despite having been duped by the Navy, I do not regret having volunteered for this experiment. If the experiment helped to save lives, then it was worth it to have volunteered. I probably would have volunteered even if we were not promised incentives to do so.

Looking back on my life, I consider myself a very fortunate man. The incidents that have touched my life, both good and bad, have convinced me that each person is placed on this earth for a specific purpose and for a limited period of time. It was during my duty aboard the USS JASON ARHI ship and prior to the invasion of Leyte in the Philippines, that my beliefs were reinforced once again.

It seems that fifty men were needed to go on a special assignment. The assignment required a man to hold a Ship Fitter's Rank. The purpose of this special assignment was to scout out the beaches prior to the invasion. I held the rank of Petty Officer Metalsmith Third Class. My insignia consisted of two hammers that crossed. It was the same insignia as the Ship Fitter's insignia.

My friend, George Worthington, and I were the only two Metalsmiths selected out of the total number of fifty men needed for this extremely dangerous assignment. It was a nerve-racking time for all of us for we knew just how deadly this assignment could be.

I can recall one of my sailor friend's telling me with tears in his eyes that he had a bad feeling about going on this assignment. He said that he had a wife and two small children at home in Brooklyn, New York, and that he had a sick feeling deep inside that he would never see them again. I tried my best to console him and to reassure him that we would make it through this ordeal together.

At 2:00 a.m. prior to our scheduled departure at 6:00 a.m., a call came in from San Francisco, California, informing the officer in charge that my friend George Worthington and I were to be removed from this special assignment because we held the rank of Metalsmith. They wanted only the rank of Ship Fitters to be on board. I greeted the news with mixed emotions. On the one hand I was relieved that I would not have to go on this dangerous assignment, but on the other hand, I was saddened that I would not be able to accompany my friend from Brooklyn.

Much to our great sadness, we later learned that about a day after they had left on this special assignment, suicide planes attacked the fifty men who were aboard the ship. The attackers dropped a bomb down the stack of the ship blowing it to pieces, killing all fifty men on board. I immediately thought of my friend from Brooklyn, and his chilling premonition that he would never see his wife and two young children ever again. Silently I prayed for him and the other men who lost their lives on that perilous assignment. I also thanked the Lord for having spared me. Once again my beliefs were reaffirmed that God has a plan for each of us. My time had not yet come. I was destined to fulfill other hopes and dreams.

Still another incident that impacted on my life occurred when I was serving aboard the USS JASON ARHI, repair ship. We were anchored in Ulithi, a small island in the Pacific. We were told that this was a safe haven from the Japanese suicide planes. One evening around 7:00 p.m., while I was sleeping in the aft end of the ship, I was suddenly awakened by the loud crash of a plane.

It appeared that a Japanese Kamikaze suicide plane had attacked our ship, the USS JASON ARHI. However, it overshot its mark by seven feet which would have been the area where I was sleeping, hitting instead, the US RANDOLPH, the aircraft carrier which was anchored nearby. There was mass confusion everywhere. At first I thought I was dreaming. Everything seemed to be happening in slow motion. It all seemed so surreal.

I immediately ran to my battle station. As I raced to my position, I crashed head on with another sailor who had been running in the opposite direction. We both fell to the ground and looked at each other, dazed and frightened. I never did find out who he was.

Once I arrived at my station, which was a lookout at the bow of the ship, I could see sailors jumping off of the ship into the pounding waters below. Flames were shooting out from every direction. Other ships in the area were sending in crews to help some of the men, but their attempts were futile. All around, charred bodies were floating in the choppy waters below, and the stench of burning flesh that filled the air was gut-wrenching. Once everything had calmed down, it was discovered that one of the suicide pilots was a female. It took several days to retrieve all of the bodies from the water. This was one of the saddest, most traumatic times in my life. Once again, I said a silent prayer for all of the brave men who sacrificed their lives that day for our country, and I thanked God for sparing me and keeping me safe.

Another incident that I recall happened when we were anchored in Ulithi and we were assigned to repair an aircraft carrier that had been hit by suicide planes. The USS JASON ARHI repair ship had pulled along side of the damaged carrier. I was among the group of men assigned to repair the damages.

In order for a man to get from one ship to another, the others would place him in a bucket and swing him on to the other ship using a derrick. I had spent the entire day aboard the damaged ship and was ready to return to my ship, the USS JASON ARHI. It was around 6:00 p.m., and I had just signaled to the operator to come and pick me up.

I was waving to the operator and he was starting to head my way. All of a sudden, before I even knew what was happening, I was at the bottom of the lower level, lying on a platform thirty feet below. I can remember seeing the Navy pilots standing over me trying to get me to lie still. I kept repeating that I was fine and that I just wanted to go back to my ship. After a few minutes they explained to me what had happened. At this point, I was completely dazed.

Apparently someone had pushed the wrong button, and the platform that I was partially standing on caused me to make a complete somersault. I was able to grab on to the one-half inch ledge for a short time. However, I could not hold on, and when my hand slipped off of the ledge, I plummeted down the landing of the platform thirty feet below.

I was extremely fortunate in that I hit the platform while it was still moving, which helped to break my fall. After convincing the pilots that I was fine, they allowed me to take the next bucket back to my ship. I did not say a word to anyone and soon realized it was a big mistake.

The next day, I tried to get out of my bunk, which was on the top third, when I felt this excruciating pain in my left chest area. My nose and the entire side of my face were swollen and bruised. I immediately went to the ship's doctor for medical attention. When I explained to him what had happened, he stared at me in disbelief. He said that it was medically impossible for me to have fallen a distance of thirty-five feet without sustaining more serious injuries. I kept repeating to him that what I was telling him was true. I could not find anyone to verify my story because the ship had already departed during the night.

After thoroughly examining me, the ship's doctor pronounced that he could not find anything seriously wrong with me except that I had contusions to my face, nose, and shoulder. For the next six months, the pain in my chest worsened. Whenever I would lie on my left side I would suffer excruciating pain that radiated throughout my chest and into the base of my skull.

My life turned around when I spoke with the well-known, former Mr. America and professional wrestler, Gene Stanley (his professional name). The son of Polish immigrants, Gene Stanley came from Cicero, Illinois. His real name is Gene Zigowich. His sister and brother were also weightlifters and professional wrestlers.

I would admire his fine physique and his deep devotion to keeping his body in top physical condition. He was offering a class aboard ship in bodybuilding that was going to be free of charge for anyone interested. I immediately jumped at the chance to train with such a fine man. I figured that if anything were seriously wrong with me following my injury, it would manifest itself once I began the strenuous physical activity of the bodybuilding sessions.

Mr. Stanley's program was excellent. He believed in repetitious weightlifting. Rather than lifting large weights once or twice, he preferred lifting smaller weights for approximately twenty-five to fifty times. This method of training enabled the muscles to develop far greater flexibility.

His program consisted of fourteen different exercises that involved every muscle in the body. In the beginning, I found that my pains were worsening. I then went back to the ship's doctor for another examination. Once again, he could find nothing physically wrong with me. I had the distinct feeling that he thought my pains were fabricated. When I advised him that I had voluntarily entered the US

Navy and that I had no intentions of seeking a medical discharge, his whole attitude towards me changed.

I decided to continue with the weightlifting program. Eventually, the pain subsided and I became more comfortable with the weightlifting routine. After one year of extensive training and practice, I had developed a forty-six inch chest and a thirty-four inch waist of solid muscle.

I began feeling physically stronger and more relaxed. Only a slight pain remained from my previous injury. When I was examined prior to my discharge from the Navy, I explained my problem to the examining physician. Once again, he could not find anything physically wrong with me.

It was not until I was examined by a doctor at John Hopkins Hospital in Baltimore, Maryland, after I had been honorably discharged from the Navy, that the real reason for my pain was diagnosed. Upon a thorough examination, the doctor concluded that I had suffered a deep muscle pull in my chest when I had fallen on my left side, all of which forced my arms into an unnatural position.

The doctor assured me that although my injury could be painful at times, it was not fatal and it would eventually disappear. After about two years, the pain finally subsided and I was greatly relieved. Once again God was watching over me, and my time had not yet come. His plans for me were just beginning, and I was grateful for the chance to pursue my dreams.

One incident that I vividly recall concerns the engagement ring that my wife, Viola, gave me in April 1949. It was a beautiful 14-karat-gold ring that had a perfect blue-white diamond in the center.

After fifteen years of wearing this ring, I awoke one morning and discovered that the diamond was missing from its setting. I was shocked and heartbroken. I could not understand how it could possibly have happened. In spite of the missing diamond, I continued to wear the ring because it had a tremendous sentimental value to me.

In May 1984, I got up early to prepare myself for work. It was a beautiful sunny morning. I raised the shades to allow the sunlight to enter. It brightened the entire kitchen. As I glanced across the room, I noticed a shining object at the base of the moulding on the kitchen tile. It was shining like a bright star in the sky. I surmised that it was the reflection of a piece of glass that had become lodged in that space. I decided to go over and retrieve it. Much to my surprise, I could not believe what I had found—the diamond that I had lost years earlier! To think that the diamond was still there despite the many times the floor had been washed and vacuumed over the years made finding it all that more miraculous. The tears began to flow down my cheeks. I called my wife, Viola to tell her the good news. We both wept as we held each other close, so overcome with joy, so elated.

I immediately placed the diamond in a safe place. The next day I took the ring to my jeweler to have the diamond reset. After 54 years of wearing the ring, it still looks like new. I will forever cherish this ring. Never in my wildest dreams did I ever think that I would see that diamond again. The odds of finding it were akin to winning the lottery. In a way, I felt that I had. It was a true miracle.

Another incident that vividly stands out in my mind concerns Boomer, my daughter, Deborah's Yellow Labrador Retriever. One summer afternoon around 2:00 p.m., when Boomer was four years old, I decided to take him out for one of our usual two-mile walks. On this particular day, the sun was beating down quite strongly, but a cool breeze was blowing.

We were about one mile into our walk when the cool breezes stopped and the beating rays of the sun had become unbearable. Suddenly, Boomer began to pant heavily. Then he lay down at my feet and refused to move. I immediately knelt down beside him and gently stroked his face. He licked my hand and rested his head against my arm. Frantically, I searched around for water, but there was none anywhere. I prayed to God to help me.

Suddenly out of nowhere, a kindly old woman appeared in a car at the side of the road. At first, I was not sure she was really there because the rays of the sun reflecting against her car made her appear almost non-existent. She called out to me and asked me if she could help. I explained to her that I needed to get Boomer home right away and give him water to cool him down.

Without a moment's hesitation, she offered to give Boomer and me a ride home. She carefully opened the back door of her car, and Boomer got up and jumped right into the back seat. I thanked her for her kindness, and she just smiled and said it was her pleasure to be able to help. She then drove us home and wished us luck. No sooner had Boomer and I gotten out of her car, when the kindly stranger disappeared from sight before I could even turn around to thank her once again.

She must have been a guardian angel sent to answer my prayers that fateful day. She appeared at the precise moment that Boomer and I needed her most. Strangely enough, I never did see this kindly woman ever again. I shall always be grateful to her for caring enough to make a difference.

As soon as I got Boomer indoors, I bathed him in cool water. He immediately began to perk up. I then held his head as he sipped cool water from his bowl. For the remainder of the day, Boomer rested in the air-conditioned house and by the next day, he was back to normal.

Boomer returned the favor when he became our true-life hero several years later. Perhaps it was a gesture of appreciation for my having helped him that day, when he saved my wife, Viola. Deborah was downstairs working in her law office when suddenly Boomer ran up to her with my wife's slipper in his mouth. He ran to Deborah and dropped the slipper by her foot. While it was unusual for Boomer to ever take a slipper, Deborah thought that perhaps he only wanted to play, and she sent him on his way.

Several minutes later, Boomer appeared again in Deborah's office, now with Viola's other slipper. He was determined to make Deborah come with him this time. Boomer grabbed the end of Deborah's sleeve and began to whine and pull her toward the door. Realizing that something had to be wrong, Deborah quickly followed Boomer who proceeded to race up the stairs to the second floor.

As Deborah rounded the top step, Boomer ran into the bathroom. It was then that Deborah realized that Viola had slipped and fallen backwards into the bathtub. Boomer had positioned himself at the edge of the bathtub so that Viola could hold onto his collar and keep her head out of the water. Boomer feverishly licked Viola's face and continued to nudge her to keep her awake.

Boomer was truly our guardian angel that day, and from that moment on, he has continued to watch over Viola as well as the rest of our family. He is and always will be our special hero and the love and joy of our lives as is Scooter, our beloved Bassett Hound.

I experienced another unusual incident on August 10, 1997, while I was traveling north on Route 46 in Clifton, New Jersey, to my daughter, Deborah's house. It was around 2:00 p.m., and the sun was shining brightly. I was traveling north at the designated speed of thirty-five miles per hour in the right lane of a two lane highway. As I was approaching my destination, I put on my left directional signal to move into the left lane.

I looked in my rear-view mirror as well as my side-view mirror. The highway was clear with the exception of one car that was quite a distance behind me. After assessing the situation, it appeared as though I would safely be able to move to the left lane a short distance from my destination.

As I was about to make my move into the left lane, I heard a woman's voice call out to me. It was loud, distinct, and exceedingly calm. It sounded as though she were right next to me in the car. I remained in my lane and immediately turned my head to see where the voice was coming from, but no one was there.

I looked back in the rear-view and side-view mirrors once more and noticed a vehicle coming towards me in the left lane at a tremendously high rate of speed. The vehicle passed by me as if I were standing still. Had I not heard the woman's voice and remained where I was, there is no doubt in my mind that I would have been hit by the speeding car. I would have been directly in the path of the speeding car had I moved into the left lane as planned.

I shall be forever grateful to the mysterious woman who called out to me at the precise moment that I would have been struck by the speeding car and no doubt killed or seriously injured. Working through my guardian angel, God once again spared my life, and in his own special way, worked yet another miracle of life. I feel blessed to have experienced his love and direction so many times in my life. I am indeed a fortunate man.

CHAPTER TWENTY-FOUR

MY MIRACLE DOGWOOD

It all began in the spring of 1959 while I was browsing around my favorite garden nursery, Richfield Farms, in Clifton, New Jersey. The moment that I spotted the small red dogwood tree hidden in the corner of the nursery, I was immediately drawn to it in the same way that one is drawn to the "runt of the litter." It had been placed off to the side of the nursery, out of public view because it was straggly and not expected to survive. The few leaves that graced its boughs were withered and riddled with small holes.

Although the tree was small in stature and deemed a loss, I envisioned how it would one day grow tall and proud in my front yard at 11 Pilgrim Drive. I imagined seeing young birds nestled in its boughs and its crimson leaves floating to the earth in autumn. Without any hesitation, I purchased the tree for the price of $4.00. Much to my delight, my wife, Viola, was equally taken with what was destined to become our "miracle dogwood tree." I could not wait to plant our new tree. After much thought, I selected a sunny spot in the front yard where it could spread without any obstacles in its way.

I was sure to give our new tree plenty of room to grow. I dug a hole and layered it with a mixture of one part peat moss and three parts of rich topsoil. After carefully placing our tree in its new home, I applied one cup of slow releasing nutrients to nourish it throughout the coming months and to give it a healthy start.

Gently, I positioned our tree until it lay straight in the ground. I filled the hole within three inches from ground level with the nutrient mixture that I had prepared and made certain to firm the soil around the base of the tree. I then filled the hole with water and allowed it to drain.

Once the hole drained, I filled the hole to ground level with the remainder of the nutrient mixture that I had prepared and added three inches of fresh cedar mulch to hold in the moisture. I then stood back proudly to admire our new addition.

Over the many years that our dogwood tree has grown, my family and I have nurtured it with patience and tender- loving care. It survived countless winters and struggles with drought. Now more than forty years later, I am happy to report that our "miracle dogwood tree" still

Miracle Dogwood Tree
May 10, 1999 Clifton, NJ

stands proud and tall despite the ravages of time that have taken so many of our other plantings. Somehow, our miracle dogwood continues to survive, a true testament to its tenacity and spirit.

Although our miracle tree never grew tall, it did grow sturdy and straight. Our family and friends have enjoyed its timeless beauty each season for many, many seasons, and it is as beautiful today as it was forty years ago when I first gazed upon it. It has never failed to blossom every spring despite the fact that ten years ago, it lost all of its bark and was not expected to survive.

Unwilling to allow our miracle tree to die, I coated it with pruning tar and applied miracle grow to it in a desperate attempt to hold onto what had become so important to us. Miraculously, the following spring, our tree not only grew back some of its lost bark, but in fact, it became even more vibrant and beautiful that year than it had ever been before. Even today, despite the loss of bark, our miracle tree continues to flourish.

Last year I graced the base of our miracle dogwood tree with colorful tulips, daffodils, and hyacinths. When they were all in bloom, the sight was truly a spectacle of beauty to behold. As I stood in front and gazed upon our miracle tree in all its splendor, my thoughts drifted back to an earlier time forty years before when I first happened upon our miracle tree. I was filled with a peace and calm that was unsurpassed. Just being near our tree brings back so many wonderful memories of the many years of pleasure it has brought not only to us, but also, to all who are blessed to share in its beauty. It is truly a "miracle tree" and one that shall always blossom and flourish in my heart forever.

CHAPTER TWENTY-FIVE

FIFTIETH WEDDING ANNIVERSARY

On October 23, 1999, my wife, Viola, and I celebrated our fiftieth wedding anniversary. It is hard to believe that fifty years have passed since we pledged our love to each other. I consider myself very fortunate to have a wife as loving and caring as Viola. We are both truly blessed to have our three wonderful children, Denise, Deborah, and Vincent, Jr., who have given us untold joy throughout the years and who continue to enrich our lives even to this day.

I believe that Viola and I have enjoyed such happiness over the last fifty years due to our mutual love, admiration, and respect for each other. We supported each other and gave of ourselves unselfishly during the hard times and continued to love and support each other during the good times. No problem was ever too difficult for us to solve as long as we were together in making

Vincent R. Saladini, Sr.
Viola Saladini (sitting)

October 23, 1999

267

decisions and supporting one other.

Throughout the years, we have tried to instill in our three children the same values that have enabled us to enjoy such a long, loving, and lasting relationship. We have demonstrated both trust and undying love for each other, always tempered with kindness and compassion. We have always taught our children to take pride in all that they do and to always remember that their word must always be honored.

Viola and I enjoy each day of life to its fullest and always try to maintain a positive outlook on life no matter what may come our way. Together we have weathered many storms, and I have no doubt that as long as we have each other and our children, we will continue to weather whatever else life may hold for us. We look forward to many more years of wedded bliss and happy times with our children. We are indeed truly blessed.

The following article appeared in the <u>Dateline Journal,</u> dated February 16, 2000.

Anniversary

Saladinis celebrate 50th

On Oct. 23, Vincent R. and Viola Saladini were honored with a surprise 50th wedding anniversary party given by their three children, Denise, Deborah and Vincent, Jr., at The Manor in West Orange.

Mr. Saladini was born and raised in Martinsburg, West Virginia. After World War II, he came to study at the American Gentlemen's School of Men's and Women's Design in New York City. Shortly thereafter, he met his wife and the couple married in St. Francis Church, in Newark on Oct. 23, 1949. Mr. Saladini was a guidance counselor at New York's Fashion industries High School and an adjunct professor of men's and women's fashion design at Fashion institute of Technology in New York City for 25 years before retiring in 1991.

Mr. Saladini graduated from Oswego State University, Oswego, N.Y. with a B.S. degree in Vocational Technical Education. He also graduated form Montclair State University, with a Masters Degree in Student Personnel Services. He is also a World War II Navy Veteran. He served aboard the USS Jason ARH1 and the USS Sibley APA, 206. He is also the recipient of four service awards including the Pacific Theater Ribbon, Americana Theater Ribbon, Victory Medal and the Philippine Liberation Medal. He is a member of the Veterans of Foreign Wars, AARP, and United Federation of Teachers.

Mrs. Saladini worked at the RCA facility in Harrison for 10 years prior to her marriage. The former Viola Russa, she was born and raised in Newark. They are the proud parents of three

Viola & Vincent Saladini

children. Their daughter, Denise, is married to Dr. Warren Ceurvels and she is a teacher of ESL at Passaic High School. She and Dr. Ceurvels have one son, Matthew James Ceurvels, 9 years old. They reside in Vernon.

Their daughter, Deborah, is an attorney at law, licensed to practice in both New Jersey and West Virginia. She maintains a private practice in Clifton.

Their son, Vincent, Jr. is an anesthesiologist at the Hackensack Medical Center. He is married to the former Dr. Linda Barra of North Haledon, also an anesthesiologist. They reside in Saddle River.

269

CHAPTER TWENTY-SIX

GROWING OLD GRACEFULLY

What really is "old age?" Is it a state of mind? Is it a state of being? Is it a combination of both? I have never been one to dwell on growing old because I have been far too busy enjoying life and focusing on the present. Yet growing old is something that we must be mindful of, however, for we will all eventually face "old age" unless some greater force ends our lives before the ravages of time take their toll on us.

Although there are fundamental needs that appear at all age levels, some needs may be more important at one particular age level than they are at another age level. Other needs are important at every age level. I believe, for example, that the need for love is important at every age level. Everyone needs to feel that he is loved and somehow special to another person.

The ability to love and be loved is one of the greatest joys that one can experience. The sharing of love with another, whether it is a parent and child, two spouses or the love between two friends, helps to create a special bond that enables us to endure whatever trials and tribulations life may hold for us. We all need to experience that special "oneness" with another.

For many, this special bond with another person can last a lifetime, serving as an anchor in times of pain and indecision, and a beacon of light in times of joy and happiness. We all need to feel that we have someone we can turn to no matter what may be going on in our life at any given moment, someone who will not judge us, but who will love us unconditionally.

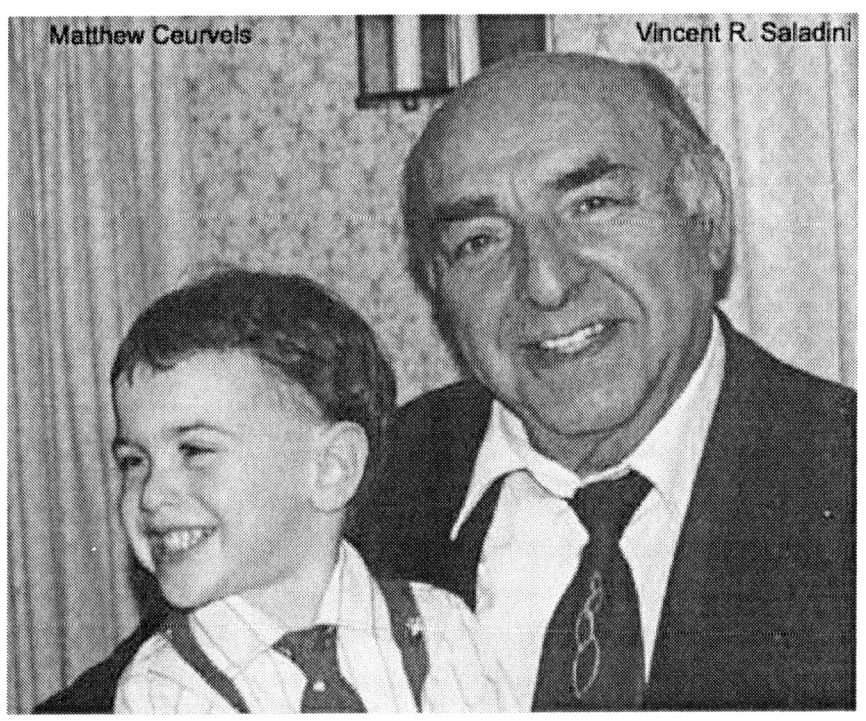

Matthew Ceurvels   Vincent R. Saladini

I have been richly blessed with the love of my family, especially my wife, children, and grandchild, Matthew. We have always been there for each other, and I know that we always will be, no matter what life may hold for each of us along the way. We can laugh together and even cry together, safe and secure in the knowledge that we are never alone. It has been this bond of love that has enabled me to endure the many hardships that I experienced in life.

For many people, in addition to establishing a bond of love with another person, they often share a special love with their pets. There is no question in my mind that pets have the ability to fill a void of loneliness that so often marks the coming of old age, a time when many of our loved ones have passed on, and we are forced to fend for ourselves.

Perhaps what is most special about a pet's love is that it is unconditional and given freely and without question. Pets have an intuitive ability to know what their owner is feeling and to somehow make it better by cuddling up to them and showing them that they are loved and never alone.

As a young boy growing up in West Virginia, I was raised during a time when animals and farming were the way of life. One of my fondest memories is caring for my cow, Bessie. Every morning, rain or shine, I would race out to the barn to brush Bessie and feed her before milking her. Bessie was more than just a cow to me—she was someone who would always listen to me. As I would stroke her back with her favorite brush, she would moo softly and turn to lick my face. Not one day passed that I did not kiss Bessie on her forehead and tell her that I loved her.

I would then take Bessie out to pasture along with my collie dog, Rex, who would watch Bessie while I napped in the shade of a soft, billowy willow tree. At three o'clock on the button, Rex would race out into the fields to bring Bessie home for the evening. He would hold his head erect with his tail waving in the breeze as though he were the shepherd and Bessie were his flock. Bessie would trail along beside Rex, and together, they would make their way back to the barn where Bessie would always be treated to a fresh bail of hay. Animals have been and always will be an important part of my life both for the joy they bring to others and for the joy they allow others to bring to them.

I began my retirement at a time when my daughter, Deborah, had just bought a cuddly Yellow Labrador Retriever puppy named Barney. Sadly, Barney's life was tragically cut short due to an incurable illness, and he would only live for one year. In the brief time that he lived, Barney was showered with untold love by our family, especially Deborah, and he in turn filled our lives with endless joy and happiness. No matter how ill he was feeling, Barney always managed to comfort us and dry our tears with a soft nudge against our cheeks. Despite the fact that we knew Barney would soon die, his death was nonetheless devastating and extremely painful for us. He will always be loved and remembered in our hearts because of all of the love that he gave to us.

Shortly before Barney died, Deborah purchased another Yellow Labrador Retriever puppy named Boomer so that Barney would not ever be alone. Boomer was Barney's constant companion, never leaving his side, right up until the moment he died. Boomer would bring his toys to Barney and lie down next to him where he would remain for hours at a time. Many times we would see Boomer licking Barney's face and nestling tightly against him. Boomer clearly sensed that Barney was not well. Often, he would nudge Barney and encourage him to move around.

When Barney died, Boomer's grief was as deep and moving as our own. He wandered around Barney's room aimlessly, stopping at times to lie down where he and Barney would often rest together, especially in Barney's final days.

Shortly after Barney's death, Deborah rescued and adopted an elderly, abused Black Labrador Retriever from the Clifton Animal Shelter. She named him Smokey.

Deborah first became aware of Smokey's plight when she visited the Clifton Animal Shelter one morning after finishing up a court matter. As she made her way through the pound, she spotted a crate that was marked with a large black "X". When Deborah inquired as to what the black "X" meant, she learned, much to her dismay, that Smokey was destined to be put to sleep the next morning. He had been at the shelter for several months. He was elderly (estimated to be 13-14 years old) and had been badly abused, all of which made him an unlikely and undesirable candidate for adoption. Deborah was devastated.

She immediately opened the door to Smokey's crate where he was lying on a torn and tattered blanket, gently stroked his head and told him not to worry. She promised him that she would take him home with her and give him all of the love that she possibly could. She vowed to him that he would never suffer abuse again, and he would forever know only gentleness and love.

Smokey was frightened and shivering. Deborah knew in her heart that she could not leave without Smokey. As Deborah cradled Smokey's head in her arms, cuddled him and told him that he was coming home with her, she noticed a tear come out of his eye and run down his face. He knew as she did, that he would not suffer any longer and that he had found a new and loving home. Deborah knew right then and there that she had made the right decision.

When Deborah took her new "baby," to the veterinarian the next day, she received the devastating news that Smokey had multiple health problems from the many years of abuse and neglect that he had suffered. Deborah was advised not to become too attached to Smokey because he had kidney, liver, and bladder problems, as well as arthritis and hip problems; it was highly unlikely that he would survive for more than a few weeks.

Undaunted by the sad news, Deborah was more determined than ever that whatever time Smokey had left, he would be loved, cared for, and never left alone. True to her word, Deborah lovingly cared for Smokey and with Boomer's help, Smokey managed to get around just fine. Boomer happily greeted his new companion, although Smokey was leery of his new friend after the abuse he had previously suffered. After painstaking attempts to comfort Smokey, Deborah was finally successful in gaining Smokey's trust and confidence, and for the next five years, Boomer and Smokey were virtually inseparable, often lying down next to each other at Deborah's feet as she worked in her law office.

Whenever Smokey would have to go outside, Boomer would come into Deborah's office and nudge the jingle bells hanging on the door to let her know. He would then grab Smokey's collar and lead him down the three steps to the backyard. When Smokey had finished his business, Boomer would grab his collar once again and lead him up the three steps and back into the living room where he would wait for Smokey to lie down in front of the fireplace.

Boomer would then lie next to Smokey and place his head on Smokey's stomach until Smokey fell asleep, and he would be right at his side when Smokey awakened. Boomer would also break up all of the dog biscuits for Smokey into tiny pieces and push them under his mouth because Smokey was unable to do so for himself.

Despite the initial grim news, Smokey lived for five years. When Smokey ultimately passed away from cancer at the ripe old age of 18, Boomer pined for weeks at the loss of his faithful companion. On the morning of Smokey's trip to the veterinarian, Dr. Louis Crupi, for what we believed was to be surgery to correct a dental problem, Boomer was especially restless and saddened.

As Deborah placed Smokey's leash around his neck, Boomer ran to the door and tried to block Deborah's way. He gently but firmly tugged at her right sleeve, all the while nestling against Smokey and refusing to let him near the door. When Deborah bent down to comfort Boomer and reassure him that Smokey would not be gone long, he let out a pitiful wail that brought Deborah to tears. Sensing defeat, Boomer moved away from the door, licked Deborah's cheek, nestled against Smokey's face, and then turned to lie down on his blanket. He heaved a sigh that was almost human as Deborah and Smokey made their way down the walkway.

As Deborah helped Dr. Crupi place Smokey into a run, a sick feeling came over her, and she hugged Smokey for what was to be the last time. As she held him to her chest and stroked his neck, he licked her face and nestled so tightly that Deborah remained frozen in place. As she turned to look once more at Smokey, he stared into her eyes, as a tear ran down his cheek. He then sank down into the blanket that Deborah had so gently placed in his run. Deborah promised Smokey that she would see him again.

Later that day, Deborah received the devastating news that Smokey was not suffering from a dental problem, as originally believed, but that he actually had cancer. In fact, the cancer was so aggressive that it had already spread to Smokey's face, back, and abdomen. Deborah knew what she had to do. With her friend Brian Lombardo at her side, she rushed to Dr. Crupi's office where Smokey was still under anesthesia from the anticipated surgery.

As Deborah entered the room, Brian noticed that the heart monitor was racing. Smokey knew that he was not alone and that Deborah had kept her promise to him. Deborah held Smokey as he drew his final breath and the monitors fell silent.

When Deborah returned home that evening, Boomer was waiting at the door to greet her. He clearly sensed her grief as she sank to the floor and held him close. He nestled closely to her and pressed his face against her cheek in a touching gesture of comfort and understanding.

After Smokey's death, Boomer became deeply depressed and seemed to lose his will to live. He no longer wanted to eat and would circle the rooms in Deborah's house searching for his beloved Smokey. We all realized that we needed to find Boomer another baby to love and care for since he had always been so gentle and nurturing to both Barney and Smokey. Within a short time, Deborah became Mom to Scooter, her precious Bassett Hound, and Boomer's new "baby brother." Scooter is a tri-colored Basset Hound with long, droopy ears, deeply set sad eyes, and a loving personality that is unmatched by any other.

Boomer perked up immediately upon Scooter's arrival, and his will and spirit soared once again. Scooter and Boomer immediately took to each other and from the moment that they met, they have been completely inseparable. In fact, on any given day, they can either be found nestled next to Deborah as she works in her law office or snuggled together in front of the fireplace.

As with Smokey, Boomer lovingly cares for Scooter and continues his tradition of breaking up the dog biscuits into small pieces since Scooter's pudgy paws are too short to hold the biscuits himself. After Scooter has eaten all of the broken biscuit pieces, he rolls over on his back, kicks his four paws in the air and whines for more! Boomer is always eager to oblige, which has resulted in both having to double their exercise routine to stay in shape. It is truly a delightful sight to behold!

It has been both a privilege and a delight to be surrounded by the love and companionship that Boomer and Scooter offer. Their love is unconditional and ever present. No matter how dreary the day, no matter what else may be going on, the one constant is the love that we can always count on from Boomer and Scooter. No amount of money in the world can replace the sheer joy and delight that we all experience from being fortunate to have Boomer and Scooter in our lives. We look forward to many more years of happiness with our two precious angels.

While we were all deeply saddened by Smokey's death, we were all consoled by the fact that Smokey's final years were filled with unending love and devotion, and we shall be forever grateful for the love and joy that he brought to our lives.

I have always been a very active person throughout my life. When the time came for me to retire, I did so with some fear and trepidation. I had always loved my work in the field of education and I immersed myself in every phase of my job. The educational field had always been challenging and inspirational to me and I was deeply concerned that the loss of such daily contact would leave me feeling empty and unfulfilled.

I knew that once I retired, I had to do something that would give me a feeling of worth and satisfaction. For years, I had always toyed around with a number of ideas that I had one day hoped to expound upon and share with others. Only then, I never had the time. Well, with retirement looming in front of me, I knew that this would be the perfect time to bring those ideas to fruition.

After much contemplation, I came up with a novel idea for a different concept in greeting cards that would allow me to remain challenged and occupied. I applied for and received a copyright for my cards in 1998 and am currently in the process of marketing my concept so that I may share part of my dream with others.

Another activity that has kept me busy during my retirement years is gardening. Nothing makes me feel more alive then when I am working close to nature and I can feel the good earth between my fingers. My daughter, Deborah, and I have spent countless hours developing, designing, and planting perennial gardens on our properties. We have planted over 300 varieties of perennial plants ranging from dwarf varieties such as miniature roses, miniature mums, and miniature daffodils, to butterfly shrubs, althea, heather and fresh herb gardens. Our trademark is to border our gardens with handpicked riverbed rocks.

On any given day, Deborah and I can be found climbing through rock quarries to find the perfect stones to compliment our gardens. Deborah and I love creating gardens that allow for color and growth all year long. From the first sign of spring through the coldest of winters, our gardens shower us with untold beauty. Life abounds all year long giving us a constant feeling of hope and renewal.

My daughter and I enjoy decorating the gardens with various types of ornaments and colorful lights to highlight the different displays. In the fall months, the gardens are alive with scarecrows, pumpkins, and goblins, while the coming of Christmas finds the gardens surrounded by snowmen, reindeer, Santa, and elves. With the coming of the spring, the gardens are filled with bunnies, chicks, colorful ribbons, and Easter eggs, all awaiting the birth of new life. The summer months enjoy a garden surrounded by cheerful welcome signs, draping flower garlands, decorated birdbaths, and colorful planters with cascading petunias, and geraniums. Throughout the year, family and friends are greeted with the sweet, whimsical tones of wind chimes that delight everyone with each breeze that gently passes through.

Old age does not have to mean the end. On the contrary, it is an ever-present reminder of just how precious every moment is and how each of us must seize the day and live life to its fullest. I do not fear growing old for with old age also come a special wisdom and a newfound peace and contentment. I now have the time to relax and enjoy all that life has to offer. I have the unconditional love of my family and friends. I have the warmth and comfort of knowing that Boomer and Scooter are ever present to shower me with their own special love and through it all, I know that I am never truly alone.

As I reflect upon my life, I realize that there were many things that I wanted to express to my parents when they were alive, but never did. Although I felt the words in my heart, I never took the time to tell my parents

Vincent R. Saladini Sr., Boomer
Clifton, NJ. 1996

280

how deeply I loved, admired, and respected them. Life has sadly taught me that young people should never be ashamed or afraid to openly show love, respect, and admiration for their parents, for hiding such feelings will deny them a second chance at developing a truly loving relationship with the two most important and influential people in their lives.

Now that I am older, I have a much greater appreciation for the hard work, devotion, and sacrifices that marked my parents' lives. I know that my parents are in heaven looking down on me and guiding me through life. As I look toward the sky, I tip my hat to the finest human beings that God has ever placed on this earth—my parents.

I have finally come to understand that each of us is placed on this earth for a purpose. It is entirely up to the individual to make the best of whatever attributes, talents, and skills that he or she possesses. Through hard work, perseverance, and many sacrifices, dreams really do come true.

Vincent Rocco Saladini, Sr.

APPENDIX

Frequently Asked Questions

Question 1: What is an Italian doing in West Virginia?

This question has been asked of me many times throughout my life. I can recall being asked this question while serving aboard ship in the United States Navy. Many men serving with me came from the northeastern part of the United States. As soon as they heard my southern accent, they would ask me where I came from. When I told them that I came from West Virginia, they were very surprised that an Italian would settle in West Virginia. I would explain to them that it was not really unusual at all for Italians to settle there. In fact, there are Italians in nearly every state of the United States.

I know of many Italians living in the following villages and towns in the eastern panhandle of West Virginia: Kearneysville, Milville, Marlowe, Charlestown, Harpers Ferry, and Martinsburg. Most of them worked in the mines and throughout neighboring farms. Many were self-employed as tailors, shoemakers, barbers, and grocery store owners. They were hardworking, honest, and decent people who struggled and survived together by being supportive of each other. I am proud of my heritage and of the fact that I am a West Virginia native.

When I came north to study in Newark, New Jersey, and later in New York City, I was repeatedly asked the same question. One incident stands out in my mind more than any other. I can recall telling a teacher at the High School of Fashion Industries that I was born and raised in West Virginia, only to be warned by him not to tell anyone because if I did, I would not get hired for the teaching position that I was applying for in the district.

I remember looking at him squarely in the eyes and calmly stating that I had no intentions of denying my birthplace, and was proud to be from West Virginia. Fortunately, the fact that I was from West Virginia did not prevent me from securing the teaching position. I was hired for the position based upon my experience, my character, and my ability to do the job in conjunction with my thorough knowledge of the clothing trade, rather than where I was or was not born.

I am proud to be an Italian-American who was born and raised in West Virginia. My parents always taught me to respect a person for who and what he/she is, rather than based upon his/her race, color or creed, and I have lived my life by those teachings. By heeding the advice of my parents, I have been able to achieve success and have never had any trouble dealing with people of all levels of our great society.

Question 2: How were the Italians treated in West Virginia?

This question was frequently asked of me. Like many other immigrant groups that came to America in the early years, the Italians were treated with skepticism. They were looked down upon by the WASP who dominated all areas of social life in their communities. It was extremely difficult for an Italian to find work outside of the mines. I can recall when my sister, Teodolinda, applied for a job at a factory. She was required to sign her name and religious preference. In the end, she was rejected for the job.

In another incident, I can recall sitting in a restaurant with my cousin, Angelo Saladini, having lunch. While we were sitting there, a gentleman from the next table came over and made an ethnic comment to us. My cousin's immediate reaction was to punch him in the face. I calmed him down, however, and we just ignored the man's ignorant comment. The owner of the restaurant, who was of Greek origin, heard what was taking place and apologized to us for his customer's ignorance. He immediately ordered him to leave. He stated that he would not tolerate such behavior in his restaurant. We thanked him and commended him for his courage.

I can also recall being barred from many clubs and dances when I was in my teens simply because I was Italian. We had difficulty meeting girls outside our ethnic group because no one wanted to associate with "Italian immigrants." As a result, the Italians of the community dated primarily from their own ethnic group.

Still another incident that stands out in my mind was the time that someone was stealing corn from a nearby farm in the village of Big Springs, West Virginia. The Italians were being blamed for these crimes without any proof whatsoever. The townspeople indicated that the Italians had to be guilty since Italians had a reputation for being a bunch of crooks and gangsters. They were apparently influenced by many of the movies of that time which depicted Italians as being thugs and gangsters. These misconceptions could not have been further from the truth.

In fact, the people of Big Springs, West Virginia, were hardworking, honest people who prided themselves on being self-reliant and self-sufficient. They would never dream of taking something that did not belong to them.

When the thefts became out of control, a group of Italian immigrants decided to form a watch in the cornfields to see who was really stealing from the neighboring villagers. They finally captured the true thieves, who were clearly not any of the Italian immigrants. The police arrested the thieves, and they were prosecuted for stealing.

This incident taught me never to jump to conclusions about any particular race of people without the evidence to back up those claims. To accuse someone of something merely because of his race or nationality is very wrong. The accusing villagers had to come to terms with the fact that their condemnation of the Italians was inappropriate, and their prejudices were demeaning and hurtful.

Another incident that vividly stands out in my mind concerns my Uncle Gus. Uncle Gus enjoyed walking from Martinsburg, West Virginia, to Big Springs, West Virginia. He would walk along the highway and take his time, delighting in being outdoors.

Because of a mining injury, Uncle Gus was left with a limp which caused him to stagger when he walked. The police were constantly picking him up and charging him with being drunk because he staggered when he walked. Because Uncle Gus did not speak any English, he was unable to explain his mining injury to the police and the fact that he limped and staggered as a result of the injury.

The situation finally reached a point where Uncle Gus was constantly being harassed by the police. The men of the village of Big Springs, West Virginia, decided that something had to be done to rectify this injustice. They all went down to city hall in a group to explain the situation to the mayor. He was very sympathetic and with his assistance, the situation was corrected. From that point forward, Uncle Gus was no longer harassed, and he was free to walk in peace without fear of being stopped by the police.

Finally, during the time that I was growing up in Big Springs, West Virginia, we were tormented with cross burnings on several occasions. Once we complained to our local Catholic Pastor in Martinsburg, West Virginia; however, the city officials put a stop to this horrific situation.

I can truthfully state that once the people of the community understood that the Italians were hardworking, honest, decent people, they began to treat us with respect. They began socializing with us and making us feel as though we were part of the community instead of unwanted outcasts. Gradually, bonds of trust grew and our lives in the community took on a more pleasant existence. I am proud to have been part of that growing community.

In my experience, I have found that once people are educated about other ethnic groups, they will soon realize that we all have the same dreams, hopes, and aspirations as any other group. The Italian immigrant is no longer looked upon as being inferior. We have come a long way in achieving equality for people of all races, colors, and creeds; all have played an integral part in the building and development of our great United States of America.

Question 3: With respect to the northern Italian immigrant versus the southern Italian immigrant, who is superior?

It has often been stated that the northern Italian immigrant is superior to the southern Italian immigrant. This premise has been set forth and argued many times. I, however, question the validity of such a statement. If we study the early history of the Italian nation, we find that the northern part of Italy was a highly developed and industrialized area. It was the home of many of our fine Italian painters, artists, educators, and skilled craftsmen.

Prior to 1870, it was these northern Italian immigrants who came to the United States. Because of their skills and educational backgrounds, they were better received by the Americans. Many of them assimilated into the American society without too much difficulty. They were able to find better paying jobs because of a demand for their skills. Furthermore, because of their diverse educational backgrounds, many were able to start their own businesses. They also settled into the farmlands of New Jersey, New York, and California.

It was not until the 1870's that the mass of Italians came to America. This group of immigrants was made up of peasants who came predominately from the southern part of Italy. They came to America with dreams and hopes of seeking a better way of life for themselves and for their children. Because of the deplorable conditions in southern Italy, they were extremely poor, illiterate, and unskilled. Lack of funds kept them in the cities where they were forced to live in crowded, unsanitary slums. The housing conditions were extremely poor.

Because this group of Italian immigrants was not too well received by the Americans, they would tend to band together and stay together. Many of them went to work as laborers on railroads and construction projects throughout the northeast. However, as the railroads were being built, many of the Italian immigrants made their way to other parts of the United States where they worked in the mines, textile mills, clothing factories, local fisheries, and anywhere else that they could secure employment.

Because of their lack of education and skills, the majority of these Italian immigrants were given the lowest paying jobs. Their workday was not limited to any particular schedule. It was not at all uncommon for many of them to work ten to twelve hour days. Because of these types of working conditions that existed, the southern Italian immigrant had all that he could do just to earn a living. He had neither the time nor the means to receive a better education. At the same time, discrimination in the work place and the housing department kept him in the so-called "Little Italys."

The southern Italian immigrant has played a significant role in the development of the America that we know and enjoy today. Through hard work, sacrifice, perseverance, and a sheer determination to succeed, the southern Italian immigrants, as well as their children, have prospered and enjoyed success in all areas of society including business, sports, music, education, and the arts.

As the son of an Italian immigrant, I am very proud of my Italian heritage. I am thoroughly convinced that there is no superior group. As recorded in history, both groups have made numerous contributions to the development of our nation. We can all be proud of these

Vincent Rocco Saladini, Sr.

courageous people, whether they came from the northern or southern part of Italy, for they struggled to overcome overwhelming obstacles in order to achieve success and good fortune in the land of opportunity.

Favorite Family Recipes

GRANDMA AMELIA CAPRIOTTI'S HOMEMADE BREAD

INGREDIENTS

4 cups flour
1 teaspoon salt
3 tablespoons sugar
2 packs of yeast
½ half stick of butter

DIRECTIONS

* Mix flour, salt, yeast and softened butter together
* Dissolve yeast in warm water—let sit until bubbly
* Add flour mixture to yeast and work mixture together
* If too soft, add more flour
* Cover with towel and place in warm area and let rise half way
* Grease pans and set aside
* beat down dough and place in greased pans
* Cover with a towel a second time, and place in warm area and let rise to top of pan
* Bake at 350 degrees for 25-30 minutes or until top is brown
Rub one tablespoon of butter on top of bread

Vincent Rocco Saladini, Sr.

Remembering

Amelia Maria Saladini Capriotti

A Loving Mother, Grandmother and Sister
A True and Loyal Friend
A Faithful Servant

AUNT MINNIE MANSPEAKER'S FRIED BREAD

INGREDIENTS

5 lbs. flour
2 cups olive oil
1 tablespoon salt
1 teaspoon sugar
3 packs yeast
3-1/2 cups lukewarm water (feels hot to touch but not uncomfortably hot)

DIRECTIONS

* Put 5 lbs. flour (holding back one cup of flour for later use) in
12 quart stock pot
* Add salt and sugar to flour
* Dissolve the 3 packs of yeast in lukewarm water
* Make crater in middle of flour mixture and pour in 2-1/2 cups of the water mixture
* Stir mixture by hand and form dough
* Add the rest of water mixture as needed while making the dough
* The mixture will be somewhat sticky. Use some of the reserved flour if necessary
* Add 2 tablespoons of olive oil to rub onto the outside of the dough and around the sides of the pan to keep it from sticking during the rising process
* Put a lid on the stock pan and cover the pan with a towel

* The dough will rise and fill the pan after a few hours and should be kneaded back down to its original size. This process should continue throughout the day over at least 6 hours or more so it would be best started in the morning and cooked at dinner. During the kneading and rising process, more olive oil can be added to keep the dough from sticking to the pan

* Knead the dough one final time and form a large mound

* Sprinkle some of the remaining flour on the table surface and sprinkle the mound of dough lightly to reduce the stickiness. Slice the mound into smaller pieces about the size of a baseball. There should be about 10-12 pieces

* Take a piece and reduce sticking by adding a little flour. Then knead the piece and keep folding it in half until it has a consistent texture with no seams. Put the piece on the table and roll it out with a rolling pin to about 3/8" thickness, like a very thick pancake. It may be necessary to add a little flour to keep it from sticking, but the less flour the better. The dough should be about 6-7" in diameter. use a fork to punch 10-15 times into the dough to allow air to escape while cooking

* Use a 10" or 12" skillet (just so the sides of the rolled out bread do not touch the sides of the skillet), and turn the heat to medium high. Pour enough olive oil in the skillet to be about 3/8"-1/2" deep. When the oil has heated, lay one piece of bread dough into the pan. Lift up the edge of the dough with a fork to allow air to escape so the center cooks as well as the edges. It is important to continually spin the dough while frying so that it does not burn. When the bottom gets a light golden brown and the bottom center looks done, flip the bread and fry the other side. When the second side is finished, set in a plate on top of a paper towel

to absorb the extra oil. Continue frying the bread one at a time. Stack the bread with a paper towel between each layer.

* Cut the bread in two and slice to make a sandwich. Do not slice all the way through and you will have a little hinge to fold over like a roll. You could also slice it without cutting through any of the edge so that you will have a pocket to make a pita.

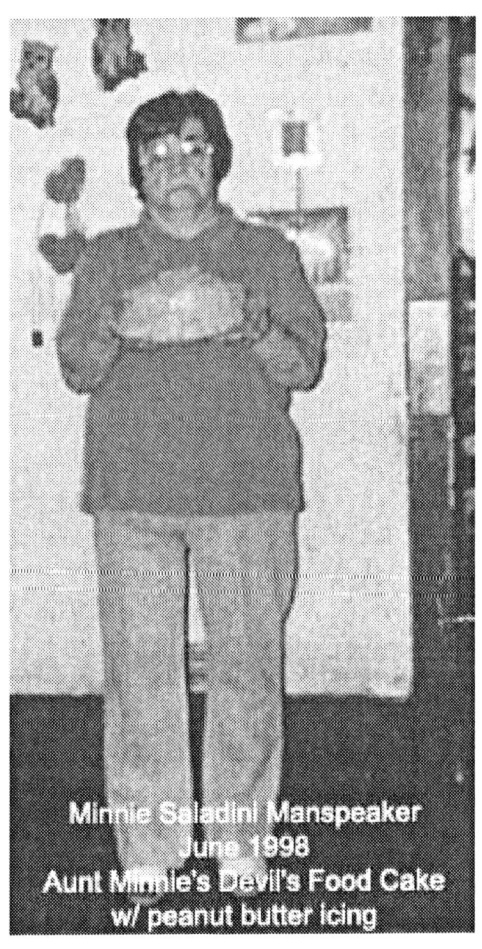

Minnie Saladini Manspeaker
June 1998
Aunt Minnie's Devil's Food Cake
w/ peanut butter icing

AUNT MINNIE MANSPEAKER'S DEVIL'S FOOD CAKE WITH PEANUT BUTTER ICING

INGREDIENTS

2 cups sifted flour
1-3/4 cups granulated sugar
3/4 cup cocoa
1/4 teaspoon baking soda
1-1/2 teaspoons baking powder
1 teaspoon salt
3/4 cup milk
1 teaspoon vanilla
1/2 milk
3 medium eggs
3/4 cup shortening

DIRECTIONS

* Into a large bowl stir together the sifted flour, sugar, baking soda, baking powder, cocoa and salt
* Drop in shortening, 3/4 cup milk, and vanilla
* Using an electric mixer, beat together for 2-1/2 minutes
* Add 1/2 cup milk and eggs
* Spread batter into two 9" round cake pans
* Bake at 350 degrees for 35 minutes

PEANUT BUTTER ICING

* 1 lb. 10x sugar
* 10 tablespoons peanut butter
* 1 tablespoon vanilla

DIRECTIONS

Mix together and add milk as needed to form a creamy, smooth icing. Spread evenly over cake.

VIOLA E. SALADINI'S ITALIAN SWEET TURKEY SAUSAGES

Viola E. Saladini
Italian Sweet Turkey Sausages

INGREDIENTS

* 8 2 oz. Italian sweet turkey sausage links
* 8 oz. can of tomato sauce
* 2 medium onions, finely chopped
* 3 garlic cloves, crushed
* 2 tablespoons of chopped parsley
* 2 tablespoons of virgin olive oil
* 1 cup water

DIRECTIONS

Vincent R. Saladini, Sr.
Enjoying Italian Sweet Sausage

1. Place 2 tablespoons of virgin olive oil in a non-stick frying pan and heat over a medium flame

2. Place sausage links in olive oil
3. Cook sausage until crisp and brown, remove from pan
4. Place chopped onion and garlic in frying pan and saute until caramelized
5. Place browned sausages back into frying pan
6. Add tomato sauce, parsley and one cup water and simmer for 20 minutes
7. Serve over spaghetti or pasta of your choice

Serves 4 people

Viola E. Saladini
Vernon, NJ

Vincent Rocco Saladini, Sr.

VINCENT R. SALADINI, SR.'S, BAKED CHICKEN A LA BIG SPRINGS

INGREDIENTS

* 4 lbs. boneless, skinless chicken breasts
* 1 cup fat free, lactose free milk or regular milk
* 2 cups crushed Rice Chex cereal
* 1-1/2 teaspoons paprika
* 3/4 teaspoon salt
* 1/4 teaspoon black pepper
* 1/4 teaspoon cayenne pepper
* 1 tablespoon crushed basil
* 1 tablespoon crushed parsley

DIRECTIONS

1. Preheat oven to 375 degrees
2. Coat a roasting pan with Pam non-stick cooking spray; set aside
3. Pour milk into a shallow bowl
4. Add chicken, turning to coat with milk
5. Refrigerate for 20 minutes, turning occasionally
6. On a plate, combine rice chex cereal, basil, parsley, black pepper, cayenne pepper, salt and paprika
7. Dip chicken breasts into the cereal mixture and coat evenly
8. Layer coated chicken breasts in roasting pan

9. Bake for 50 minutes turning the pieces one or two times until they are brown and crispy
10. When pricked with a fork, the juices should run clear.

Serves 6 people

Vincent R. Saladini, Sr.
Vernon, NJ

Vincent Rocco Saladini, Sr.

VINCENT R. SALADINI, SR.'S, CREAMY VANILLA MILK PIE

INGREDIENTS

* 1 cup sugar
* 1 cup milk (Fat free-lactose free or regular)
* 1/4 cup all purpose white flour
* 1 egg
* 3 egg whites
* 2 tablespoons melted butter or margarine
* 1-1/2 teaspoons pure vanilla extract
* 1 frozen 9" deep dish pie shell, thawed

DIRECTIONS

1. Preheat oven to 375 degrees
2. In a medium bowl, combine sugar, vanilla, milk, flour, egg whites, egg and melted butter/margarine
3. Beat with fork or whisk until smooth
4. Pour into thawed piecrust
5. Bake for 45 minutes or until lightly browned
6. Allow to cool completely in a rack

Serves 8 people

DEBORAH J. SALADINI'S BAKED TURKEY THIGHS WITH SPRING VEGETABLES AND HERB POCKETS

INGREDIENTS

* 8 large turkey thighs with the skins removed
* 2 14 oz. cans of baby corn nuggets, drained
* 2 14 oz. cans of artichoke hearts, drained
* 2 14 oz. cans of hearts of palm
* 3 lbs. of fresh baby carrots
* 5 large Yukon gold potatoes, cut into cubes, with the skins on
* 1 loaf of fresh bread, grated
* 2 beaten eggs
* 1/2 cup melted butter
* parsley, basil, onion powder, garlic powder, oregano, poultry seasoning
4 cups of water

DIRECTIONS

1. Season skinless turkey thighs with parsley, basil, onion powder, garlic powder, oregano
2. Layer thighs, meaty side up, in a roasting pan that has been sprayed with Pam non-stick cooking spray
3. On top of the seasoned turkey thighs, layer the baby carrots, artichoke hearts, hearts of palm, potatoes and baby corn nuggets

4. Sprinkle liberally with parsley, basil, onion powder, garlic powder, oregano, and poultry seasoning
5. In a separate large bowl, combine fresh grated bread, parsley, basil, onion powder, garlic powder, oregano, poultry seasoning, beaten eggs and melted butter and form into round balls
6. Layer round herb balls around the roasting pan on top of the layered vegetables
7. Cover with tinfoil and bake at 300 degrees for 4-6 hours until the turkey thighs are fork tender and the juices have caramelized

Serves 8 people

Deborah J. Saladini's baked turkey thighs with spring vegetables and herb pockets

VINCENT R. SALADINI, SR.'S, HOMEMADE CHICKEN VEGETABLE SOUP

INGREDIENTS

* 3 lbs. boneless, skinless chicken breasts
* 1 lb. fresh baby carrots
* 4 large potatoes cut into small cubes (with the skin left on)
* 2 tablespoons onion powder
* 2 tablespoons garlic powder
* 2 tablespoons each of basil, parsley
* 3 cups frozen peas
* 3 cups uncooked rice
* 1/2 cup ketchup
* 3 quarts water
* One large onion, cut in half
* 4 stalks celery

DIRECTIONS

1. Place all ingredients except rice and peas, in a large stock pot and simmer for 2-3 hours on a low flame.
2. When the chicken is fork-tender, add the uncooked rice and peas and simmer for 15 minutes.

Serves 6 people

DEBORAH J. SALADINI'S CHEESY CHICKEN OMELETTES

INGREDIENTS

* 3 lbs. boneless, skinless chicken breasts, trimmed of all fat and cut into small pies
* 5-6 slices of fat free American or cheddar cheese cut into pieces
* 8 eggs, beaten in a bowl
* 3 tablespoons each of basil, parsley, onion powder, garlic powder
* 1 cup of crushed premium saltine crackers or breadcrumbs
* 1/2 cup milk
* 1/2 cup I Can't Believe It's Not Butter liquid butter spray or melted butter

DIRECTIONS

1. Combine all ingredients in a large bowl and stir together until all ingredients are well blended; add more breadcrumbs if mixture is too liquidy or add more milk if mixture is too dry
2. Drop 1/4 cup size scoops into a hot, non-stick pan that has been sprayed with Pam cooking spray
3. Brown on each side until the cheese is melted and the chicken juices are no longer pink when pricked with a fork

Serves 6 people

DEBORAH J. SALADINI'S SAUTEED CHICKEN BREASTS

INGREDIENTS

* 2 lbs. boneless, skinless chicken breasts, trimmed of all fat and cut into cubes
* 2 tablespoons each of basil, parsley, onion powder, garlic powder

DIRECTIONS

1. Spray frying pan with Pam cooking spray
2. Place cubed chicken into hot pan and season with remaining ingredients
3. Saute until the chicken is golden brown
4. Serve with fresh peas and carrots and a crisp salad.

Serves 4 people.

Deborah Saladini
Montclair, NJ 7/29/01

AUNT ROSIE CRABTREE'S SCRUMPTIOUS RUM CAKE

INGREDIENTS

* 3 cups sifted cake flour
* 2-1/2 teaspoons double-acting baking powder
* 1 teaspoon salt
* 1/2 cup plus 2 tablespoons soft shortening
* 1/2 cup rum
* 1-3/4 cups plus 2 tablespoons sugar
* 2 large eggs, unbeaten
* 1-1/4 cup milk
1-1/2 teaspoons vanilla

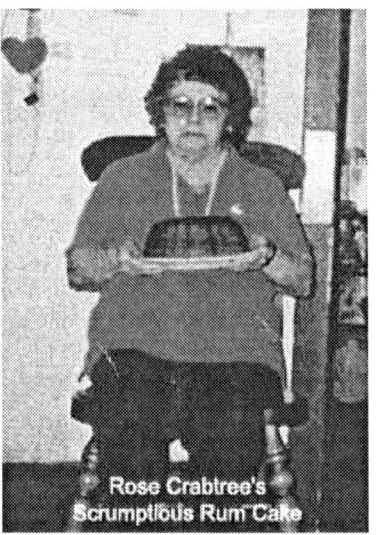

Rose Crabtree's Scrumptious Rum Cake

DIRECTIONS

1. Preheat oven to 350 degrees
2. In a bowl, cream together the butter and sugar
3. Add eggs and mix well
4. Add the flour a pinch of salt
5. Add vanilla and rum and mix well
6. Spray 8" bundt pan with Pam cooking spray
7. Pour mixture in prepared bundt pan
8. Bake in 350 degree oven for 3/4 hour

GLAZE

INGREDIENTS

* 1 cup sugar
* 1 stick butter
* 1/2 cup rum
* 1/4 cup sugar

DIRECTIONS

1. Melt butter in pan
2. Add sugar and water and boil until it looks like syrup
3. Pour in rum and stir
4. Prick cake with a fork all around the top and spoon the hot icing over the cake into the holes
5. Allow cake to cool and settle before serving so that the rum flavor sets in.

Serves 8-10 people

DENISE ANN CEURVELS' ANISETTE SPONGE COOKIES

INGREDIENTS

Denise Ann Ceurvels
Anisette Sponge Cookies

2 1/2 cups flour
3 teaspoons baking powder
1 cup sugar
1 stick of butter at room temperature
3 large eggs
1 1/2 ounces anisette
1 teaspoon vanilla
Confectioner's powdered sugar (optional)

DIRECTIONS

1. Preheat oven to 350 degrees.
2. Combine flour and baking powder in bowl and mix well.
3. Cream the sugar and butter in large bowl until mixture is fluffy. Add the eggs, one by one, and beat well by hand or with a mixer. Stir in anisette and vanilla.
4. Blend flour mixture into egg mixture until well combined.
5. Use a teaspoon or small ice cream scoop to drop the mixture onto a non-stick cookie sheet. Bake for 15 minutes. Remove cookies from oven and place on wire rack to cool thoroughly. If desired, powdered sugar may be sprinkled on cookies when cooled.

What's In A Name?

PASQUALE SALADINI

P... is for the many pleasures and joy we derived from being in your presence.

A... is for the admiration, love and respect we have for you.

S... is for the satisfaction you derived from being kind to others.

Q... is for the many questions we asked, which you always answered with such patience and understanding.

U... is for the understanding and tolerance you exhibited to those less fortunate.

A... is for the ability to make everyone feel comfortable in your presence.

L... is for the true love you shared with your family.

E... is for the effort you expended to keep the family together in times of deep crisis.

S... is for the many sacrifices you made for the family.

A... is for the positive attitude you exhibited in spite of hardships.

L... is for the true love you shared with your family.

A... is for your many achievements despite the many obstacles.

D... is for being a devoted, loving and caring father.

I... is for the inspiration you instilled in us by your actions and deeds as well as your words.

N... is for the numerous words of encouragement and hope you gave to each of us to lift our spirits.

I... is for your intelligence and ability to recognize a problem and go about solving it.

Put them all together and they spell **PASQUALE SALADINI**, our devoted, loving and caring father who left this Earth all too soon, but who unquestionably continues to love and guide us from above in the peace and solitude of God's heavenly kingdom.

Pasquale Saladini

JOHANNA DI MARIA SALADINI

J... is for the joy and comfort she brought to her family.

O... is for the openness, honesty and compassion she projected.

H... is for her heart as pure as gold.

A... is for the admiration, love and patience she had for her family.

N... is for the many sleepless nights she spent caring for her family.

N... is for the numerous meals she prepared with love.

A... is for her uncanny ability to make everyone comfortable in her presence.

D... is for her endless devotion to her family.

I... is for her initiative and involvement in raising her children.

M... is for the mercy she showed to family and friends alike.

A... is for the adoration we all have for her.

R... is for the rights she fought so hard to protect.

I... is for her inner beauty which glowed from within.

A... is for the admiration we feel for you.

S... is for the satisfaction she derived from helping others.

A... is for her positive attitude no matter what life held for her.

L... is for the true love she shared with her family.

A... is for her keen ability to cook delicious meals from the simplest ingredients

D... is for her untimely death with so much life yet to live.

I... is for her innate ability to love and be loved.

N... is for the nicest woman one could ever hope to know.

I... is for her keen insights into the feelings of those around her.

Put them all together and they spell **JOHANNA DI MARIA SALADINI**, our loving, caring and devoted mother who met an untimely death while still in the prime of her life. I know that she goes with God and keeps watch over us in death as she did in life.

Johanna DiMaria Saladini

CESARINA SALADINI

C... is for a caring, loving and devoted mother.

E... is for the tremendous energy you always exuded.

S... is for the satisfaction you derived in helping others.

A... is for the deep adoration we all feel for you.

R... is for the right we had to be ourselves in your presence.

I... is for your keen insights to make wise choices.

N... is for the nights you sat with us to calm our fears.

A... is for your positive attitude despite your own fears.

S... is for the sanity you brought to the chaos around us.

A... is for your ability to make everyone feel at home.

L... is for the true love you shared with your family.

A... is for your many achievements despite such adversity.

D... is for your tireless devotion to your family.

I... is for your interest in all that we did.

N... is for the sleepless nights you watched over us.

I... is for your intellect which you freely shared.

Put them all together and they spell **CESARINA SALADINI**, our loving and caring stepmother who loved and respected us as though we were her own. We thank you for your years of love and devotion. We know that you enjoy the Kingdom of God and guide us still.

TEODOLINDA SALADINI

T... is for Teodolinda, my father's first loving wife.

E... is for her eagerness to help those less fortunate.

O... is for her positive outlook on life despite so many obstacles to overcome.

D... is for a devoted, loving mother who was always there.

O... is for her optimism in times of doubt and fear.

L... is for the true love she had for her devoted family.

I... is for your inspiration and innermost beauty.

N... is for your never-ending ability to give to others.

D... is for your determination to keep us together as a family.

A... is for the admiration and love you always had for your family.

S... is for the many sacrifices you made for us.

A... is for your positive attitude despite the obstacles ever present.

L... is for the true love you bestowed upon your family.

A... is for your uncanny ability to adapt to a new way of life.

D... is for always being a devoted, loving wife and mother.

I... is for your inspiration to all of us during the hard times.

N... is for the nature you taught us to love and respect.

I... is for your ingenuity and ability to thrive.

Put them all together and they spell **<u>TEODOLINDA</u> <u>SALADINI</u>**, a loving, caring, devoted wife and mother who continues to inspire us from the heavens above.

<u>JOHN RUSSO</u>

<u>J...</u> is for the joy you brought to us each day of our lives.

<u>O...</u> is for the optimism you always shared with others.

<u>H...</u> is for a heart of gold forever filled with love.

<u>N...</u> is for your natural ability to nurture those around you.

<u>R...</u> is for the respect you commanded and received.

<u>U...</u> is for your genuine understanding and compassion.

<u>S...</u> is for the many sacrifices you made for your family.

<u>S...</u> is for the sense of security you gave to your loved ones.

<u>O...</u> is for the openness you exuded and your timeless sincerity.

Vincent Rocco Saladini, Sr.

Put them all together and they spell **JOHN RUSSO**, a devoted, loving father filled with love and compassion who watches over us still, from Heaven above.

ANTOINETTE RUSSO

A... is for the genuine adoration and love we have for you.

N... is for the many sleepless nights you cared for your family.

T... is for your unending tolerance and patience for others.

O... is for your optimism in the face of adversity.

I... is for your ingenuity in times of pain and struggle.

N... is for your natural ability to survive despite the odds.

E... is for your heroic efforts to keep the family together.

T... is for the tenderness you lavished upon the family.

T... is for the tasks you performed without ever complaining.

E... is for your boundless energy and ever-present love.

R... is for the respect you commanded and received from others.

U... is for your compassionate understanding for the family.

S... is for the unselfish sacrifices you made for the family.

S... is for the superb suppers you prepared for the family.

O... is for always being outgoing and orderly.

Put them all together and they spell **ANTOINETTE RUSSO**, a loving, devoted and caring wife and mother who guided us in life, and now watches over us peacefully from above in the Kingdom of God.

EMIDIO SALADINI

E... is for Emidio, a man we all hold in the highest esteem.

M... is for the memories that he shared with us over the years.

I... is for the inspiration he was to all who loved him.

D... is for your undying devotion to your family and friends.

I... is for your keen insights to make wise and lasting choices.

O... is for your endless optimism in the face of adversity.

S... is for the satisfaction you derive from helping others.

A... is for the positive attitude you always exhibited.

L... is for the love you shared with your wife and children.

A... is for the admiration you received from others each day.

D... is for always being devoted and giving to your family.

I... is for the tremendous inspiration you were to others.

N... is for the many nights you calmed your family's fears.

I... is for the initiative you had to be successful.

Put them all together and they spell **EMIDIO SALADINI**, a devoted, kind, loving and caring husband and father who always showed endless compassion for his family and friends. I am deeply proud and honored to have called him my uncle. I know that he continues to love and guide us from Heaven above.

ALBA SALADINI

A... is for the admiration everyone had for you.

L... is for the love you always gave to your family and friends.

B... is for the inner beauty which made you glow.

A... is for your positive attitude despite the hardships.

S... is for the satisfaction your presence gave to others.

A... is for the aura of love that surrounded all you did.

L... is for being that special link that kept the family together.

A... is for the many achievements you accomplished in life.

D... is for your devotion to your family and friends.

I... is for your inspiration to others.

N... is for the nights you spent caring for your family.

I... is for your insights into life that you freely shared.

Put them all together and they spell **<u>ALBA SALADINI</u>**, a caring and loving wife and mother who loved deeply and with great compassion. You continue to love from above where your days are filled with peace.

JOSEPH SALADINI

J... is for the joy you bring to others.

O... is for your sense of optimism.

S... is for your sense of humor.

E... is for your boundless energy.

P... is for the sense of peace you give to others.

H... is for the happiness you derive from each day of life.

S... is for the satisfaction your presence gives to others.

A... is for the aura of love that surrounds all you do.

L... is for the love you give to others.

A... is for the many achievements you accomplished in life.

D... is for your devotion to your family and friends.

I... is for your inspiration to others.

N... is for the nights you spent caring for your family.

I... is for your insights into life that you freely shared.

327

Put them all together and they spell **JOSEPH SALADINI**, a loving and caring brother, husband, and father who fills those around him with joy and love.

ENASE SALADINI

E... is for the boundless energy you have.

N... is for all the nice things you do for others.

A... is for your ability to help others.

S... is for the sweet disposition you have.

E... is for the eternal love we have for you.

S... is for the satisfaction you give to others.

A... is for the admiration we feel for you.

L... is for the love and adoration we have for you.

A... is for the absence we all feel when we are apart.

D... is for the dear things you do for others.

I... is for the inspiration you give to all of us.

N... is for the nights you cared for your family.

I... is for your insights into the world around you.

Put them all together and they spell **ENASE SALADINI**, a loving and devoted wife and mother whose love for her family and friends have endeared her to us forever.

Enase Saladini
Big Springs, West Virginia

DOLLY SALADINI

D... is for Dolly, a person we all love.

O... is for her optimism in the face of adversity.

L... is for the true love she has for her family.

L... is for her love of life.

Y... is for her youthful attitude towards life.

S... is for the satisfaction her presence brings to others.

A... is for her ever positive attitude.

L... is for her love of music.

A... is for her ability to prepare excellent meals.

D... is for her being such a devoted and loving sister.

I... is for her interest in all that we did.

N... is for her natural ability to nurture those around her.

I... is for her keen insights into life.

Put them all together and they spell **DOLLY SALADINI,** a loving and caring sister who fills those around her with love and joy.

WARREN CEURVELS

W... is for your willingness to help those around you.

A... is for the admiration we all have for you.

R... is for the respect you command from and receive from others.

R... is for your right to always be yourself.

E... is for the great effort you display in all that you do.

N... is for the many nights you spent caring for your family.

C... is for the care and concern you have for your family.

E... is for your boundless energy in keeping up with Matty.

U... is for your intelligent understanding of others.

R... is for the logical reasoning you successfully apply to all situations.

V... is for your veracity and vigor.

E... is for the many evenings you spend with your loved ones.

L... is for the love you give to and receive from others.

S... is for the selflessness you display to your family.

Put them all together and they spell **WARREN CEURVELS**, a devoted, loving and caring husband and father whose zest for life and compassion towards others fills our lives with untold joy.

Warren Ceurvels

DENISE ANN CEURVELS

D... is for your devotion to your family and career.

E... is for the endless effort you expend for others.

N... is for the nice things you do each day.

I... is for the inspiration you give to your family and friends.

S... is for the sacrifices you have made for your family.

E... is for your boundless energy.

A... is for your ability to achieve success.

N... is for your pleasant nature.

N... is for the newness you bring to each day of life.

C... is for the care and concern you show for your family.

E... is for your eagerness to please your family and friends.

U... is for your genuine understanding of the needs of others.

R... is for the respect you command and receive from others.

V... is for the variety of hobbies you enjoy with your family.

E... is for the many evenings you spent caring for your family.

L... is for the love you give and receive from others.

S... is for the satisfaction you derive from being a wife and mother.

Put them all together and they spell **DENISE ANN CEURVELS**, our precious firstborn child, and devoted, loving and caring wife and mother who fills us with pride and untold joy.

Denise Saladini Ceurvels

FRANK CEURVELS

F... is for the funny things you do to make us smile.

R... is for your keen sense of right and wrong.

A... is for your ability to achieve success in all you do.

N... is for the nights you spent working towards your goals.

K... is for the kindness you show to family and friends alike.

C... is for always being caring and considerate of others.

E... is for genuine efforts to help those around you.

U... is for the understanding you show others in all you do.

R... is for the respect you command and receive from others.

V... is for the personal victories you have come to know.

E... is for your boundless energy and drive for success.

L... is for the love you give to and receive from others.

S... is for your keen sensibilities and many successes.

Put them all together and they spell **FRANK CEURVELS**, a caring, loving son and grandson who has brought joy to those around him and who has enriched our lives in many wonderful ways. We are proud to have him in our lives.

MATTHEW JAMES CEURVELS

M... is for Matty, the joy of our lives.
A... is for your ability to grasp new ideas each day.
T... is for the times we spent hugging and loving you.
T... is for your tender and loving touch.
H... is for the happiness you bring to us just being near you.
E... is for your boundless energy and zest for life.
W... is for the warmth we feel having you near.

J... is for the utter joy you give us each day of life.
A... is for always being the apple of our eye.
M... is for the many moments of happiness you bring to us.
E... is for effort you put into all that you do.
S... is for one smart boy whose smile lights up our lives.

C... is for a caring, compassionate child whom we adore.
E... is for the many evenings we enjoyed playing with you.
U... is for your keen understanding of the world around you.
R... is for the respect you receive from others.
V... is for the vim and vigor you always show.
E... is for the excitement we feel just being near you.
L... is for the deep and abiding love we have for you.
S... is for the satisfaction we derive watching you grow.

Put them all together and they spell **MATTHEW JAMES CEURVELS**, our precious firstborn grandson, the joy of our lives, the light of our lives, our hope and inspiration for the future. You cannot even begin to imagine how much we love and adore you and cherish each moment that we are together. A glorious future awaits you.

VINCENT ROCCO SALADINI, SR.

V... is for Venanzio, the Italian name for Vincent.

I... is for the inspiration I received from my parents.

N... is for the many nights I spent attending college.

C... is for the caring, loving, devoted father and spouse I pledged to always be.

E... is for the enjoyment I derive each day of my life.

N... is for the numerous weekends I spent studying for my college classes.

T... is for the tolerance and patience I have for others.

R... is for the right to be oneself without being judgmental.

O... is for my openness and ever present optimism.

C... is for my being a conscientious, caring human being.

C... is for my care of and concern for others.

O... is for the optimism I share with others.

S... is for the satisfaction I derive from being kind to others.

A... is for the admiration and love I have for my family.

L... is for the tender love and care I receive from my family.

A... is for my ability to enjoy life to its fullest.

D... is for my devotion to my family and friends.

I... is for my insights into the world around me.

N... is for my need to be an active role model for my family.

I... is for my ingenuity in surviving life's troubling moments.

S... is for the satisfaction I derive from my wife and children.

R... is for the respect I give to and receive from my family.

Put them all together and they spell **VINCENT ROCCO SALADINI, SR.,** a devoted, loving and caring husband and father, loved and treasured forever, admired and respected, always and forever in our hearts.

Vincent R. Saladini

VIOLA ESTHER SALADINI

V... is for Viola, the vibrant love of my life.
I... is for the inspiration she instilled in me.
O... is for the optimism she always shares.
L... is for the true love we have for each other.
A... is for the adoration I have for her always.

E... is for everything that we share.
S... is for the satisfaction I derive just being near her.
T... is for the tenderness she shares with me always.
H... is for her heart of gold.
E... is for the eternity we shall share.
R... is for her regalness in all that she does.

S... is for the many suppers that we have shared.
A... is for her ever positive attitude.
L... is for the love she has for our family.
A... is for her acceptance of others.
D... is for her endless devotion to our family.
I... is for the intimacy that we share.
N... is for the nights that she cared for us all.
I... is for the loving interest she takes in each of us.

Put them all together and they spell **VIOLA ESTHER SALADINI**, the love of my life, my sole inspiration, my precious wife, friend and lover, the devoted and loving mother of our three children. You are treasured and loved forever.

Vincent Rocco Saladini, Sr.

ADAM CAPRIOTTI, SR.

A... is for the immense admiration we feel for you.

D... is for your dedication to your family and friends.

A... is for your ability to make everyone feel comfortable.

M... is for the memories of you that live on in each of us.

C... is for the compassion and concern you showed to others.

A... is for the admiration we each have for you.

P... is for the pleasure we feel when you are near.

R... is for the right to always be yourself without judging.

I... is for your initiative and drive to succeed.

O... is for your optimism in the face of adversity.

T... is for your tolerance of others at all times.

T... is for the thanks we owe you for your selfless sacrifices.

I... is for the inspiration you gave to each of us.

S... is for the many sacrifices you made for your family.

R... is for the respect you commanded and received from others.

Put them all together and they spell **ADAM CAPRIOTTI, SR.** a devoted, loving and caring husband and father whose selfless acts and sacrifices for his family enabled them to endure the many hardships that they faced. I know that he is resting peacefully in the glorious kingdom of Heaven above.

AMELIA CAPRIOTTI

A... is for the immense admiration we feel for you.

M... is for the moments of pleasure you brought to us.

E... is for your endless effort to help those around you.

L... is for the true love you show to your family and friends.

I... is for your keen insights into everyday life.

A... is for the many activities that you engaged in.

C... is for your care of and concern for others.

A... is for the admiration you receive from others.

P... is for the pleasure we feel when you are near.

R... is for the right to always be yourself without judging.

I... is for your initiative and drive to succeed.

O... is for your optimism in the face of adversity.

T... is for your tolerance of others at all times.

T... is for the thanks we owe you for your selfless sacrifices.

I... is for your instinctive ability to comfort others.

Put them all together and they spell **AMELIA CAPRIOTTI**, our devoted, loving and caring sister, whose sacrifices enabled our family to remain together after our mother died. We are indebted to you forever. May you find eternal peace and happiness in the kingdom of God.

DEBORAH JEAN SALADINI

D... is for your devotion to your family and law career.

E... is for the great effort you put into all that you do.

B... is for the brilliance you bring to our lives.

O... is for your optimism despite what life may bring.

R... is for your readiness and willingness to help others.

A... is for your ability to solve problems for others.

H... is for your heart of gold and compassion for others.

J... is for the joy you bring into our lives each day.

E... is for your eagerness to always be there for others.

A... is for your ability to love and be loved.

N... is for the nights you spent caring for others.

S... is for your sensitivity to the needs of others.

A... is for your positive attitude in the face of adversity.

L... is for the love and joy you bring to our lives each day.

A... is for your many accomplishments and achievements in life.

D... is for always being our "Darling Debbie."

I... is for your insights into solving life's little problems.

N... is for the new hope you bring to each day.

I... is for your instinctual ability to understand others.

Put them all together and they spell **DEBORAH JEAN SALADINI**, a highly intelligent, kind, loving and compassionate sister and daughter who continues to fill our lives with untold joy and happiness that is never-ending.

PAUL ALLAN MASSARO

P... is for the passion which you bring to life.

A... is for your incredible artistic abilities.

U... is for your unsurpassed writing talent.

L... is for your love of life around you.

A... is for your animal charm.

L... is for the intense love everyone feels for you.

L... is for the unending love and joy you give to Debbie.

A... is for your ability to delight those around you.

N... is for your never-say-die attitude towards life.

M... is for the man who has brought untold joy to Debbie's life.

A... is for the many accomplishments that adorn your life.

S... is for the sparkle in your eyes.

S... is for your sensitivity to others.

A... is for your ability to love and be loved.

R... is for your readiness to help others.

O... is for your optimism and positive outlook on life.

Put them all together and they spell **PAUL ALLAN MASSARO**, a man who has earned our complete love and respect, a man who shall forever have our trust and admiration, and a man whose brilliance and zest for life, and whose caring and loving nature has filled our lives, and most importantly, Debbie's life, with untold joy and happiness. You shall forever be an integral part of our lives and you shall forever be loved and welcome in our hearts.

VINCENT ROCCO SALADINI, JR.

V... is for Vincent, our son who fills us with pride and joy.

I... is for the inspiration you bring to those around you.

N... is for the countless nights you devoted to saving lives.

C... is for the care and concern you show to your family.

E... is for your eagerness to help those less fortunate.

N... is for your nurturing nature and compassion towards others.

T... is for the tolerance and tenderness you show to others.

R... is for the reason you use to solve everyday problems.

O... is for your sense of eternal optimism.

C... is for your noble sense of conscience and compassion.

C... is for the comfort and love you give to others.

O... is for your beautiful openness to your family and friends.

S... is for your sensitivity in times of pain and doubt.

A... is for your keen ability to sense the needs of others.

L... is for the love you share with your wife and family, especially Harrison Cole.

A... is for your admirable achievements despite the adversity.

D... is for your tireless devotion to your family and patients.

I... is for your keen insights into the needs of others.

N... is for the need others have to love you and be near you.

I... is for your innate instinct to know others intimately.

J... is for the sheer joy you bring to our lives each day.

R... is for the respect you command and receive by just being you.

Put them all together and they spell **VINCENT ROCCO SALADINI, JR.**, a devoted and compassionate son, father, brother, uncle and husband who fills our lives with untold joy and pride, and who has enriched us a hundredfold just by loving us and letting us love him.

Vincent R. Saladini, Jr.

LINDA VICTORIA SALADINI

L... is for the love we have for you now and forever.

I... is for being an inspiration to your family and friends.

N... is for the nights you spent caring for your family.

D... is for your devotion to your husband, family and patients.

A... is for the admiration we all feel for you.

V... is for your vivacious personality.

I... is for your inspiration and zest for life.

C... is for your genuine care, compassion and concern for others.

T... is for your tenderness to those around you, especially Harrison Cole.

O... is for your openness and eternal optimism.

R... is for your regal beauty and charm.

I... is for your keen insights into others.

A... is for your agility and fond aspirations.

S... is for the sense of serenity you bring to others.

A... is for your remarkable ability to love and be loved.

L... is for the love you share with your family and friends.

A... is for the many acts of kindness you shower upon others.

D... is for daring to dream and finally realizing that dream.

I... is for your innate intelligence in all that you do.

N... is for your unselfish need to give to others.

I... is for your innocence.

Put them all together and they spell **LINDA VICTORIA SALADINI**, a caring, compassionate, kind and loving wife, mother and daughter-in-law who shall be forever loved and adored by all of us.

HARRISON COLE SALADINI

H... is for Harrison, our precious new grandson.

A... is for the admiration we all feel for you.

R... is for your right to love and be loved.

R... is for your right to seek and find peace, love and happiness.

I... is for the inspiration you will bring to others.

S... is for the son who will bring joy to our family.

O... is for a rosy outlook for a happy and healthy life.

N... is for our never-ending love for you.

C... is for the care we delight in giving to you.

O... is for the positive outlook we know you will have.

L... is for the endless love we all feel for you.

E... is for your boundless energy and enthusiasm.

S... is for the many bright and sunny days that await you.

A... is for always filling our lives with so much peace and joy.

L... is for a life that is filled with wonder and zest.

A... is for the aura of love you inspire.

D... is for the delight you have given to us.

I... is for your insights sure to come.

N... is for the never-ending love you will receive from all of us.

I... is for the interesting and exciting accomplishments that await you.

Vincent Rocco Saladini, Sr.

Put them all together and they spell **HARRISON COLE SALADINI**, our adorable, precious new addition to the Saladini family. May you always carry your name with the greatest dignity and honor and may you realize all of your dreams. We love you with all our hearts.

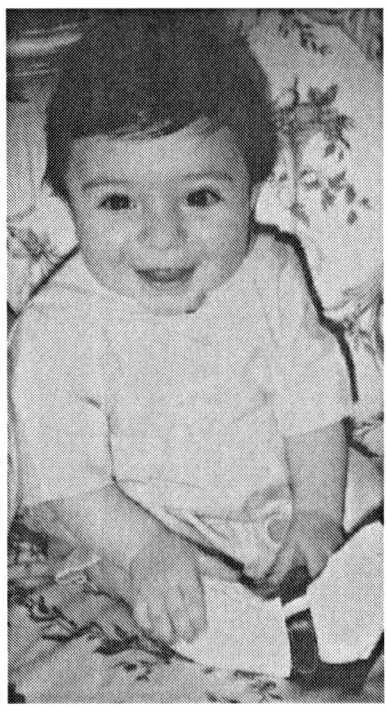

<u>MINNIE MANSPEAKER</u>

<u>M...</u> is for being such a caring and devoted mother.

<u>I...</u> is for you keen insights into the world around you.

<u>N...</u> is for your numerous words of encouragement.

<u>N...</u> is for your good nature and compassion towards others.

<u>I...</u> is for your innermost beauty and love of life.

<u>E...</u> is for your eagerness to always help others.

<u>M...</u> is for the many moments of joy you bring to others.

<u>A...</u> is for our deep admiration and respect for you.

<u>N...</u> is for the nights you spent caring for your family.

<u>S...</u> is for the many sacrifices you always made for your family.

<u>P...</u> is for the joy and pleasure you bring to others.

<u>E...</u> is for your efforts to keep your family always safe.

<u>A...</u> is for your positive attitude in times of adversity.

<u>K...</u> is for your keen ability to understand others.

E... is for your boundless energy and zest for life.

R... is for the high school ring you unselfishly bought me.

Put them all together and they spell **MINNIE MANSPEAKER**, our devoted, caring and loving sister who sacrificed throughout her life for her family so that we would never be without. We love you dearly.

Hagerstown, Maryland
Minnie Saladini Smith

ROSIE WOLFENSBERGER

R... is for Rosie, who makes us all proud.

O... is for your openness and honest.

S... is for the satisfaction you derive from helping others.

I... is for the inspiration you give to others.

E... is for your eagerness to help your family and friends.

W... is for you willingness to go out of your way for others.

O... is for your eternal optimism throughout life.

L... is for the true love you share with your family.

F... is for your friendliness to others.

E... is for the evenings of pleasure we shared growing up.

N... is for the nights you spent caring for your family.

S... is for the delicious suppers you prepared for your family.

B... is for the beauty of your smile.

E... is for your tireless effort to help others.

R... is for the great respect we all feel for you.

G... is for your goodness and generosity to those around you.

E... is for your boundless energy.

R... is for the way you rejoice in each day of life.

Put them all together and they spell **ROSIE WOLFENSBERGER**, our loving and caring sister whose love and devotion carried us through the hard times. We love you dearly.

Hagerstown, Maryland
Rosie Saladini Crabtree

LUCY CUTRONE

L... is for the love you give to others.

U... is for your understanding of those around you.

C... is for the care you give to others.

Y... is for the many years you sacrificed for your family.

C... is for your concern for those around you.

U... is for your unique ability to love and beloved.

T... is for the many times you sacrificed for your family.

R... is for the respect you receive from others.

O... is for your openness to others.

N... is for the many nights you spent caring for your family.

E... is for your eagerness to help others.

Put them all together and they spell **LUCY CUTRONE**, a loving, caring sister and devoted mother whose zest for life shall not be forgotten. May she rest in peace in the Lord's kingdom.

1947 Big Springs, West Virginia
Lucy Saladini

ANGELO SALADINI, SR.

A... is for the admiration we all feel for you.

N... is for all of the nice things you do for others.

G... is for the goodness you always find in others.

E... is for your tireless efforts to care for your family.

L... is for the tremendous love you always give to your family.

O... is for your eternal optimism even in the face of adversity.

S... is for the many sacrifices you made for your family.

A... is for your many worthy achievements in life.

L... is for the love and respect we all have for you.

A... is for your positive attitude in all that you do.

D... is for your devotion to your family and friends.

I... is for your keen insights into the world around you.

N... is for the many nights you spent caring for your family.

I...   is for the inspiration you give to others.

S...   is for your selflessness in all that you do.

R...   is for the respect that we have for you now and forever.

Put them all together and they spell **ANGELO SALADINI, SR.**, a loving, caring brother and a devoted father and husband whose guidance and strength throughout the years sustained us and helped us to grow. We love you dearly.

April 24, 1944 Big Springs, West Virginia
Angelo Saladini

LOUISE SALADINI

L... is for a loving, caring mother and wife.

O... is for your optimistic outlook on life.

U... is for your understanding and compassion.

I... is for your innermost beauty and love of life.

S... is for the satisfaction you bring to others.

E... is for your eagerness to help others.

S... is for the many sacrifices you made for your family.

A... is for the admiration we have for you.

L... is for the true love you share with your family.

A... is for your ability to make those around you feel comfortable and loved.

D... is for your devotion to your family as a loving wife and mother.

I... is for your keen insights into the world around you.

N... is for the nice things you do for those around you.
I... is for your ingenuity and constant source of inspiration.

Put them all together and they spell **<u>LOUISE
SALADINI</u>**, a loving, caring mother and wife who earns
the respect of all who come in contact with her.

MARY SALADINI

M... is for Mary, our precious angel child.

A... is for your ability to accept God's will.

R... is for the respect we all had for you.

Y... is for the years of life you never knew.

S... is for the satisfaction you gave to us.

A... is for the beautiful little angel we called Mary.

L... is for the love and adoration we had for you.

A... is for the absence we all felt when you died so young.

D... is for the untimely death of our beautiful angel.

I... is for the inspiration you gave to all of us.

N... is for the nights we cried when you were taken from us.

I... is for your insights that we shall never know.

Put them all together and they spell **MARY SALADINI**, our beautiful baby sister who died tragically at birth. Your brief time on Earth filled us with love and joy and a peaceful calmness that has sustained us all of these years. I know that you are one of God's precious angels looking down upon us with the same love in death that you shared with us in life. So often I ponder what dreams you would have accomplished, what mysteries you would have unraveled, what destiny would be yours. We will love you forever.

<u>CARLO ROSSI</u>

<u>C...</u> is for the care and compassion you show to others.

<u>A...</u> is for your ability to make others comfortable near you.

<u>R...</u> is for the respect you give to and receive from others.

<u>L...</u> is for the love you receive from family and friends.

<u>O...</u> is for your eternal optimism even in the face of adversity.

<u>R...</u> is for the way you rejoiced in each day of life.

<u>O...</u> is for your openness and sincerity.

<u>S...</u> is for the many sacrifices you made for your family.

<u>S...</u> is for your sincerity and warm smile.

<u>I...</u> is for your innate ability to bring joy to others.

Put them all together and they spell **CARLO ROSSI**, a kind, compassionate and caring brother and son whose untimely death in the prime of his life shattered our lives forever. We shall never forget you and shall remember you always with love and warmth. Rest peacefully in God's sacred Kingdom until we meet again.

JOHN S. FERRO

J... is for a just and compassionate man.

O... is for the optimism you always displayed.

H... is for the many hours you patiently spent teaching me the basics of fine tailoring, and the hope and encouragement you always gave me.

N... is for your good nature and compassion towards others.

S... is for the satisfaction you derived by being kind to those around you.

F... is for the faith and trust you had in my ability to learn the tailoring trade.

E... is for your eagerness to help those less fortunate.

R... is for the respect you earned and received from those around you.

R... is for the way you rejoiced in each day of life.

O... is for your openness in dealing with others.

Put them all together and they spell **JOHN S. FERRO**, a man who has earned my utmost respect and admiration. He gave me an opportunity to pursue a career in the fashion trades and he never stopped believing in me. He instilled in me a zest for life and a work ethic to always do my best and to never settle for less. He taught me to take pride in my work and to follow my heart no matter what obstacles I may face. I have faithfully followed throughout my life and career, all that he has instilled in me. I shall be forever grateful for his patience, kindness and understanding and his teachings shall remain with me forever.

John S. Ferro (retired)
Martinsburg, West Virginia
"My first tailoring teacher"

BARNEY

B... is for Barney, our cherished and loved puppy.

A... is for the admiration we all had for you.

R... is for your radiant and regal beauty.

N... is for the nights we spent holding you and loving you.

E... is for the energy you exhibited despite being terminally ill.

Y... is for the most precious year we spent with you.

Put them all together and they spell **BARNEY**, our precious Yellow Labrador puppy whose brief life on this Earth taught us how precious life really is and who gave us unconditional love despite his pain and suffering. Many were the tears we shed when you died in Deborah's arms and many more were the tears we shed knowing that at last you were at peace in God's Kingdom, awaiting our loving arms once again.

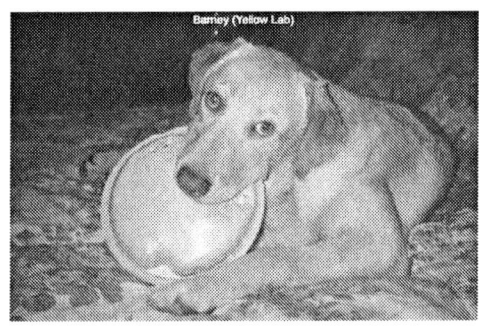

SMOKEY

S... is for the many smiles you brought to our faces.

M... is for the many nights we spent loving and caring for you.

O... is for the way you openly showed your love for us.

K... is for the kindness we gave to you each day of life.

E... is for the eternal love we have for you.

Y... is for the yearning we feel since you were called home.

Put them all together and they spell **SMOKEY**, a loving and loyal dog who enriched our lives and who taught us what it means to give, to love and to be loved each day of life. We miss you more than words can ever express and we await the joy of being with you once again.

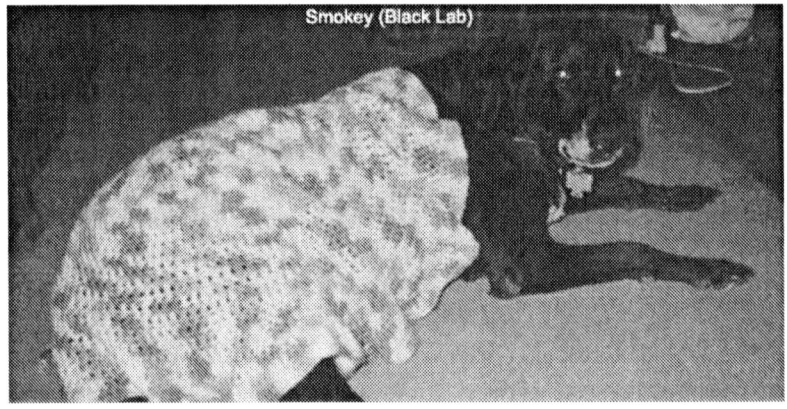

Smokey (Black Lab)

BOOMER

B... is for the joy and beauty you bring to us each day.

O... is for your ongoing drive to make us happy.

O... is for the way you openly show your love for us.

M... is for the many hours you spend loving us.

E... is for your boundless energy and enthusiasm.

R... is for the real love and devotion you give to us each day.

Put them all together and they spell **BOOMER**, our loving and devoted dog whose unconditional love for each of us has filled us with a sense of true joy that will remain with us forever. You are our precious guardian angel always watching over us.

Boomer
Clifton, NJ

SCOOTER

S... is for Scooter, our precious little hound.

C... is for the caring ways you show us your love.

O... is for the way you openly care for us.

O... is for your ongoing need to love and be loved.

T... is for the many times we spend hugging and cuddling you.

E... is for your boundless energy and sense of enthusiasm.

R... is for the real love and devotion you give to us each day.

Put them all together and they spell **SCOOTER**, our precious, lovable little hound who brings untold love and joy into our lives each day. Your unconditional love is real and forever and we will love you until the end of time and beyond.

Scooter (Basset Hound)
Born July 18, 1996

Personal Quotes

1. "Life is like a puff of smoke. There is a fine line between life and death. One moment it is visible and the next moment, it disappears into eternity."

2. "Success is most appreciated when it is achieved through hard work, sacrifice, perseverance, and honesty of purpose."

3. "The manner in which we utilize our time is of vital importance. We should make our journey on this earth enjoyable and fruitful. A kind word of encouragement or a smile to our fellow human beings will help one to achieve this goal."

4. "Dreaming is living in the state of the unconscious mind. In this state, life becomes a fantasyland. One can dream of goals, hopes, and aspirations far beyond the depths of the conscious human mind. I, too, have experienced vivid dreams of fantasies that I thought were impossible to achieve. However, many of my fantasy dreams have become a reality. So, close your eyes, lean back, and relax. Perhaps you, too, may dream a fantasy that will one day become a reality for you. Dream on...dream on..."

5. "Each of us is placed on this earth for a specific reason. God has a blueprint for each of us that only he can interpret. Some will leave this earth early on in life while others will remain for what seems like an eternity. Who makes the final decision? God will, of course, because he holds our destiny in the palm of his hands and in his infinite power and wisdom, he will never let us falter."

6. "Why are the majority of human beings so obsessed with material things in life? Is it greed or just plain ignorance? Accumulating material wealth can be a positive factor, a benefit to all mankind if the one who amasses such wealth shares it with those less fortunate who are unable to help themselves."

7. "A friend is a person who accepts you for what you are and acknowledges you as a human being, good or bad. A friend is a person with whom you can share your hopes, goals, dreams and aspirations, your innermost thoughts, feelings, and secrets without fear of being judged. A friend is a person with whom you can share a mutual trust and respect that will endure forever."

8. "Do not be too hasty in passing judgment on another until you have first assessed your own positive and negative qualities."

9. Be not too free with the 'facts', for the truth will eventually be a prevailing force."

10. The world is not entirely flat. There are hills and valleys in every landscape. Be prepared to travel over any and all terrain in order to reach your destination. Do not be discouraged. Meet challenges head-on; do not be afraid to face whatever life has to offer."

Getting the Most Value When Selecting Your Wardrobe, Table of Proportions for Rises and Inseams, Trouser Classifications, Drafting Trousers and Jerkins

A. <u>FABRIC</u>:

Suits are made from all types of fabric. Federal labeling laws require that the content of fabrics be indicated by displaying a tag or label on the garment. Most commonly used fabrics are wool, polyester and polyester/woolen blends. There are two types of wool—woolens and worsteds.

1. Woolens are generally soft with some bulkiness. They have a noticeable nap that resists wrinkles. Loosely woven fabrics, however, lose their shape easier and they need more frequent pressing. Tweed and flannel, for example, do not shine and they are made from short woolen yarns.

2. Worsteds are made from long woolen yarns. They are very smooth fabrics with tightly woven fibers that hold their shape and creases longer. They are lighter in weight and they can be used year round. Some examples are 10-12 oz. tropical serge and gabardine.

3. Polyester: (dacron, nylon, darvan) These fabrics have been created to mimic wool; however, they lack the soft drape of wool. They feel rather lifeless, "plastic feeling" and stiff.

4. Cashmere: Luxury fabric that has soft, fine yarns from the kashmur goat. Other animal fabrics such as camel's hair, alpaca, vicuna and llama lend themselves to various uses in the textile industry.

B. FIT: Fit is very important. A good fit can compensate for slight shortcomings in the quality and construction of the fabric. A poor fit can make the most expensive garment look sloppy and cheap. It is important to select a style and proportion that feels comfortable and that enhances your appearance.

Men's sizes commonly come in long, regular, short, stout, stub and corpulent. Women's sizes commonly come in petite, regular, and half sizes. There is a wide selection of size ranges. If a garment requires extensive alterations, then it is best to try on another size and style. If you opt to select plaids or stripes, you must make sure that the patterns match at the center back, sleeve front, lapel edges, collar edges, pockets, side seams of trousers, and center.

C. BASIC STYLES:

1. EUROPEAN CUT
   a. Fitted at chest/hips
   b. Exaggerated shoulders
   c. High cut armholes
   d. Low gorge line
   e. No vent
   f. Trousers pleated and cuffed

2. AMERICAN CUT
   a. Full cut, broad chested
   b. Straight coat sometimes
   c. Nipped at waist
   d. Low cut armholes
   e. Soft shoulders
   f. Single-breasted, two buttons

g. 3 1/2" lapels

h. Center vent

i. Trousers without pleats or cuffs

3. **<u>BRITISH CUT</u>**
   a. Slightly padded shoulder
   b. Two side vents
   c. Pinched waist
   d. Peaked lapels
   e. 3 1/2" wide lapels
   f. Trousers pleated and cuffed

D. <u>LAPELS:</u> Edges should be thin and roll softly towards the body.

E. <u>LININGS:</u> They should be stitched down at the armholes, bottom of coat, and inside and outside of seams. The best lining is Bemberg (rayon) since it does not stain easily and it is durable. Lining should be cut larger to allow movement of the body without resistance.
   1. Pleat at front of shoulder
   2. Pleat at center back
   3. Bellow pleat at bottom of fully lined coat

F. <u>INTERFACING:</u> This is called the skeleton (inside holdup) or inner soul of the garment. It consists of three components:
   1. Hymo
   2. Haricloth
   3. Flannel

This type of garment construction allows the garment to breathe and it gives shape. Some garments are made with fusible-woven and unwoven.
1. Very stiff
2. Locks moisture in, preventing evaporation
3. Feels cold in winter
4. Warm in summer

G. <u>SEAMS:</u>
1. Open seams at pocket, less bulky
2. Shoulder seams should be concave, better fit
3. Outlets for enlargement of garment
   a. Center coat back
   b. Side coat front
   c. Center back trouser
   d. Back trouser panel inseam

H. <u>BUTTONHOLES:</u>
1. They should look evenly stitched without loose thread
2. Hand buttonholes are softer and wear longer
3. Made with buttonhole silk twist, size D or ten
4. Buttons—Decorative or functional
   a. Functional—should be sewn with a stand to prevent puckering
   b. Decorative—flat
   c. Buttons sewn to garment with size 30 linen thread (waxed)

I. <u>SLEEVES:</u>
1. Should hang so that front of sleeve falls at center of hip (side) pocket
2. If sleeve is too far back, will wrinkle at front

3. If too far forward, will wrinkle at back
4. To check sleeve balance, hold coat with hand underside of sleeve at shoulder
5. Sleeve length:
   a. According to individual preference
   b. Check for accuracy of sleeve length by having tailor measure from knuckle at thumb to desired length. Match opposite sleeve using same procedure
   c. Knuckle position is more accurate—stationary point

J. SLEEVE HEAD:
1. Check to see if seam at shoulder has a sharp, square edge. If it does, sleeve head has been omitted
2. Sleeve head:
   a. A soft strip of material that extends beyond shoulder pads
   b. Provides smooth continuous line from shoulder to sleeve
   c. Takes up fullness that is applied to sleeves

K. SHOULDER PADS:
1. Lift coat by the shoulder
2. Should feel soft, not lumpy
3. Sleeve seams should be sewn to canvas to prevent shifting

L. SHOULDERS:
1. Slightly concave to relieve pressure from front of armhole

2. Back shoulder cut larger than front shoulder, fullness worked in
3. If shoulder is too tight, diagonal breaks will form; very uncomfortable

M. ARMHOLES:
1. Should feel comfortable
2. Too deep if you raise your arms and coat lifts up
3. Too shallow if uncomfortable

N. COLLAR:
1. Collar should fit the neck
2. French canvas sewn to undercollar melton to retain shape
3. If collar is too long, lapels roll short
4. If collar too short, lapels roll long

O. VENT:
1. Should lie flat—not open

P. TROUSERS:
1. Length breaks slightly at front and slanted to back
2. Pockets—deep, clean finish on the inside. Check if tape has been applied to opening. Should not stretch
3. Lining sewn at crotch area to prevent wear—front part only; back part optional

Q. VEST:
1. Fit snuggly at neck
2. Lies flat around chest area
3. Check if tape has been applied to front and button edge by grasping edge and pulling slightly

R. SKIRT:
1. Skirt length—depends on style
2. Classic look—slightly below knees
3. Skirt lining—attached at waistband, free hanging, hemmed separately
4. 2"-2 1/2" hem at bottom

TRIVIA:
1. 130 different operations in making a coat—over half are hand operations in custom made clothes
2. 3 types of garment constructions
   a. Ready made
   b. Made-to-measure
   c. Custom made
3. Garments are graded on a scale 1-6, 6+
   a. 1 equals all machine operations
   b. 6-6+ over half hand operations
4. Just as a sculptor molds clay, a tailor molds fabrics through the use of shaping, pressing, darts, fullness, etc.

CLOTHIERS:

1. MEN'S WEAR:
   a. Brooks Brothers
   b. Harve Bernard
   c. Oxford
   d. Giorgio Armani
   e. Austin Reed
   f. Yves Saint Laurent
   g. Hart Schaffner & Marx

h. Daks
i. Bill Blass
j. Haggar
k. Pierre Cardin
l. Adolfo Alfred
m. Calvin Klein
n. Evan Piccone
o. Hickey Freeman
p. Freeman (Philadelphia)
q. Faberge Clothing
r. Christian Dior
s. Nik-Nik Clothing

2. WOMEN'S WEAR:
a. Brooks Brothers
b. Larry Levine
c. Kirkland Hall
d. Ashley Brooke
e. Harve Bernard
f. Sasson
g. Saville

Please note that I have included only a partial list of clothiers for your selection. I am certain that there are many more such clothiers that exist. Whichever clothier you choose, you should make certain to select a reputable organization that will stand behind its work product and service.

SALADINI
TABLE OF PROPORTIONS
FOR
RISES AND INSEAMS
BY
HEIGHTS AND SEATS

	SEATS	34	35	36	37	38	39	40	41	42	43	44	45	46	47	48	49	50	
	HEIGHTS	7⅞	8	8⅛	8¼	8⅜	8½	8⅝	8¾	8⅞	9	9⅛	9¼	9⅜	9½	9⅝	9¾	9⅞	RISE
	5' 4"	27½	27¾	28	28¼	28½	28¾	29	29¼	29½	29¾	30	30¼	30½	30¾	31	31¼	31½	INSEAM
SHORTS	5' 5"	8	8⅛	8¼	8⅜	8½	8⅝	8¾	8⅞	9	9⅛	9¼	9⅜	9½	9⅝	9¾	9⅞	10	RISE
		27¾	28	28¼	28½	28¾	29	29¼	29½	29¾	30	30¼	30½	30¾	31	31¼	31½	31¾	INSEAM
	5' 6"	8⅛	8¼	8⅜	8½	8⅝	8¾	8⅞	9	9⅛	9¼	9⅜	9½	9⅝	9¾	9⅞	10	10⅛	RISE
		28	28¼	28½	28¾	29	29¼	29½	29¾	30	30¼	30½	30¾	31	31¼	31½	31¾	32	INSEAM
	5' 7"	8¼	8⅜	8½	8⅝	8¾	8⅞	9	9⅛	9¼	9⅜	9½	9⅝	9¾	9⅞	10	10⅛	10¼	RISE
		28¼	28½	28¾	29	29¼	29½	29¾	30	30¼	30½	30¾	31	31¼	31½	31¾	32	32¼	INSEAM
	5' 8"	8⅜	8½	8⅝	8¾	8⅞	9	9⅛	9¼	9⅜	9½	9⅝	9¾	9⅞	10	10⅛	10¼	10⅜	RISE
		28½	28¾	29	29¼	29½	29¾	30	30¼	30½	30¾	31	31¼	31½	31¾	32	32¼	32½	INSEAM
REGULARS	5' 9"	8½	8⅝	8¾	8⅞	9	9⅛	9¼	9⅜	9½	9⅝	9¾	9⅞	10	10⅛	10¼	10⅜	10½	RISE
		28¾	29	29¼	29½	29¾	30	30¼	30½	30¾	31	31¼	31½	31¾	32	32¼	32½	32¾	INSEAM
	5' 10"	8⅝	8¾	8⅞	9	9⅛	9¼	9⅜	9½	9⅝	9¾	9⅞	10	10⅛	10¼	10⅜	10½	10⅝	RISE
		29	29¼	29½	29¾	30	30¼	30½	30¾	31	31¼	31½	31¾	32	32¼	32½	32¾	33	INSEAM
	5' 11"	8¾	8⅞	9	9⅛	9¼	9⅜	9½	9⅝	9¾	9⅞	10	10⅛	10¼	10⅜	10½	10⅝	10¾	RISE
		29¼	29½	29¾	30	30¼	30½	30¾	31	31¼	31½	31¾	32	32¼	32½	32¾	33	33¼	INSEAM
	6'	8⅞	9	9⅛	9¼	9⅜	9½	9⅝	9¾	9⅞	10	10⅛	10¼	10⅜	10½	10⅝	10¾	10⅞	RISE
		29½	29¾	30	30¼	30½	30¾	31	31¼	31½	31¾	32	32¼	32½	32¾	33	33¼	33½	INSEAM
	6' 1"	9	9⅛	9¼	9⅜	9½	9⅝	9¾	9⅞	10	10⅛	10¼	10⅜	10½	10⅝	10¾	10⅞	11	RISE
		29¾	30	30¼	30½	30¾	31	31¼	31½	31¾	32	32¼	32½	32¾	33	33¼	33½	33¾	INSEAM
LONGS	6' 2"	9⅛	9¼	9⅜	9½	9⅝	9¾	9⅞	10	10⅛	10¼	10⅜	10½	10⅝	10¾	10⅞	11	11⅛	RISE
		30	30¼	30½	30¾	31	31¼	31½	31¾	32	32¼	32½	32¾	33	33¼	33½	33¾	34	INSEAM
	6' 3"	9¼	9⅜	9½	9⅝	9¾	9⅞	10	10⅛	10¼	10⅜	10½	10⅝	10¾	10⅞	11	11⅛	11¼	RISE
		30¼	30½	30¾	31	31¼	31½	31¾	32	32¼	32½	32¾	33	33¼	33½	33¾	34	34¼	INSEAM
	6' 4"	9⅜	9½	9⅝	9¾	9⅞	10	10⅛	10¼	10⅜	10½	10⅝	10¾	10⅞	11	11⅛	11¼	11⅜	RISE
		30½	30¾	31	31¼	31½	31¾	32	32¼	32½	32¾	33	33¼	33½	33¾	34	34¼	34½	INSEAM

PROPORTIONAL FORMULAS

RISE= 1/2 Seat on 1/4 division + 4-1/4 inches + or -
1/8 inch for every inch below or above 5' 9".
INSEAM= 1/4 height + 1/2 seat on 1/2 division + 3 inches
OUTSEAM= inseam + rise
STOUTS OR CORPULENTS reduce inseam 1/2 inch
AVERAGE HEIGHT = 5' 9"
AVERAGE SEAT = 40"

Vincent Rocco Saladini, Sr.

TROUSER CLASSIFICATIONS

Two basic classifications will be used for the identification of trousers: Drop classification and Height classification.

DROP CLASSIFICATION

This classification is based on the difference between the waist and seat measurements.

A normal drop is six (6) inches. For example: Waist 34"
Seat 40"

To illustrate the comparison in drops, a 40" seat will be used in all categories.

CATEGORY	SMALL WAIST	NORMAL	STUB	STOUT	CORPULENT
DROP	8"-10"	6"-7"	4"-5"	2"-3"	0"-1"
WAIST	32"-30"	34"-33"	36"-35"	38"-37"	40"-39"
SEAT	40"	40"	40"	40"	40"

HEIGHT CLASSIFICATION

This classification is the proportional measurements based on various heights. This classification can be combined with the Drop classification. An individual may have a regular height but have a stout drop. Hence, a regular stout. This concept can be applied to all of the various proportions. For example: Regular stout is a person 5'9", waist 38, seat 40.

EXTRA SHORT- Below 5' 1"

SHORT-   5' 5"

REGULAR-   5' 9"

LONG-   6'

EXTRA LONG- Above 6' 4"

REGULAR TROUSER

Measure forward 4 inches from edge of paper. Form a right angle at right side of paper. Draw a line approximately length of outseam measurement.

DRAFTING FRONT SECTION:

1   is the starting point.

2   down from 1 is the Rise Measure (9¼") (CROTCH LINE).

3   down from 2 is the Inseam Measure (30½") (BOTTOM LINE).

4   is midway between 2 and 3.

5   up from 4 is 2 inches. (KNEE LINE)

6   up from 2 is raised seat (41") on 1/6 division. (SEAT LINE).
Square forward points, 1, 2, 3, 5 and 6. These are basic construction lines.

7   forward from 2 is raised seat (41) on 1/2 division.
Square up to waist line locating points 8 and 9 as shown.

10   forward from 8 is 3/16 inch.
Draw a line from 9 through 10 to crotch line.

11   forward from 7 is 2-3/8 inches. Increase or decrease 1/8 inch for each size smaller or larger than 40 seat. Dress is equally distributed. Shape from 10 to 11 as shown.

12   is midway between 2 and 11.

13   forward from 2 equals distance 12 to 2 plus 1/4 inch.
Draw a line from 13 through 12 to top of waist line (CREASE LINE)

14   is located at knee line.

15   is located at waist line.

16   back from 9 is raised waist (35") on 1/2 division (8-3/4").
Square a short line up from 16.

17   up from 16 is 1/4 inch. Shape from 17 to 15 and 17 to 6 as shown.

18   forward from 14 is Knee Measure (19") on 1/4 division - 1/4 inch/

19   back from 14 is the same.

20   forward from 13 is Bottom Measure (20") on 1/4 division - 1/4".

21   back from 13 is the same.
Connect points 11 to 18 to 20 as shown. Connect points 2 to 19 to 21 as shown.

391

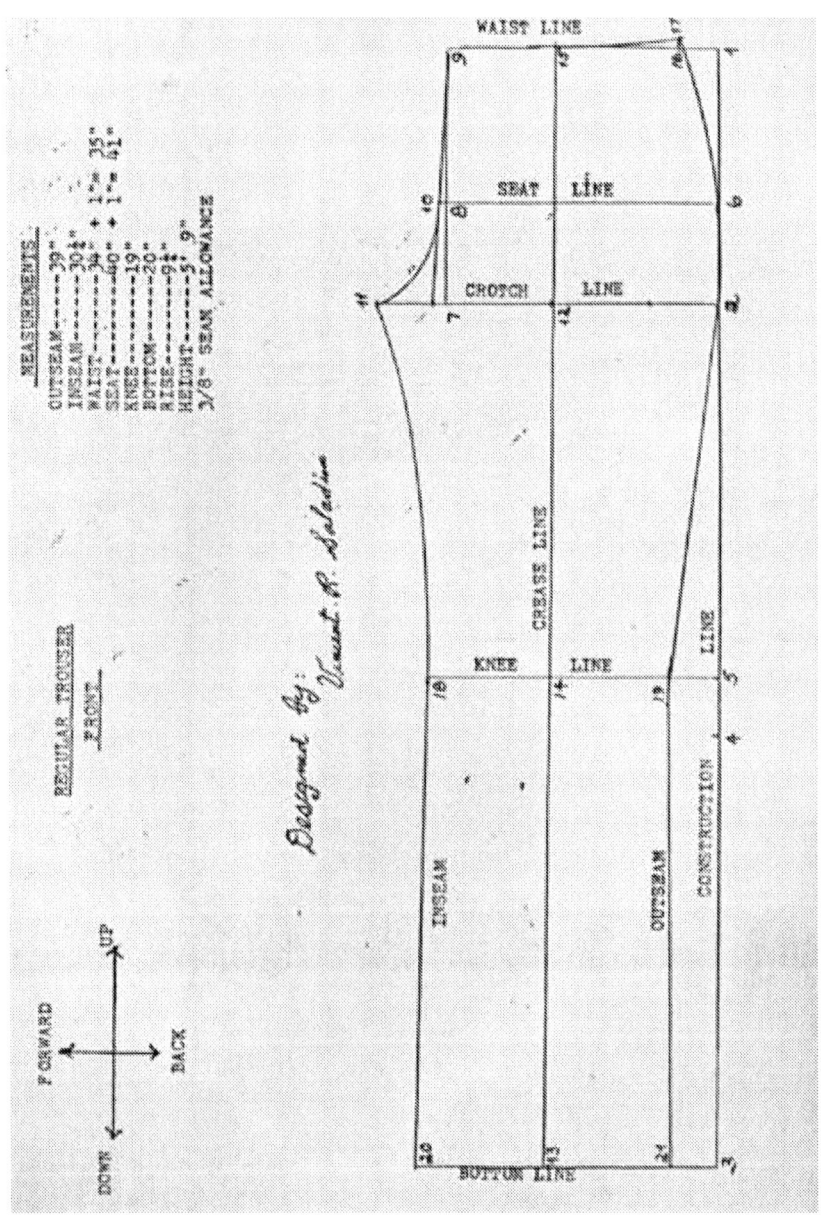

PREPARATION FOR DRAFTING BACK

METHOD- I - Cutting out front section to draft back

1. Cut out front section neatly and accurately starting at point 17 to 9 to 11 down to 20 to 21 and back to 17.

2. Place trimmed front section on another sheet of pattern paper allowing about 5 inches around entire front section. Pin front section to pattern paper on crease line at 12 and 13.

3. Extend lines forward and backward at waist, crotch, knee, bottom and backward only at seat line. Indicate drafting numbers on front section.

****

METHOD- II - Picking and tracing front section to draft back

1. Place drafted front section on sheet of paper allowing about 5 inches around entire front. Pin front section to paper on crease line at 12 and 13.

2. Pick or pierce with an awl or pin at points 17, 15, 9, 10, 11, 18, 20, 21, 19, 2, 6 and 13.

3. Remove pins and front draft section. Connect and shape all points as original front draft. Indicate front section drafting numbers.

4. Extend lines forward and backward as in Method I.

****

METHOD- III - Drafting back on front section using original front draft

1. Extend construction lines forward and backward.

2. Draft back on front section draft.

3. Place drafted back section on sheet of pattern paper. Pick and trace back at points H, F, D, 11, M, I, K, 13, L, J, G and back to H.

4. Connect and shape all points as original back draft.

5. Cut out front section as in Method I.

393

REGULAR TROUSER

DRAFTING BACK SECTION:

A forward from 7 is raised seat (41") on 1/6 division (3-1/2").

B forward from A is 2-1/2 inches. Decrease or increase 1/8 inch for each size smaller or larger than 40" seat. Square a short line down from B.

C up from 7 is raised seat (41") on 1/8 division (2-5/8"). Increase or decrease 1/8 inch for each size larger or smaller than 40" seat. Crossmark at C locating D.

Draw a line from D to 2. Square up on line D-2 locating center back.

E is located at waist line as shown.

F up from E is the same distance as E to 9.

G back from point where line D-F intersects at seat line is raised seat (41") on 1/2 division + 1-1/2 inches + 1/4 inch for ease (12").

H back from F is raised waist (35") on 1/2 division + 1 inch dart allowance + 1-1/2 inches for four (4) 3/8 inch seams (11-1/4"). Connect H to F.

I forward from 18 is 1 inch.

J back from 19 is 1 inch.

K forward from 20 is 1 inch.

L back from 21 is inch.

M up from I is the same distance as 11 to 18.

Connect points H-G-J-L.

Connect points K-I and M.
I to M should be shaped as shown using a curved ruler.

Shape from points D to M as shown.

Complete front and back sections by adding pocket positions, outlets, notches and back dart.

394

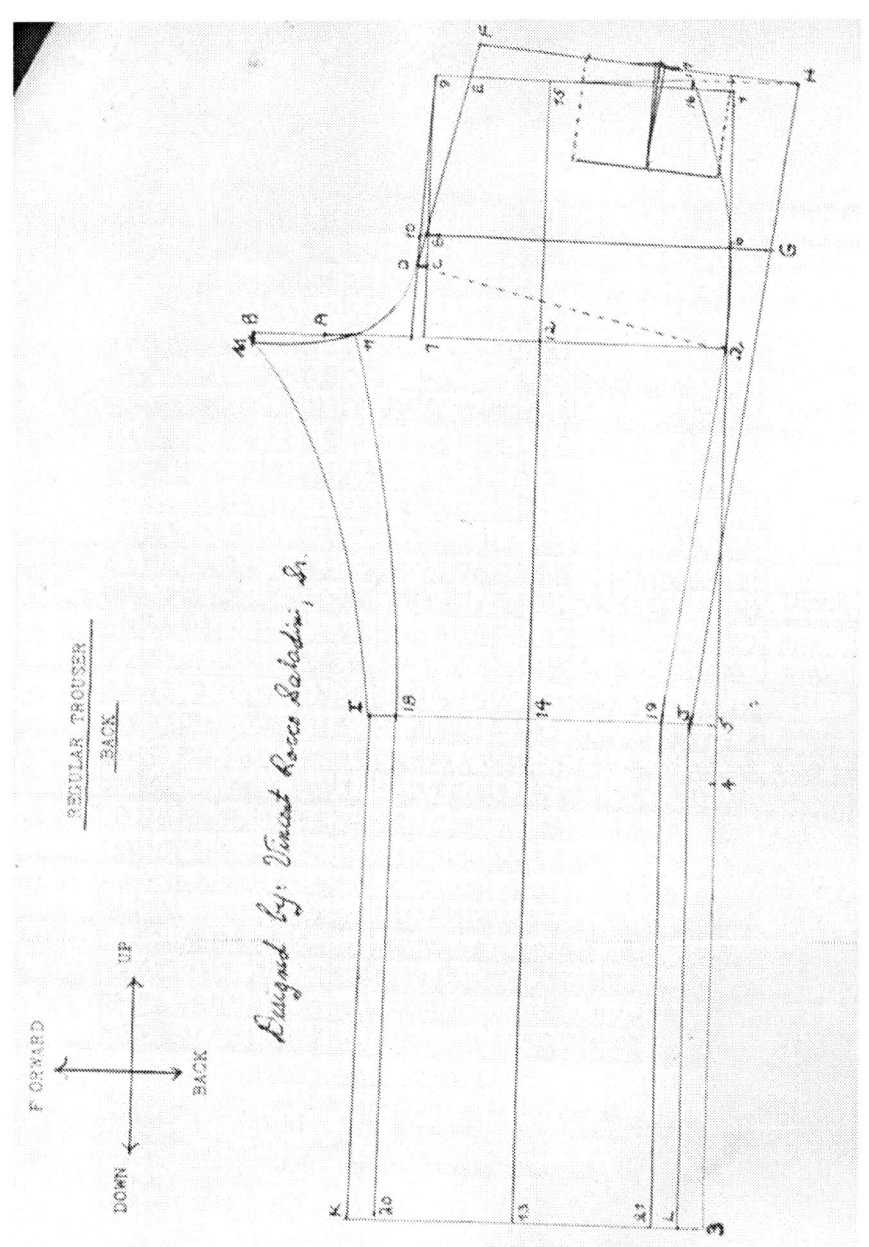

REGULAR TROUSER
BACK

Designed by: Vincent Rocco Saladin, Sr.

FORWARD

UP

BACK

DOWN

Vincent Rocco Saladini, Sr.

REGULAR STOUT
PLAIN FRONT

Measure forward 4 inches from edge of paper. Form a right
angle at right side of paper. Draw a line approximately length
of outseam measurement.

DRAFTING FRONT SECTION:

1   is the starting point.

2   down from 1 is the Rise Measure (9¼") (CROTCH LINE).

3   down from 2 is the Inseam Measure (29-3/4") (BOTTOM LINE).

4   is midway between 2 and 3.

5   up from 4 is 2 inches. (KNEE LINE).

6   up from 2 is raised seat (41") on 1/6 division. (SEAT LINE).
Square forward points, 1, 2, 3, 5 and 6. These are basic
construction lines.

7   forward from 2 is raised seat (41") on 1/2 division.

8   forward from 7 is 1/2 inch (1/8" for each size above normal
drop- 4 sizes). Square a dotted line up to waist line
locating points 9 and 10 as shown.

11   forward from 8 is 2-3/8 inches. Increase or decrease 1/8"
for each size smaller or larger than 40 seat. Dress is
equally distributed.

12   is midway between 2 and 11.

13   back from 12 is 1/4 inch. (1/16" for each size above normal
drop- 4 sizes).

14   forward from 3 equals 13 to 2 plus 1/4 inch. Draw a line
from 14 through 13 to top of waist line. (Crease line).

15   is located at knee line.

16   is located at waist line.

17   forward from 15 is Knee Measure (20") on 1/4 division.

18   back from 15 is the same.

19   forward from 14 is Bottom Measure (20") on 1/4 division.

20   back from 14 is the same.

396

<u>REGULAR STOUT</u>
<u>PLAIN FRONT</u>

<u>DRAFTING FRONT SECTION</u> (Cont'd)

21   up from 2 is 1 inch. (1/4 inch for each size above normal).
      Draw a dotted line from 21 to 8. Place long arm of square
      on line 21- and square up approximately 1-1/2 inches
      above waist line.

22   is located at seat line.

23   is located at waist line.

24   up from 23 is the same distance as 10 to 23.
      Draw fly line from 22 to 11.

25   back from 24 is raised waist (39") on 1/2 division (9-3/4").
      Square a short line up from 25.

26   up from 25 is 1/4 inch.
      Connect 24 to 25 for new waist line.
      Shape 26 to 16 as shown.

27   back from 9 is raised seat (41") on 1/2 division + 1/4 inch
      for ease.
      Shape from 26 to 27 to 18 as shown.
      Connect 18 to completing outseam.
      Connect points 19 to 17 to 11 as shown completing inseam.

REGULAR STOUT
PLAIN FRONT

DRAFTING BACK SECTION:

A   forward from 8 is raised seat (41") on 1/6 division (3-1/2").

B   forward from A is 2-1/2 inches. Decrease or increase 1/8 inch for each size smaller or larger than 40" seat. Square a short line down from B.

C   up from 8 is raised seat (41") on 1/8 division (2-5/8"). Cross mark at C locating D. Draw a line from D to 21. Square up on line D-21 locating center back. Point E is located at waist line as shown.

F   up from E is the same distance as E to 24.

G   back from point where D-F intersects at seat line is raised seat (41") on 1/2 division + 1-1/2 inches + 1/4 inch for ease (12").

H   back from F is raised waist (39") on 1/2 division + 1 inch dart allowance + 1-1/2 inches for four (4) 3/8 inch seams (12-1/4"). Connect H to F.

I   forward from 17 is 1 inch.

J   back from 18 is the same.

K   forward from 19 is 1 inch.

L   back from 20 is the same.

M   up from I is the same distance as 17 to 11.

Connect points H-G-J and L.

Connect points K-I and M.
I to M should be shaped as shown using a curved ruler.

Shape from points D to M as shown.

Complete front and back sections by adding pocket positions, outlets, notches and back dart.

398

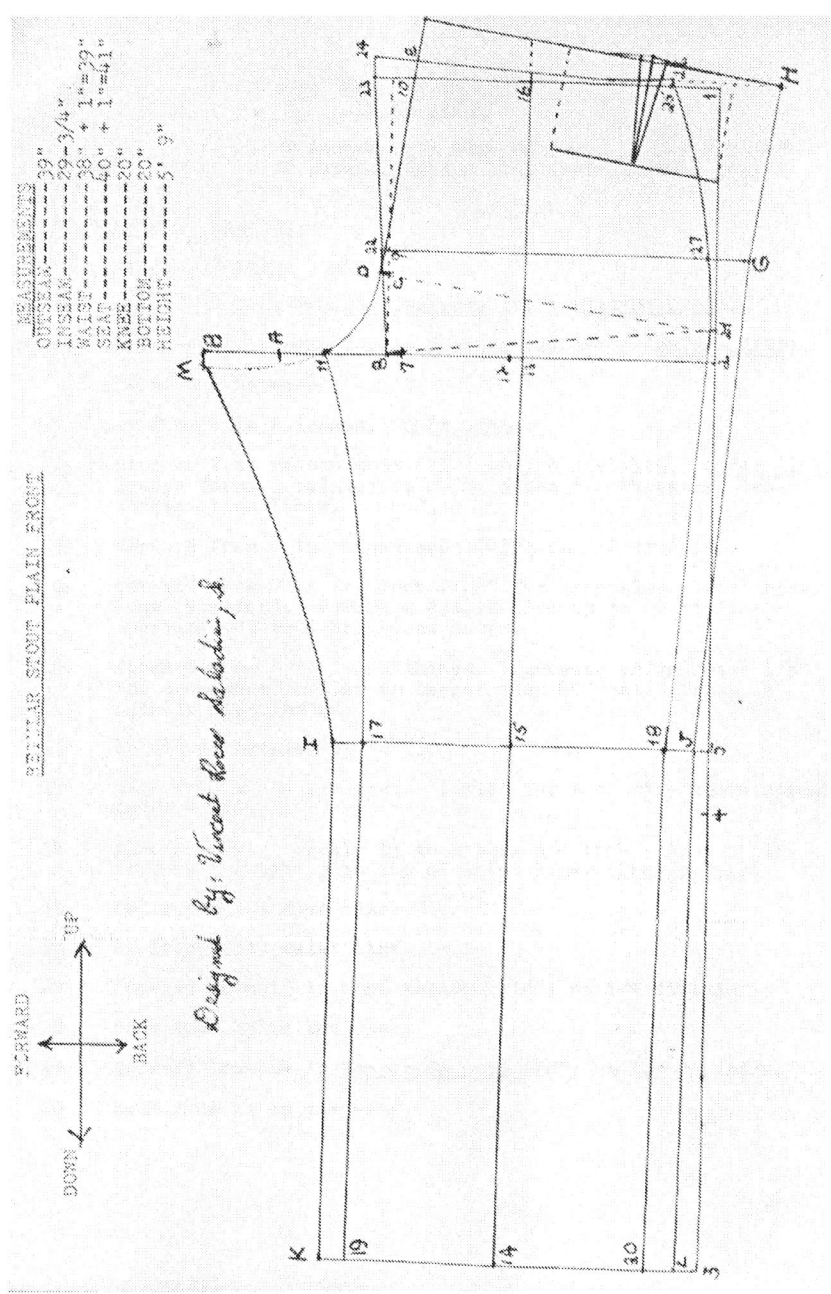

REGULAR STOUT PLAIN FRONT

MEASUREMENTS
OUTSEAM ------ 39"
INSEAM ------ 29-3/4"
WAIST ------ 38" + 1"=39"
SEAT ------ 40" + 1"=41"
KNEE ------ 20"
BOTTOM ------ 20"
HEIGHT ------ 5' 9"

Designed by: Vincent Rocco DiBartino, Sr.

DRAFTING A JERKIN

1. Square down and forward.

2. Is 1/2 division of breast down from 1, square forward.

3. Is 1/4 height in inches down (68 divided by 4 =17) from 1, square forward.

4. Is 3 inches down from 3, square forward.

5. Is 1/6 division of breast forward from 1, square up.

6. Is 1 inch squared up from 5, shape midway between 5 and 1 as shown.

7. Is 4 inches forward from 5, square down to breast line.

8. Is indicated at point where lines 8 and 2 meet.

9. Is 1 inch down from 7, connect straight line to 6.

10. Is 1/2 division of breast plus 1 1/2" from 2.

11. Is indicated at point that lines 10 and 4 meet.

12. Is 1 inch down from 2, connect straight line 6 to 12.

13. Is 1/2" forward from 3.

14. Is indicated by placing long arm of square on 12-13 and short arm on 11, square back from 1.

15. Is indicated at point lines 4 and 11, cross 12-14.

16. Is 1 inch down from 10.

17. Is midway between 7-8.

18. Is 1 inch back from 17, shape 16-8-18-9 as shown.

19. Is 1 1/4 inch back from 11, square up and mark 1 inch and 3 inches.

20. Is 5 inches back from 19, square up and mark 1 inch and 4 inches, round corners at bottom of patch pockets as shown.

BOTTOM OUTLET:

Square down and connect straight line 1 1/4 inch at 11 and 14 for front and at 11 and 4 for back.

FRONT:

Pick and trace points 12-6-9-8-16-11-14. Pocket marks and bottom outlet. Fold paper on 12 and 14 to cut a one-piece front.

BACK:

Pick and trace points 1-6-9-18-8-15-11-14 and bottom outlet.
Connect straight line 1 to 4.

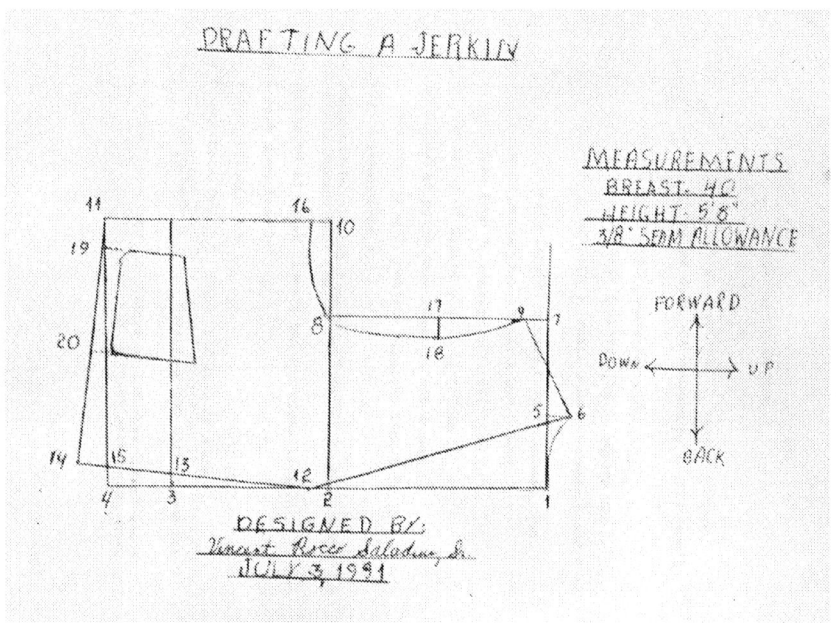

Big Springs Descendants Who Served in the Military

During our country's time of need, I am proud to report that the men of Big Springs, West Virginia, as well as their relatives and descendants, bravely and valiantly answered the call of duty without a moment's hesitation. A large number of representatives served in World War II. In fact, fourteen men out of a total of fourteen families with a population of eighty-eight people served in the military.

Vincent R. Saladini
U.S.S. Sibley (APA206)
Anchored in San Francisco Bay
February 20, 1946

We did proudly have representatives who served honorably during World War II, the Korean War, the Vietnam War, the Lebanon War, and peacetime as well. In spite of our many men who served in the military during such combat duty, fortunately, all returned home safely. We had only one casualty. Carlo Rossi was tragically killed in a bus accident while stationed at the United States Naval base in Roanoke, Virginia. His untimely death devastated the families of Big Springs, West Virginia, as he was greatly loved by those who knew him.

Speaking for the men of Big Springs, West Virginia, we are all proud and honored for having had the opportunity to serve our country during its time of need. The sacrifices that we had to make were worth the effort to preserve our valued freedom. I commend all of those brave men and women who served in the past and who are presently serving in the military. Without their brave efforts and unselfish willingness to make sacrifices, we would not enjoy the liberties that we do today. It is truly an honor for me to have served with such outstanding individuals. The following is a compilation of the original families and/ or descendants of Big Springs, West Virginia, who served in the armed forces from World War II to the present.

WORLD WAR II

1. Vincent Rocco Saladini, Sr.—Navy
2. Angelo Peter Saladini, Sr.—Navy
3. Carlo Rossi—Navy
4. Chris Piccolomini—Navy
5. Tito Orsini—Navy
6. Sam Piccolomini—Army
7. Italo Bigiarelli—Army
8. John Piccolomini—Army
9. Orlando De Stefano—Army
10. Louie De Stefano—Army
11. Tom Smith—Army
12. Elio Bigiarelli—Air Force
13. Patsy Saladini—Air Force
14. Louie Rossi—Air Force

KOREAN WAR
15. Jim Crabtree—Army
16. Anthony Petrucci—Army

VIETNAM WAR
17. Grayson Smith, Jr.—Marines
18. Bobby Joe Smith—Army

LEBANON WAR
19. Patsy Capriotti—Marines

PEACE TIME
20. Adam Capriotti, Jr.—Air Force
21. Anthony Petrucci—Army

22. John Wolfensberger—Navy
23. Salvatore Saladini—Army
24. Steven Lee Wolfensberger—Army

Vincent R. Saladini, Angelo P. Saladini
August 1945   Big Springs, West Virginia
World War II

Cpl. Patsey A. Saladini
World War II
United States Air Force

Italo Bigiarelli
World War II
India

Pfc. Elio Bigiarelli
World War II
United States Air Force

Vincent Rocco Saladini, Sr.

Bobby Smith
Vietnam War Verteran
United States Army

Grayson Smith Jr. (holding Vietnamese orphan)
U.S. Marines   Vietnam War

Vincent Rocco Saladini, Sr.

Pfc. Elio Bigiarelli
May 1945 Germany
United States Air Force

Jim Crabtree
U.S. Army
Korean War Veteran

Alonzo De Stefano
United States Army
World War II

ABOUT THE AUTHOR

Born December 23,1924, the third youngest of ten children, Vincent Rocco Saladini, Sr. learned tailoring at the tender age of twelve. At forty-two, he returned to college and received a Bachelor of Science Degree in Vocational Technical Education and a Master of Arts Degree in Student Personnel Services. Vincent also holds licenses and certificates as a Principal, Private Trade School Teacher, Guidance Counselor and Teacher of Men's Clothing Manufacturing, and in Administration, Supervision and Tailoring. He worked as an Adjunct Professor of Men's and Women's Design at Fashion Institute of Technology and an educator and full-time guidance counselor at the High School of Fashion Industries until he retired in June 1991.

Printed in the United States
22313LVS00002B/15